EXPOSURE *of* MALICE

SECRETS OF BEAVER CREEK

Book 3

LILA FERRARI

For more information on books by Lila Ferrari, or to subscribe to her newsletter, visit her website here: https://www.lilaferrariwrites.com

Paperback ISBN: 979-8-9933360-1-5

Praise for Lila Ferrari

Secrets of Beaver Creek

The mystery brought them together.
The past threatens to tear them apart.

Every town has secrets.

Beaver Creek does a better job of hiding them.

Secrets of Beaver Creek weaves together mystery and

romance with a strong sense of place and where love really does conquer all.

Because sometimes, the biggest surprises aren't just about solving the crime. They're about finding the courage to face the past, the strength to begin again and the kind of love that shows up anyway even when you're not sure you deserve it.

Praise for the series

"It was definitely a page turner with amazing plot going on. A small town with a dashing sheriff and a recently moved mystery writer Jane, found themselves between murder and chaos. Things take a twist when the body is found in Jane's pond. A Mystery Suspense Romance that will keep you hooked, so definitely try it out and find the person behind all this."—Reviewer

"This is the exact type of book I was trying to find all my life! Cozy mystery meets spice. Ethan and Jane don't care much for each other at first and as the mystery surrounding her farm intensifies, Ethan can't deny the strong attraction he has had for Jane from the start. Set in Vermont, a great small town setting, wonderful characters, romance, and a good mystery to keep you reading until well past your bedtime. I'm looking forward to reading the next in the series."—Reviewer

"I love it when I find an author who writes in the genre that I love and in such a compelling manner that you simply do not want to stop reading the story. That's a difficult thing to do with so many authors in the marketplace now. It is sometimes very hard to find that special spark that an author brings to keep you addicted to reading, but Ferrari has it! This story has numerous elements that keep you engaged, including suspense, murder, romance, friendship, and fun.

"The setting is highly detailed and sounds like a wonderful small town you would want to live in, too! The two main characters are beautifully matched and complement each other. Dylan was a surprise character with his grumpy exterior but passionate and protective interior. Savannah was humble, strong, and sweet. Ferrari blends in a community that is strong, supportive, and protective of their family, found and real. Exposure of Obsession is emotional, sexy, suspense-filled, and full of chick-lit vibes, all rolled into one. I could not stop reading and loved it! I will be reading more from Ferrari soon!"—Reviewer

KnightGuard Security

Mission:
Courage ~ Redemption ~ Second Chances

Motivated by a sense of justice and driven by her own personal tragedy, Sam Knight creates **KnightGuard Security**—an organization composed of ex-cops, retired military heroes, and special-ops veterans, all dedicated to safeguarding others.

Using the skills they learned, and armed with courage and resilience in the face of life's greatest challenges, each will risk it all to help courageous women in peril while discovering the transformative power of love.

Recurring themes of courage, redemption, and second chances are interwoven throughout each book.

PRAISE FOR THE SERIES

"Lila Ferrari has written a fast-paced romantic suspense with strong characters and a complex plot."—Reviewer

"I've read all the books in this series and I honestly loved every one of them! Lila Ferrari has the ability to keep the reader enthralled by keeping the story moving along and making you want to keep reading and wanting to get to the next page as fast as possible."—Reviewer

"There is suspense, drama, danger, villains, and romance. I want to read more in this series."—Reviewer

"What a sweet, romantic, and exciting book. I couldn't put the book down. Through the book I was smiling. The characters have great details and descriptions of their history. You feel like you are a part of their love story. If you like military romance and Happily Ever After endings this is your story!"—Reviewer

BROTHERHOOD ALLIANCE

(Special Forces, Operation Alpha)

MISSION:
COURAGE ~ HONOR ~ PROTECT

The **Brotherhood Alliance** is made up of ex-military and special forces finding their way in a world vastly different from the one they left.

They served their country with honor.

As they seek to find their place in this new world and use skills acquired in the military, they will honor and defend the most vulnerable clients who have no resources to protect themselves.

Haywood Lake is the perfect location for their headquarters—quiet, peaceful, and secluded.

PRAISE FOR THE SERIES

"This is a well written story which has loss, grief, suspense, danger, intrigue, healing, twists, and love, which leads to a thrilling and addictive page turner."—Reviewer

"This book is so full of action and romance you won't want to put it down."—Reviewer

"This was my first book by this author. It had a great amount of suspense and it was an easy read that keeps the pages turning. I liked the main characters and the military background of the male lead."—Reviewer

"It was an edge of my seat read me not able to put it down it was very well written in full detail all of the characters worked great as a team. The villains were very cunning, but the heroes were slicker than the villains gave them credit for and were able to catch them and save the day.. definitely worth the read."—Reviewer

"Omg this the first book I read of this series. I am hooked!!!! I now have to go back and read the first 5!!!!! Is there nothing better than an Alpha male? Omg 😲 😱 😲 love them all."—Reviewer

"I absolutely love Lila Ferrari's series, and this latest book did not disappoint. From start to finish, it is packed with twists, turns, and an exciting plotline that kept me on the edge of my seat...What really stands out to me is this author's ability to balance heart-pounding action with meaningful character development.

"It was also a treat to catch up with other characters from the previous books, the camaraderie and brotherhood between the members of the Brotherhood Alliance, along with the strong bond they share with their women, adds a layer of depth and warmth that makes this series even more enjoyable. Overall, this book was a brilliant read that exceeded my expectations. The characters, the tension, and the storyline were all top-notch. I can't wait to see what Lila Ferrari has in store for us next!" —Reviewer

Exposure Of Malice

Secrets of Beaver Creek, Book 3

COURAGE, REDEMPTION, SECOND CHANCES

Emily Harper thought she'd left the chaos behind when she opened Serenity Spa in quiet Beaver Creek. But her sense of safety unravels the night she finds a woman's body in the locker room. The death isn't random. Someone brought danger and darkness into her world on purpose.

Deputy Sheriff Adam Sadler never planned on staying tangled in anyone's life, but protecting Emily becomes more than just part of the job. She's strong, guarded, and caught in something far more calculated than it seems.

As suspicion spreads and the danger creeps closer, Adam must decide if he's willing to risk everything—including his heart—for a woman who may already be in the crosshairs.

Exposure of Malice is a stand-alone book with a HEA, but it's recommended you read the books in order to get maximum enjoyment.

For Ray,
Always

One

The comforting scent of lavender and eucalyptus greeted Emily Harper as she unlocked the front door of Serenity Spa. The polished wooden floors gleamed in the early morning light. Soft harp music played in the background. Everything looked just the way it should.

Peaceful. Welcoming. Safe.

She needed that illusion of calm almost as much as her clients did.

For a moment, she almost hummed a melody she used to warm up with before gigs but stopped. That part of her life belonged to Boston, and she'd left all that behind.

Emily let out a long sigh, rolled her shoulders and smiled. For once, things were almost going her way. The spa was hers. Business was steady.

And she had a boyfriend.

Emily laughed to herself. *Boyfriend.* Was that even a word adults used today? What else could she call Adam Sadler? Deputy Dreamboat? Her significant other? Boy toy?

Nah, now she was just being silly.

Boyfriend would have to do.

"Morning, Emily," called out Morgan Tate, her bubbly receptionist and one of the few original team members who hadn't jumped ship—yet. She leaned over the front desk, holding a smoothie in one hand. "It's your lucky day. Yoga this morning and afternoon plus back-to-back massages in between."

Emily placed her tote bag down and took the offered drink. "I'll take lucky any day. Did the towels finish drying?"

"Folded, fluffed and put away."

Emily grinned. "Thanks. You're a lifesaver. One less thing I must worry about."

She unlocked her office and the drawer she kept her purse in. Then ducked into the staff locker room they'd added last winter. It wasn't fancy, just a row of full-size lockers, a bench and a full-length mirror.

She opened her locker and traded her boots for the comfortable pair of slip-ons she kept inside. On the shelf was a soft headband and a protein bar she kept forgetting to eat. On the hook hung a spare zip-up hoodie and a tote bag. The lockers were deep enough for a small duffel or winter coat. At the time, she'd wanted her staff to feel like they had space, not just a cubby. Now it just felt like one more thing she had to clean.

The first hour passed calmly, just the way she liked it. Morning yoga classes were her favorite. Time to stretch out the kinks, breathe deeply and ease into the day.

Then, the first client arrived. Then another. Both left in that post-massage daze she loved watching. The steady flow of business settled her nerves, and she was in her element. The spa was humming. The schedule was full. She should have felt grateful.

But it didn't quite smooth out the nagging worry she hadn't managed to shake.

After checking in with her last client, Emily ducked into

the break room to refill her water bottle and paused. Two of her newer massage therapists, Lauren and Megan, huddled over their phones, whispering.

Like she couldn't hear them. Like she didn't know that Aspire Day Spa was offering new sign-on bonuses.

Like she didn't know they were about to jump ship.

As if she hadn't already lost her cleaning person and three staff members in the past three months to them.

"Everything okay over there?" she asked, keeping her tone light.

Lauren glanced up too quickly. "Oh, hey. We were just checking the weather. Supposed to be heavy rain later."

"Well, that's Vermont in the fall for you," Emily said with a tight smile. "Sunshine in the morning, rain by dinner."

They laughed a little too quickly, then left the room.

Emily stood alone in the silence.

Aspire had sleek branding, an aggressive social media campaign, a juice bar in the lobby and now bonuses big enough to lure even her most loyal employees.

It wasn't personal, she told herself.

People came and went. Careers changed. Priorities shifted.

Still, she couldn't compete with places that looked like a luxury resort instead of rural Vermont. Serenity Spa was in an old Victorian house nestled downtown, just past the firehouse and Harvest Moon Diner. Quaint, homey and now, maybe a little too quiet.

Although Beaver Creek had been seeing a lot of out-of-towners lately. People who came for the foliage, the art galleries, the small-batch cider and beer, and the farm-to-table dinners.

She could still carve out a niche. Maybe there was still a market for something grounded. Something real.

She just had to hold on long enough to figure out how.

THE INTERVIEW for the cleaning position was the last thing Emily had to do before closing. Only one person had applied, and honestly, she was too tired of picking up the slack to be picky. Still, she gave a little prayer that this person would work out.

At six o'clock on the dot, a petite woman in her mid-forties stepped through the door. She wore tailored slacks and a soft gray sweater. Her gray hair was pulled into a tidy low bun.

"Celeste, welcome," Emily said, offering a smile as she rose. "Thank you for coming in."

"My pleasure," the woman replied. "I saw your posting at the coop and took a chance the position was still open. I just moved into town."

"Well, welcome." Emily walked into her office and gestured to the chair opposite her desk. "Have a seat. Make yourself comfortable."

Celeste Miller sat gracefully, folding her hands in her lap. There was something about her. She wasn't cold. More like restrained, careful, maybe too careful. Emily couldn't put her finger on it.

Emily ran through the job description, the pay, then asked about prior experience. Celeste answered each question succinctly. She slid a single sheet of paper across the desk with handwritten references from places that Emily didn't recognize.

Nothing in Montpelier, Barre, Stowe, not even Burlingham or Middleton.

Instead, there were towns called Greenfield Heights and Ridge Hollow.

She frowned. Those didn't ring any bells.

She glanced up. "Are these places in Vermont?"

Celeste tilted her head slightly. "Oh no. Mostly out of state." She lifted her hands in a small shrug. "I've moved around a bit."

"Military?"

There was a pause.

Celeste smiled. "Something like that."

The answer was too smooth. But it wasn't a deal-breaker. People relocated all the time for work, family, fresh starts. But something about the answer felt vague.

Emily pushed the thought aside. She needed help, and Celeste was the only one answering her ad.

"How long were you at your last job?"

Celeste gave her a small smile. "Almost a year. But the owner sold the business. I've cleaned private homes and yoga studios before."

"Good." Emily nodded. "Then you know what has to be done. The job's not hard. The hours are eleven to seven weekdays and eleven to five on Saturday. During the week, we close at six, so that gives you time to finish after the clients are gone. Laundry, bathrooms, floors, locker room, wiping down and disinfecting the treatment rooms. On Saturdays, you'll be out the door at five, same as the rest of the staff."

Emily leaned back in her chair. "You okay with essential oils? They tend to linger."

"Scents don't bother me," Celeste said. "It's noise I have trouble with."

Emily blinked. "Noise?"

Celeste's eyes met hers. "Big crowds. Busy places. Places where everyone is talking at once. Serenity Spa sounds like the perfect kind of quiet."

Something about that answer bothered Emily, although she couldn't say why. The words were harmless enough.

Emily cleared her throat. "You'd be working alone most

evenings. Well, alone in the spa. I live upstairs, so I'm close if anything comes up. I'll be walking you through the sanitizing routine first. It's kind of my thing."

For a fraction of a second, Celeste's smile faltered. Her eyes flicked toward the ceiling, then back at Emily. Her smile returned. "I understand. I'm a bit of a clean freak myself."

Emily nodded. The woman was polite and a little formal, but she seemed capable. And God only knew she needed the help.

"Great," Emily said, standing. "Meet me here tomorrow night at six, if that works for you. I'll go over everything, and if it sounds like a good fit, you can start on Thursday."

"I'll be here." Celeste rose. "Thank you for the opportunity."

As Celeste left, Emily watched her get into an older model sedan and drive away. She let out the breath she hadn't realized she'd been holding.

Please let this work out. Just once.

Still, as she turned and locked the front door, Emily couldn't shake the unease that settled on her shoulders. She stepped into her office, pulled out the folded sheet of references, and made a couple of quick calls. One woman rushed through a vague "great employee, she did fine work" before hanging up. The second rang to voicemail.

It wasn't bad, but it wasn't quite right either.

Emily tapped her pen against her desk. Not exactly reassuring, but not bad enough to call the whole thing off. She shoved the paper into a drawer and told herself she'd circle back.

For now, she just needed someone who showed up.

Two

Adam Sadler cut the siren but left the lights flashing as he eased behind the gray Honda CR-V sitting crooked on the shoulder ahead. Generic, late-model. The kind of vehicle that could blend in anywhere in a town like Beaver Creek. It wasn't flashy or beat-up. Just forgettable. Which made it all the more odd to see it speeding along a mountain road with no guardrails, lined with bare trees and moose crossing signs every few miles.

He climbed out, tugged his hat down against the wind. The air held a hint of moisture. Late fall in Vermont—it could mean anything. Rain. Sleet. Snow. Or all three.

He gave his sidearm a quick pat before heading toward the car. Habit, mostly. Still, this was a deserted stretch of road. No houses nearby. No reliable cell service either. It was spotty here in the mountains. If something happened, they'd be here for a long while before anyone found them. And after the day he'd had, he wasn't ruling anything out.

It started with a missing livestock call. Jeff Candles's black Angus bull Ralphie had gotten out again and was "visiting" the neighbor's heifers. Then he had to intervene in a domestic dispute over who got to keep the dog. Followed by a flat tire on his cruiser and a delay on paperwork when the county server went down.

By the time he spotted the CR-V hauling ass up Black Bear Notch, Adam had a tension headache starting at the base of his skull and quickly working its way upward. He rubbed at the spot and muttered under his breath. Seriously. What the hell was wrong with people?

Going eighty miles an hour over winding mountain roads with hardly any guardrails? One bad decision and they'd be in a ravine or tangled around a tree. Especially now when a sudden freeze could turn the road into black ice without warning. It wasn't smart. It was stupid. More than stupid, it was suicidal.

As he approached, the driver-side window rolled down. The woman behind the wheel leaned toward him with a pleasant smile, like they were meeting for coffee, not a speeding ticket. Adam mentally shook his head. Some women thought all they had to do was flash a nice smile and they could get out of a ticket. She was going to be sadly disappointed.

Mid-thirties, glossy hair, smooth skin, polished but not flashy. Not local. She wore a lightweight jacket zipped up to her chin and smelled faintly of lavender. Her eyes were sharp and assessing. Made him feel more like she was sizing him up, not flirting.

"Afternoon," Adam said, even but firm. "Any reason you were tearing up this stretch of County 34 like it was the Indy 500?"

Her smile was sheepish. "Sorry, officer. I lost track of the speed. I'm still learning the back roads out here."

"Visiting Beaver Creek?"

"Yes," she said a little too quickly. "I'm writing a piece

about wellness tourism. You know, spas, farm-to-table retreats, that sort of thing that people eat up, and Beaver Creek has a lot of potential."

Adam kept his face neutral. Interesting choice. He didn't know much about spas, but it would seem like she'd head for the bigger cities like Burlingham or Middleton. Beaver Creek wasn't exactly the first place most people thought of for wellness getaways. Not yet, anyway.

She handed over her insurance card and license. *Jennifer Bishop.* New York plates. He gave the ID a longer look than necessary. Not because she looked suspicious, but something about her felt off.

He stepped back and headed to his cruiser and called it in. Waited. Nothing. Clean. No priors. Not even a parking ticket. Just a woman from New York in a practical car and a tidy backstory.

He walked back to the CR-V. "These roads get slick this time of year. You need to slow down."

Jennifer laughed lightly. "I'll be careful."

He didn't laugh back. Adam issued a warning this time. Just enough to make her think twice about speeding.

She rolled up the window, shifted into drive, and pulled away. Her taillights faded into the shadows.

He watched the car until it vanished around the bend.

Something about her didn't feel right. Maybe it was nothing. But she'd been smooth—too smooth, name-dropping tourism buzzwords. Like she practiced them on the drive up.

He let out a long breath, shook it off and headed back to his cruiser.

Just another out-of-towner passing through. Another person thinking that just because this was a rural area, the rules didn't apply to them.

No matter. It wasn't his job to read minds. Just license plates.

Besides, tonight he had plans. He was meeting a few friends at the Bottom-Up Tavern—a couple of beers, a few laughs, something fried and a game on TV in the background. Normal. Predictable. Safe.

And if he was lucky, maybe Emily would swing by afterward.

The idea of her curled up on his couch cuddling with him settled something restless in his chest. After a day like this, that was all he wanted.

Her.

Home.

A few hours when nothing felt off.

THE BOTTOM-UP WAS TUCKED AWAY in a corner off Falls Road near the train station. It'd been around for decades and hadn't changed much. The siding was faded, the sign half-lit, and the front door stuck when the humidity was too high, when it rained or just because. You had to kick it just right.

Outside of the jukebox, there wasn't much in the way of entertainment unless you counted the occasional bar fight. Adam used to come here on the weekends when he was younger, when that kind of thing felt exciting. But now it was just sad.

He didn't come here often, but tonight his friend Levi Barrett was bartending. Levi was a former military cop who worked there part time. The rest of his time he spent fixing up a beat-up motorcycle in his garage, giving shooting lessons at a local range and occasionally serving as an off-the-book sounding board to Adam when a case started to twist sideways.

Levi also ran a small side business installing security cameras, mostly for locals.

Adam stepped through the front door and was immediately greeted by the familiar scent of fried food and stale beer. The jukebox was playing a mournful country tune about a woman, a truck and a dog, although Adam didn't want to know in what order.

Behind the bar, Levi was pouring beers and sending them toward regulars.

"Busy tonight," Adam said as he slid onto a stool.

"Yeah, it's surprisingly decent for a weeknight." Levi handed off a pint and reached for a bar towel. "Everything okay on the sheriff's side?"

Adam huffed. "Same ol', same ol'. Speeders, loose bulls, a couple fighting over who gets the damn dog in the divorce."

Levi smirked as he wiped down the counter. "So glad I don't have to worry about that. Hey, you up for bow hunting?"

"Hmm. Let me think about that. It's been a while since I've been. Although it all depends on my schedule," Adam replied.

From the other side of the bar, he could hear the sharp clack of pool balls and a lot of swearing. Someone was losing, hopefully not badly enough to throw punches. He just wanted to relax with his friends.

A sharp whistle cut through the noise. Adam turned and spotted his friends sitting at one of the scarred wooden tables beneath the dusty vintage moose head. He made his way over, nodding to a couple of off-duty deputies and EMTs. This was their spot. A lot of the lawmen, firefighters and EMTs came here to sit, gripe and drink.

"Bro!" Nic Garcia grinned and raised his beer. He and Reed Samuels, both firefighters, were halfway through a plate of wings. Charlie Anderson, who owned Chuck's Garage, nursed a pint with grease still under his fingernails.

Charlie lifted his beer in greeting. "Thought you got abducted."

"Busy day." Adam pulled out a chair and dropped onto it. "Ethan is running late and will be here in a few."

"Heard Candles's bull, Ralphie, got loose again." Charlie grinned. "When can we expect little Ralphies?"

"Ha ha." Adam rubbed a hand over his face. "That damn bull is going to be the death of me. Candles better hope his neighbor doesn't sue. Most folks don't breed heifers until they're at least a year and a half."

"Ralphie is one of the friendliest bulls I've ever seen," Charlie replied. "But Candles knows better. He needs to get that fence electrified."

The front door groaned open and slammed against the frame. Sheriff Ethan McQueeney stepped inside and spotted the group in the corner.

He made his way over and slid into a chair. "Damn, it's cold out there. You'd think people would stay indoors, but no. Had a call about some guy's neighbor blowing leaves into his firewood stack. And another from a woman who thought someone was trespassing. Turned out it was her last year's Halloween decorations hanging from a tree."

That caused chuckles all around. Nic raised his bottle. "To Vermont. Where the weather's got mood swings worse than my ex."

Reed snorted. "Fifty degrees yesterday, frozen windshield this morning. I'm done guessing."

Ethan reached for a wing. "First heavy frost and people are going to start panic-buying salt like it's the end of the world."

"Wait until the first snow." Charlie leaned back in his chair. "Half the town forgets how brakes work."

Levi set a tray of beers and a big plate of nachos on the table. "Enjoy."

He wandered back toward the bar while the group dug in, the table filling with easy sounds of chewing, half-finished stories and good-natured ribbing between sheriffs and firefighters. It was the kind of noise that reminded Adam why he stayed in this town.

Someone yelled in the back room, followed by a thud. "You scratched the felt."

Ethan didn't even turn around. "Twenty says that's Weller and he's about to lose again."

"No bet," Adam said. "That man has never made a clean shot."

Reed raised his beer. "To long days and short tempers."

Everyone clinked bottles.

The jukebox switched tracks from a country ballad to something faster, racier. Adam leaned back in his chair and looked at his good friends, laughing and sharing stories. This was small-town life. Some people couldn't hack everyone knowing everything about you. And yeah, sometimes it was a bit much.

But looking around the table, surrounded by men who'd drop everything for him without needing to be asked, Adam knew one thing for sure—each and every one of them had his back.

EMILY TURNED onto the narrow gravel drive, tires crunching as she crept past the tree line. The oaks and maples had lost their leaves, and the bare branches looked like solemn sentinels standing guard.

Adam had called earlier, casually wondering if she might

stop by after drinks with the girls. Truth was, she was still keyed up, tired, stressed and had told him she wasn't sure. He mentioned he was meeting some friends at the Bottom-Up, but he'd be home by nine. He said it had been a long day.

Their relationship was still new, but Emily had a good feeling about the direction it was going. They hadn't slept together yet. They were still circling, checking each other out. But after all that happened today, she didn't want space or to be alone. She just wanted to be near him. Maybe have him hold her. Maybe kiss the bejesus out of her.

The modest A-frame came into view. Its weathered siding blended so well into the trees, it looked like it had grown there instead of being built. It was a sweet house, not what Emily had envisioned Adam owning. She'd been here before and loved the open concept, the mismatched furniture that was heavy on comfort. The small but efficient kitchen. It wasn't fancy. Just his. Quiet. Safe.

She pulled up, turned off the engine. Sat in the car for a moment. She hadn't called, so she hoped Adam wasn't in bed. It was only a little after nine.

He always parked his cruiser and truck in the garage, so she couldn't tell if he was home.

Taking a deep breath, she stepped out into the chilly air and made her way toward the screened-in porch that wrapped around the front. Wind chimes clinked softly in the breeze. She knew from previous visits that a battered canoe leaned against one side of the house, and on the other, a narrow trail cut through the brush toward a small, spring-fed pond that Adam liked to fish in.

She knocked on the door. Waited.

A light was on in the kitchen, but the house was still.

She stood there for a long minute, debating whether to knock again or leave.

Just as she was about to turn, the door opened.

Adam stood there in low-slung gray sweats, barefoot, bare-chested, and looking absolutely yummy. The light from the kitchen behind him gave him an almost ethereal glow.

She stared.

He stared back.

Then he reached for her, his voice low and rough around the edges.

"You came."

Three

Emily left Adam's house just after dawn, as the soft gray light cast long shadows across the quiet road. Her body was still warm from being curled against his. They'd started a movie that neither of them paid attention to.

At some point she'd fallen asleep in his arms, warm and safe, her cheek pressed against his chest.

She smiled to herself. They weren't sleeping together. Not yet. And it wasn't because she didn't want to. She did.

But Adam wasn't ready.

He told her once that if he didn't care about her, she'd already be in his bed.

But he did care. And that changed everything.

He wanted it to mean something.

So did she.

So for now, she'd take the closeness. The safety of his arms. His sweet kisses that left her breathless.

And she'd wait.

Because whatever was happening between them was worth getting right.

EMILY PULLED into the parking lot of the Harvest Moon Diner just as the scent of fresh-brewed coffee hit her through the vents.

The sweet smell of cinnamon and applewood bacon drifted through the door as she stepped inside. The place was already half full. It was a popular spot for farmers who had already milked the cows in the early morning, town workers and a few regulars chatting over coffee.

She spotted Savannah Jones and Jane Goodwin in a corner booth with two steaming mugs in front of them, a third waiting.

"You're late," Jane teased, nudging the mug toward her.

Emily slid into the booth. "I was detained by a very handsome and sexy deputy. Couldn't be helped," she said, wrapping her hands around the warm mug.

Savannah raised a brow. "Detained, huh. Do tell."

"It was very PG, thank you very much. We watched a movie, cuddled and fell asleep."

"Wow." Jane smirked. "You're way more disciplined than I am."

"Hmm," Emily murmured. "Not me. But Adam wants to wait. Says it should mean something."

"That's not the Adam I know," Jane said. "But I think you've got yourself a keeper."

Emily nodded. "I think so too."

Savannah caught her eye for a moment and smiled. Last fall's nightmare still lingered between them after Emily was forced to run for help alone, leaving Savannah behind in the hands of her kidnapper. It had been the only choice, one that saved them both.

Emily couldn't shake the guilt of leaving her behind. But

Savannah had never seen it that way. She'd called Emily brave. Said she owed her life to her.

A girls' retreat helped. It gave them space to breathe, to heal and to move forward. They didn't speak about that day anymore, not directly. But the bond it forged between them in those terrifying hours had never faded.

They sipped their coffee, ordered breakfast, and then caught up with their lives. Savannah, a famous watercolorist and a recent Beaver Creek resident, shared news about her latest art gallery exhibit featuring Moose, the enormous shelter puppy she adopted. He was part wrecking ball, part charm. The kind of dog who could knock you flat just to smother you in kisses. He was also the unexpected hero who attacked Savannah's kidnapper, giving Dylan McQueeney, the love of her life, the opening to rescue her.

Savannah paused to take a sip of coffee, then added casually, "Oh, Dylan and I are living together now."

Emily's brow lifted. "That's quite an aside and honestly not unexpected. Congratulations!"

Jane, a best-selling author, lived outside town on a farm. She gave them an update on the newest addition to her menagerie and the plot twists she threaded into her latest manuscript. She wrote crime fiction with very thinly veiled versions of her husband, Ethan McQueeney, and Adam as heroes who save the day. Ethan, who happened to be the town sheriff and her first beta reader, was equal parts appalled and secretly proud.

The conversation drifted into talk about the upcoming winter festival, and both offered to help Emily finish the holiday baskets she was putting together for the women's shelter fundraiser.

By the time they had finished breakfast and their second cup, Emily felt lighter. It reminded her that was one reason she moved to a small town. Close friends, people who had her back, the comfort of knowing she wasn't alone.

But it wasn't the whole truth. She'd needed to get out of Boston, away from the whispers and the things she'd witnessed at the spa that kept her awake at night. She never understood how it happened. She'd only asked about missing consent forms, unusual booking blocks—the little things Shay had whispered about before she left. And somehow those questions ended up in the hands of someone Emily had never met. After that, the atmosphere turned icy, and she knew it was time to leave.

Sometimes, in the quiet moments, she missed her old life and the way music used to settle her. She still had a box of old notebooks upstairs with half-written lyrics, scraps of who she used to be. She didn't let herself open it anymore. Not when it hurt that much.

Then Shay vanished. She'd always been restless, drifting between jobs, sometimes disappearing for days when life got too hard. And then there was the email, saying she needed space and was chasing the next adventure, which sounded like her and yet ... not quite. Emily tried to believe it. Tried to believe her friend had simply given in to her wanderlust. But the silence that followed left a hollow she didn't know how to fill. Emily didn't talk about that part. Not yet. Maybe not ever.

But here, surrounded by people who made her feel like she belonged, it almost felt like the broken pieces of her life were finally beginning to fit back together again.

BY THE TIME she made it to Serenity Spa, the sun had climbed higher in the sky and the air had warmed.

She parked out back, stretched the morning out of her

shoulders and stepped inside. The familiar scent of eucalyptus and lavender wrapped around her like a warm hug.

Flipping the sign to open, she double-checked the treatment schedule. Busy as usual.

She was in her office going over paperwork when Morgan arrived, smoothie in hand and full of energy.

The day moved in a steady rhythm of massages, laundry and the usual flow of yoga clients.

Just after six, Celeste arrived, right on time.

"Evening," she said, hanging her coat on the hook. She had on a pair of slacks, a long-sleeved top and sturdy walking shoes.

"Hey, come on back," Emily said, motioning her down the hall. "Do you want a cup of coffee before we begin?"

Celeste shook her head. "No. I'm fine."

"Okay, then."

Emily spent an hour giving her a crash course in spa upkeep, sanitizing towels, her preferred way of folding towels, and which oils to use in which diffusers.

Celeste listened quietly, nodding occasionally.

"This must seem like Spa Maintenance 101," Emily said with a small laugh. "But I have a particular way I like to do things."

Celeste shrugged. "It's no more difficult to do things the way you want than not."

She peeked into the linen closet and then shut the door slowly. "So ... will anyone be here while I clean?"

"During the day, of course. But at this time of the year, it's slow, so by six, we're all ready to go home. I have a key for you in the office. It shouldn't take too long to do; everyone is pretty neat."

Emily smiled, but it was an odd question unless Celeste forgot she told her everyone left at six during the week.

"Not a problem." Celeste's smile didn't quite reach her eyes.

Emily led her back to her office and unlocked the bottom drawer of her desk. There was a small box labeled "extra keys."

She fished out two small brass keys and held them out.

"One is for the side door that the staff usually uses. Just make sure it's locked when you leave, and be careful. We don't have a security system, and there aren't any cameras." Emily shrugged. "I've looked into it, but between insurance hikes and renovations, it hasn't been in the budget. The other key is for the supply closet. You and I are the only ones who have access to that."

Celeste reached out and took the keys. "Understood."

"Great. There's a checklist in the supply closet. If we are running low on supplies, let me know."

"I will." Celeste slipped the keys into her coat pocket. "Thank you again for the opportunity."

Emily nodded. "Welcome aboard."

Celeste turned and headed down the hallway, then stopped and looked back. "One more thing—would you mind paying me by check or cash for the time being? I haven't switched over my bank yet, and direct deposit's a hassle until I do."

Emily blinked, then shrugged. She'd had contractors who preferred checks before. "That's fine. I'll just note it in the ledger until we get the paperwork sorted."

"I appreciate it," she said as she walked out the door.

The spa still smelled like lavender and eucalyptus, but Emily felt unsettled. She stood in her office staring out the dim hallway long after Celeste left.

Celeste had said all the right things. She seemed capable. Professional. On paper, she was exactly what Emily needed.

But something didn't sit right.

It was nothing obvious, just a flicker of a thought she

hadn't been able to shake since they first spoke. Not enough to call it a red flag—more like a missing puzzle piece she couldn't find.

It started during their first conversation, a thought easy to brush aside at the time. *What if she's not really here for the job? What if she were a spy?*

The more Emily thought about it, the more it bothered her. Aspire Wellness had already poached three of her staff members, dangling sign-on bonuses like candy. And now this woman, out of the blue with out-of-state-references, just shows up, ready to start immediately.

Emily hated doubting people. She wanted to believe people were who they said they were.

But trust was harder these days.

She turned back to the desk and shook her head. *You're being paranoid.*

Still ... the questions lingered.

Four

By Wednesday evening, Emily had talked herself out of the weird feeling.

Celeste had shown up on time and gone straight to work folding laundry and wiping down the mats and massage tables.

Still, she had checked on Celeste twice before climbing the back stairs to the converted apartment she lived in. It wasn't much. Just a one-bedroom flat tucked into the eaves. She'd painted the walls soft green and pale gray, colors that made her feel calm even on days she didn't.

The kitchen was little more than a nook, compact but efficient, every surface within arm's reach. It had a farmhouse sink, an equally old refrigerator and an electric oven that wouldn't hold a small turkey. The living room had mismatched furniture she had collected over the years: a couple of secondhand chairs, a slip-covered couch, a coffee table and a TV. She added lavender candles, throw pillows and prints of the Boston skyline. A quiet reminder of where she'd been and why she wasn't going back.

Her small bedroom contained a queen-size bed, a side

table, and a narrow dresser with a deep closet tucked along one wall. An arched window looked out over the trees. In the fall, the leaves turned flaming red, gold and orange, although right now they were bare-limbed. Through the trees, she could see the twinkle of the town lights below.

It was mostly peaceful. Other times, too quiet.

But for now, it was home. She was grateful she had it even if she never quite stopped listening for the next shoe to drop.

IT WAS BARELY DUSK by the time Emily left to drive to Jane's house, an 1850s farmhouse about eight miles outside town that she shared with Ethan.

She followed Mills River Road to Old Mill, passing Tanner McQueeney and Leah Farley's farm on the right. It was early evening, and the lights glowed in the cow barn, though she knew Tanner milked at three thirty in the afternoon and again twelve hours later. She wondered how he did it. Just the thought of getting up in the middle of the night to milk cows had no appeal for her.

She passed Jane's pond, the same one where they'd found the body of David Thornton not long after Jane moved in. The water shimmered like glass, catching the last of the day's light. Peaceful now, despite the mystery it had once kept.

Then the old farmhouse came into view, picture-perfect with its white clapboards, big red barn standing proud and greenhouse tucked neatly beside it. She pulled into the long driveway, gravel crunching under her tires, passing curious sheep grazing in the fading light and the chicken coop quiet at the edge of the pasture. Jane had recently added a Morgan horse to pull the sleigh she'd bought and also acquired a potbellied pig named Chloe, who had a knack for escaping her pen. She was canning up a storm and making her own bread. For a city girl, Jane was sure embracing country life as well as investigating the secrets of a small town.

Emily parked her car next to Savannah's and stepped out. She took a deep breath and inhaled the brisk night air that carried the faint scent of woodsmoke and something earthy from the fields. She gave a little shiver, reached for the cheese board she had made earlier and walked up to the front door.

Before she could answer, it swung open.

Savannah stood there grinning, eyes landing on the board in Emily's hands. "You brought cheese! I love you."

"You'd love me even if I didn't bring cheese."

"True," she said with a laugh. "Come in. Lily and Leah beat you here, and Jane's expecting Claire and Olivia any minute."

Emily stepped into the house. A fire snapped and crackled in the fireplace, giving everything a soft glow. She set the appetizer on the coffee table and stepped back to admire it. Cheddar cheese from a local creamery, blue cheese from the next town over, goat cheese from Goats R Us, some fig and cranberry nut jam, and assorted salami. It was her first cheese board, and she was really pleased with the way it came together.

Then she caught the scent of basil and fresh mint as she followed Savannah through the cozy space.

Laughter spilled in from the kitchen.

Jane stood at the counter making mojitos in a blender. Her brown hair was pulled into a ponytail, her cheeks flushed from laughing. When she spotted Emily, she cut the motor.

"Hugs first," Jane ordered, wiping her hand on a towel, hugging her and then handing Emily a drink. "So glad you could get away from Adam for the night."

"Adam?" Lily lifted a brow over warm brown eyes, her sun-kissed skin now softened to a pale gold under the late fall light. She'd traded her usual jeans for a long, earth-tone skirt that swayed around her boots as she moved. A grin tugged at her lips. "Ohhh, that's a story I haven't heard."

"And you won't either," Emily huffed. "There's nothing going on."

"Not what I hear," Jane teased. "Has he handcuffed you yet?"

Emily snorted. "Nothing of the sort is going on, and I don't want to hear the sordid details of your and Ethan's love life either."

Just then the front door opened, letting in a gust of cold air.

Claire Martinez, forty-five with dark hair streaked in silver, stepped inside, clutching two wine bottles to her chest and a bag in the other. From the bag, the curve of a hand-thrown ceramic bowl peeked out. She shivered. "Sorry I'm late. Had to talk down a panicked artist who thinks her entire career hinges on getting better wall space." She handed the bottles to Savannah.

"We're all divas," quipped Savannah, winking as she set the bottles on the counter.

Savannah reached for the bag and pulled out a ceramic bowl, tilting it so the light caught the glaze, a swirl of deep blue and mossy green. Inside, it was already filled with a salad.

"Fresh from the kiln this morning," Claire said with a hint of pride in her voice.

"It's beautiful. And you made farro salad." Savannah peered into it. "I see dried cranberries, crumbles of feta and arugula. Oh yeah, I smell bread from Crumb & Co."

"Yummy!" exclaimed Lily. "What was Vanessa offering this time?"

Vanessa Crumb was their go-to baker.

"Oh, rosemary focaccia and savory pumpkin muffins with cheddar and chives," replied Claire as she pulled off her scarf and hat, letting her dark curls free. She pulled a paper-wrapped loaf and a bakery box from the large bag, the warm herby scent of bread filling the space.

"Are we still waiting for Olivia?"

"Right behind you," said a voice from behind her. Olivia Metcalfe scurried into the kitchen. At thirty-five, the journalist had the sharp, alert gaze of someone half chasing the next lead, half in the moment. Her auburn hair was wind-tossed; a well-worn leather crossbody bag bumped against her hip as she moved. "Sorry I'm late," she said breathlessly. "Breaking news. You know how it is."

"Well, the *Beaver Creek News* is lucky to have a dedicated journalist like yourself," said Lily.

Olivia grinned. "So true!"

She placed a container of date bars she was famous for on the kitchen counter, hung her coat and draped the strap of her bag over the back of a chair.

Jane glanced up from slicing limes. "Anything juicy I should know about?"

Olivia's smile was quick and sly. "Always."

Jane laughed, shaking her head as she poured another splash of rum into the blender. "Claire, Olivia, help yourselves to a mojito, and let's all go into the living room."

They gathered around the crackling fire. Emily chose to sit on one of the off-white love seats in front of a square wooden coffee table. The room was pleasant, with wooden ceiling beams and built-in bookcases around the fireplace that featured a selection of books as well as a watercolor of the farm, most likely painted by Savannah.

A few minutes later, they were all finally sitting in the living room. "Now that we're all here, a toast," Jane began, lifting her mojito. "To good friends and even better drinks."

"Hear! Hear!" They all clinked glasses and then got down

to bringing everyone up on what was going on in their lives and demolishing the cheese board.

An hour later, Emily's stomach rumbled just as Jane stood and announced they should eat.

The buffet on the island looked inviting. "Leah made the butternut squash mac and cheese. Lily brought garlic-roasted baby potatoes and rainbow carrots from her garden. I made the pork sliders," Jane said, bringing plates to the island. "And we have Claire's harvest grain salad and assorted breads." She looked around. "Oh, Olivia's date bars, plus I made mini pecan tarts."

"There's enough food here for twenty more people," said Olivia.

Jane laughed. "Well, Ethan and Tanner will eat all the left-overs, for sure."

They filled their plates and carried their wineglasses back to the living room to enjoy the fire.

Emily was just bringing a potato to her mouth when Olivia leaned forward.

"So," she said lightly, "any of you checked out Aspire Day Spa yet?"

Claire wrinkled her nose. "That's in the next town over, right?"

"Yeah," Olivia replied. "They've been running those splashy ads in the *Beaver Creek News*. You know the type. Give us ninety minutes and we'll transform your life."

Jane shook her head. "Why would we want to go there when we have the best spa right here in Beaver Creek?" She raised her glass. "To Serenity Spa."

They all cheered.

"Taryn Keene owns it. She's a former consultant, influencer and now wellness entrepreneur," Emily said.

Olivia raised a brow. "Sounds like you've done your homework."

Emily huffed. "I should know. She's poached several of my people. A yoga instructor and two massage therapists. Oh, and my cleaning woman."

"Crap." Jane shook her head. "I'm sorry you're going through that. All the more reason to boycott her place."

"That's sweet but not necessary," Emily replied. Then she thought about it. "Forget I said that. I'm too nice. I hope all her clients get rashes and their eyebrows are waxed crooked."

The girls started laughing and couldn't stop. After a minute, Savannah said, "That's the spirit. Maybe we should go over there in the middle of the night and put a few frogs and glitter bombs in her hydrotherapy tubs."

"Ha." Emily took a sip of wine. "The good news is I've hired a cleaning person to come in from eleven to seven. At least I don't have to do that in addition to everything else."

"Wow! That's great," Savannah said. "How did you find her?"

"Funny thing is, she found me. She showed up on time, didn't bring her emotional support hamster. So it's a win-win."

"What's her name?" Olivia asked too casually, or maybe she was imagining that slight pause. "Maybe I've met her around town."

"Celeste Miller," Emily replied, placing her glass on the table. "She's new to the area, has moved around a bit, has experience and so far is a good worker."

Olivia gave an easy nod. "Gotcha. Hopefully she sticks. Turnover's been crazy everywhere lately."

"Tell me about it," Leah muttered. "We had a server quit because she didn't like the way our aprons fit. Said they were too restrictive."

That earned a round of groans, and then the conversation veered toward flaky hires and funny customer service disasters.

But as the evening wore down, dessert was consumed and

dishes were done and put away, Emily caught herself thinking about the spa.

She wasn't sure why. Nothing felt wrong. Still, saying Celeste's name out loud had stirred something she couldn't define.

BY THE TIME Emily pulled into the lot behind the spa, the moon was hidden behind a dark cloud and the street was quiet.

Her headlights cut across the back door, and she sat for a moment, still high from the friendship and laughter of the night.

She grabbed the wooden cheese board, closed the car door and headed up the side stairs to her apartment.

Halfway up, she paused.

A light was on downstairs.

Not the front porch light or the reception area lamp she sometimes left on after closing, but the hallway.

The one that ran past the laundry room toward the back treatment rooms.

She frowned and looked at her watch. Almost eleven.

Celeste mentioned wanting to finish restocking the towels and a few other tasks she was behind on. Maybe she forgot to turn the light off.

Emily hesitated at the top step and sighed. She didn't want to come off as picky, but with all that was going on, she didn't need a higher electric bill.

She let herself into her apartment, set the board on the counter and headed back down.

The spa smelled of lavender and eucalyptus, scents that were familiar and comforting. The stillness didn't bother her.

She walked down the hall toward the light at the far end.

"Celeste?" she called out. No answer.

The laundry room door was open, the folding table clear. Towels were stacked neatly on the shelf. Nothing out of place. The treatment room at the end of the hall was cracked open.

Emily paused.

That door was supposed to be closed. She was surprised because Celeste, who seemed borderline obsessive, would have double-checked.

She entered the space. Everything looked normal. The table was freshly made. A folded cardigan was on a stool next to a half-finished bottle of sparkling water.

Celeste must have been here recently. She flicked off the overhead light.

Back in the hallway, she moved to retrace her steps toward the stairs and stopped cold.

Her office door was open just a crack.

She stared at it, her heart beating a little faster. It was probably nothing, but still. She never left her office door open after she left for the day. And she distinctly remembered checking it before she left earlier.

Emily stepped closer. The lock wasn't broken. No sign of damage.

She nudged it farther.

Her office was tidy. Desk untouched. Her laptop was closed. The filing cabinet drawers shut. But one desk drawer was open half an inch. Barely noticeable unless you were looking for it. Inside there were only sticky notes, paper clips and a couple of pens. Nothing worth touching. But Emily was certain she'd closed it before leaving.

A faint draft blew past her. She glanced toward the window. It was locked tight. The hair on the back of her neck prickled.

She couldn't put her finger on it, just a creepy feeling that someone had been in her space.

Her throat tightened as she closed the drawer. Locked the door. Stood there for a minute, listening.

Nothing.

Maybe Celeste had come in to grab a cleaning checklist or check the linen order. Maybe she'd been distracted before leaving. She wanted to believe that.

Either way, as she climbed the stairs to her apartment, she couldn't shake the feeling that something was amiss.

And for the first time since she'd moved upstairs, she locked the deadbolt behind her.

Five

Late Thursday morning, the bell over the door to the spa jingled, drawing Emily's attention from the appointment schedule.

The woman who stepped inside was dressed casually in slacks, ankle boots, and a soft jacket in a muted plum color. She looked to be in her early thirties, with chestnut hair tucked behind one ear and a leather tote slung over her shoulder. A slim notepad peeked from the bag's side pocket, the sort that people often used to jot down concerns or questions.

She offered a small smile as she approached the desk.

"Hi there," she said. "I was walking through town and saw your sign. I could seriously use a massage. Any chance you have an opening today?"

Emily scanned the screen. "Actually, yes. We just had a last-minute cancellation for eleven. It's just a thirty-minute slot, but if that works ..."

The woman's smile was quick, almost relieved. "Perfect."

Emily clicked through to the booking form. "And your name?"

"Jennifer," the woman replied.

"Great." Emily tapped in the name. "Morgan will take you back in a few minutes. You can fill out this form while you wait. Then I'll be in."

Jennifer took the clipboard and settled in the small waiting room, legs crossed, glancing around the room. She smiled slightly.

Emily knew exactly what she was experiencing. The fountain bubbling softly in the corner, the low hum of instrumental music overhead, hints of lavender and eucalyptus lingering in the air. On a small round table, a pitcher of cucumber water was surrounded by a neat stack of paper cups. Green plants filled the corners, and the chairs were deep and inviting.

She'd always judged other spas by their reception areas. Were they formal and stiff? Or thrown together with bargain-store finds? She wanted something different. A place clients would find inviting but polished. A place that felt calm the second you stepped inside.

A few minutes later, Emily walked into the massage room. The diffuser was already scenting the air. Jennifer was face down on the table, with her hair tucked to one side and a sheet covering her back.

"Do you have any knots or special areas you want addressed?" she asked.

"Always the shoulders," Jennifer's muffled voice replied.

Emily smiled. "Isn't that the truth?" She squirted oil onto her hands and rubbed them together to warm it. Then she started to work the tension from Jennifer's upper back.

"Have you been here a while?" Jennifer murmured. "Spa looks so fresh. Did you remodel?"

Emily chuckled softly. "Oh, lordy, yes. The place was in disarray when I bought it, but the bones were solid, and the apartment was already in place. I did the usual—paint, fixtures and a few other minor changes."

"I can see that. Mmm ... that feels good."

Emily continued down Jennifer's shoulder blades, loosening stubborn knots.

"Were you always a massage therapist and yoga instructor?"

"I was a massage therapist first, then got into yoga," Emily replied.

"Did you start here in Beaver Creek?"

"No, I was in Boston."

Jennifer lifted her head slightly. "That's quite a change from a big city to a small town. Do you have any competition?"

Emily blinked. Wow. This woman was quite chatty. Most of her clients just wanted to lie there and concentrate on the massage.

"Not in town. There are other spas around, of course."

"I heard there's a new spa next town over offering bonuses. Are you losing staff?"

Emily bit back a sigh. This was too much like a business interview.

Before she could answer, Jennifer let out a sudden *oof*.

Emily pulled her hands back. "I'm sorry, was that too much pressure?"

"No." Jennifer laughed lightly. "Just tight muscles. You're good."

Emily forced a smile, but the woman was just too nosy. Was Jennifer simply curious, or was there a reason for the questions?

Emily finished the massage in silence, telling Jennifer that when she was ready, Morgan would check her out. She stepped into the hall and walked toward the reception area, pausing near the side counter to jot a note.

At the front desk, Morgan met Jennifer with a smile. "Everything okay?"

"Oh, it was amazing," she replied, pulling her jacket on. "Can I make an appointment for Saturday?"

Morgan looked at the schedule. "You're in luck. Emily has an opening at four. Is that okay?"

"Yes, that's perfect."

As Jennifer headed for the door, Emily caught movement out of the corner of her eye. Celeste stood near the corner, frozen mid-step, holding a bucket of cleaning supplies.

Her eyes locked on Jennifer as she walked out the front door.

For a second, Celeste looked like she'd seen a ghost.

Then, just as quickly, she turned and disappeared down the hallway without a word.

Emily frowned. *What the heck was that all about?* Did Celeste know her? Or think she did?

She turned to Morgan. "That was weird, right?"

Morgan looked up from the appointment book. "What?"

"Celeste. She stared at Jennifer as if she had come back from the dead."

Morgan shrugged. "Maybe she just spaced out."

Emily didn't buy it but let it go for now.

She leaned against the counter and lowered her voice. "Jennifer's giving me a weird vibe. Asking all sorts of questions about me, the spa, where I used to work. Just unusual questions for a client."

Morgan blinked. "You think she's undercover or working for ..." She lowered her voice. "Aspire Day Spa? A spy?"

Emily laughed. "She could be anything. It just felt ... off."

She didn't say it out loud, but her stomach was starting to twist again. And even though Celeste had walked away, Emily couldn't help wondering if she had heard any of that.

EMILY LINGERED behind the desk pretending to double-check the schedule, but her eyes kept drifting down the hallway.

Celeste's reaction hadn't been just surprise. Or fear. Emily was sure she recognized Jennifer.

A few minutes later, Celeste returned, her cleaning bucket empty. She set it behind the front counter without a word.

Emily closed the appointment book and gave a small smile. "Hey. You okay?"

Celeste blinked. "Of course. Why?"

"You looked startled earlier. When that client left."

Celeste paused. "Oh. I thought she looked familiar, that's all."

Emily tilted her head. "From where?"

"I don't know. Maybe she reminded me of someone. I've moved around a lot." Celeste gave a quick shrug and turned to grab the cleaning spray from the shelf below. Her fingers fumbled with the nozzle before she got a grip. "I'm sure I'm mistaken."

Emily studied her, trying to read between the lines. Celeste's face was calm, too calm, and gave nothing up.

"Did she say something to you that bothered you?"

"No." Celeste gave her a tight smile. "She has one of those faces."

Emily nodded slowly. "Could be."

But the way Celeste had gone still—the way she stared at Jennifer—didn't feel like a simple case of mistaken identity.

Emily tapped her fingers against the counter, watching Celeste move through her cleaning routine like nothing had happened.

She didn't know what Jennifer was really doing here. Maybe it was nothing. She didn't know why Celeste looked like she'd seen a ghost.

But the truth was, her gut didn't buy it.

And lately, her gut had been right more times than not.

Six

On Saturday, the spa was humming. Emily barely had time to wolf down a protein bar between appointments. Being down two massage therapists and a yoga instructor hurt. She was crossing her fingers that the ads she placed would garner attention and draw in some qualified applicants.

She couldn't keep working long hours, skipping meals and pretending she wasn't bone-tired. If something didn't give soon, she'd burn out, and that wasn't going to help anyone.

She had only one appointment left. Her last massage was with that woman Jennifer. Emily still wasn't sure what to make of her. She was pleasant enough but asked way too many questions.

And after that, dinner with Deputy McDreamy. Then maybe some kissing—hopefully more. She was ready to take their relationship to the next step, but she didn't want to force Adam into something he wasn't ready for.

He was a good man. And she wanted him, but she didn't want to ruin the best thing she'd had in years by rushing it.

At quarter to four, Jennifer checked in. Morgan brought

her back to the massage room and quietly shut the door behind her.

Emily stepped in a few minutes later. "What would you like tonight? Soft or deeper pressure? Any areas I should concentrate on?"

"A combination would be perfect," Jennifer replied, settling on the table. "Mostly shoulders. It's been a taxing week."

She nodded, pulled down the sheet to expose Jennifer's back. Then she warmed oil in her hands, the faint scent of lavender from the corner diffuser mixing with the eucalyptus in the lotion, and began long, practiced strokes across the woman's upper shoulders.

She hoped Jennifer was all out of questions after their last session and would just relax and enjoy.

No such luck.

"I really like the vibe here," Jennifer mumbled. "It feels kind of boutique-y, like the places you'd find in larger cities."

And there it was. Twenty questions, round two.

"That's what I was aiming for," Emily replied. Even though she didn't want to engage, this was a client, someone she couldn't afford to offend.

"You ever think about expanding your services?" Jennifer asked lightly. "Offering Botox? Fillers? Micro-needling?"

Emily's hands hesitated for a moment. "No. We're more focused on massage, skin care, yoga. Wellness, not injections."

"Humph." Jennifer was quiet for a moment. "Makes sense. I just remember an upscale spa I went to once that offered all kinds of extra cosmetic procedures. Surprised me at the time."

Emily kept her voice even. "Those procedures are heavily regulated. You need the right licensure, medical supervision. It's not something you just casually add to the menu."

Her stomach tightened. The last time someone tried that,

it hadn't ended well. She'd only heard the whispers, the stories her roommate Shay told her before she vanished. Botched procedures. Hushed payouts. Clients who never came back. Shay had been asking questions, the kind that made people nervous. *"If you only knew what really went on there, you'd run and never look back,"* she'd warned. The memory was enough to make her blood run cold.

"Are there places around here that offer them?"

Oh. My. God. This woman was driving Emily crazy.

"Not that I know of," Emily said, smoothing her hands down Jennifer's arm. "If you're looking, you can check with a dermatologist or plastic surgeon's office. Some of them have med spa divisions."

Jennifer chuckled into the face cradle. "Nah. With my luck, I'd probably get someone who failed injections 101 and end up looking like a trout."

Her laugh was muffled by the cushion, but there was something in the way her shoulders shifted, like she was pleased with the answer, that made Emily's fingers still for a moment before she forced herself to keep working.

Emily let out a small laugh, hoping that would be the end of it.

But Jennifer continued. "I read this article a while back about a spa in Boston that was closed down after a couple of women died. Unlicensed staff doing injections in back rooms. Did you ever read about that?"

Emily's breath caught. For a heartbeat, the room seemed to tilt. She forced herself to keep moving. Her fingers pressed just a little harder into the tight muscles of Jennifer's shoulder before she eased up.

This was hitting too close to home.

"No," she said lightly. "I don't read much of the news these days. Hardly have time, plus it's too depressing."

"Guess that's smart," Jennifer said into the face cradle, her voice muffled.

Emily didn't respond. Her hands kept moving, but inside, her pulse picked up. What was Jennifer really after? Most clients didn't reference spa scandals unless they were fishing. And Emily wasn't getting caught in that net.

She didn't know if Jennifer was just talkative. Or digging for something.

Either way, she didn't like it.

When Jennifer finally left, the quiet felt heavier than it had. Emily cleaned the room, more to steady herself than anything else, before shutting off the lights.

Emily grabbed her coat and bag. The spa would close in less than ten minutes. She passed Morgan on her way out. "Thanks again for today," Emily said. "Lock up?"

"Got it. Oh, Celeste had to leave early. Around four. I saw her head out with her purse. She said she'd be in early Monday to make up for the time," Morgan replied with a smile. "Have fun tonight."

THE SUN HAD DIPPED LOW in the sky by the time Emily drove out of town, passing the Callahan B&B and turning onto the winding back road to the Log & Lantern Tavern.

The light was on in Ivy's addition, and Emily wondered if she was prepping for a party or just testing recipes, something Ivy confessed to doing in her spare time. Ivy Callahan ran Savory Seasons, the town's go-to catering business, along with the B&B.

The sky was awash in lavender and peach, colors she used to find comforting—used to. Now they reminded her how quickly peace could turn fragile.

She gripped the steering wheel tighter as Jennifer's voice echoed in her mind.

"You ever think about expanding your services? ... Offering Botox? Fillers?"

Emily's stomach clenched. Not from guilt, exactly, but from memory.

She hadn't lied to Jennifer. She had kept to herself, focusing on massages and yoga. But she'd seen things, heard whispers. Locked treatment rooms. Late appointments that didn't show up on the books. And Shay's voice warning her about what went on behind closed doors.

Emily blinked hard and forced herself to think about something lighter. Ivy in her kitchen stirring a pot just because she could. It was comforting—creating something warm and beautiful for no other reason than joy, unlike her own past.

That was behind her. Beaver Creek was her fresh start. Her second chance.

And tonight? Tonight was dinner with Adam and whatever followed.

An old tune played on the radio, one she used to sing on stage, and her throat tightened. She reached to turn it down before the memories could find her.

She let out a slow breath and pulled onto the gravel road to the Log & Lantern. The parking lot was full, and the windows glowed with warm light. She stepped out, locked the door and headed for the entrance. The faint sound of a guitar drifted across the parking lot.

Emily hadn't been here since that night almost a year ago when the group of friends ate at the Notch—a secret speakeasy in the basement that almost everyone knew about. She'd stood at the mic singing a song with the Ellis Graham Quartet that she'd written so many moons ago. But that was then. There was no way she was singing tonight.

She stepped inside, and the warmth of the room wrapped

around her. It smelled of cedar and woodsmoke and something sweet from the kitchen. Adam was already in a booth in the corner and stood when he saw her. He gave her a chaste kiss on the cheek. "I just got here and grabbed the last booth," he said.

"Good. I love sitting here." Emily looked around the rustic interior. They hadn't spent much time here upstairs; usually they had gone to the Notch, in the basement.

She took in the hand-carved wooden bar and massive fireplace. Its original structure was built for the loggers who worked the forests surrounding Beaver Creek and sent the logs down the Callahan River. Loggers no longer cut trees, but the walls were covered with vintage tools and black-and-white photographs of river drives. It was the kind of place built on stories, old and new.

A server brought menus and water. "I'll be back in a minute," she said.

Adam scanned the menu. "What do you think you're ordering?"

"Hmm." Emily glanced at the menu. "It's chilly out, so I'm going to have their famous Lumberjack Stew. And a Lantern Ale to go with it. How about you?"

"Everything sounds good," he said, setting the menu down. "But I'm in the mood for the smoked brisket sandwich with sweet potato fries and a Lantern Ale, too."

The server came back, took their orders and returned a few minutes later with their beer, frosty and amber in the firelight.

"How was work?" he asked.

Emily thought about Jennifer's probing questions, but she wasn't ready to go there. Not yet. "You know, same ol', same ol'. Women get naked. I rub their shoulders. They leave happy."

Adam choked on a laugh. "Sounds like my dream job."

"Yeah?" Emily smirked. "I'd pay good money to see you keep a straight face."

Their food arrived, and Adam offered Emily a bite of his sandwich and some fries.

"Mmm. You can taste the stout." She made a production of licking her lips slowly as she caught him watching her mouth.

His blue eyes darkened just a shade. "Careful, Em."

"Oh, we're playing dangerous now?" she teased, then scooped up a spoonful of stew and offered it to him. "Your turn."

He leaned in, took a bite and then made a big show of slowly sucking on the spoon as he pulled back.

Emily burst out laughing. "You are such a tease."

"Takes one to know one," he quipped.

This was what she wanted. A relationship that felt easy. One where they could tease each other and laugh. And one that promised something deeper waiting on the other side of dessert.

They talked and laughed, shared an apple cobbler with Calvados, lingering over every bite. It was the kind of night she wanted to keep in her memory forever.

When the check came, he beat her to it.

As they stepped out into the cool mountain air, he reached for her hand.

"Come home with me," he said softly, his eyes turning dark and filled with want and something deeper she didn't dare name.

She told herself not to overthink it. Not tonight. Some chances were worth the risk.

Seven

Emily followed Adam's truck down the narrow gravel drive. The moon was full and cast a silvery light through the bare trees, illuminating the otherwise dark path. The stillness of the night made every sound sharper —the crunch of the gravel, the faint hum of his engine— heightening the anticipation curling low in her belly. Just as the woods opened up, his sweet A-frame came into view.

He parked, and she pulled in next to him.

By the time she opened her door, he was standing there. When she stepped out, he pulled her into a hug that made her knees weak. Then he leaned in, kissed her cheeks, her nose and finally her lips with just a brush of his tongue before he deepened the kiss.

He tasted of beer and cinnamon gum. His mouth was hot against hers. His tongue swept past her lips in a way that left her breathless and wanting more. Then he slowly broke the kiss. Emily felt the loss of his warmth. Her heart thudded so loudly, she was sure he could hear it.

"I've been waiting all night to do that," he murmured.

“Mmm.” She licked her lips, still dazed. “That was worth the wait.”

He smirked.

They walked hand in hand into the open-concept living room, where the faint smell of woodsmoke from the fireplace still lingered.

He took her jacket and hung it on a hook, then shrugged off his own.

“Drink?” he asked, turning toward the small kitchen as he flicked on soft jazz.

“White wine, if you have it.”

He gave her a wink. “Be right back.”

She sat on the oversize sofa, kicked off her shoes and tucked her legs under her. The whole space felt like Adam—comfortable, masculine and welcoming. A place that felt safe without trying too hard.

Adam returned and handed her a glass of wine. He had a bottle of beer in his other hand.

“To fresh starts,” he said softly.

She lifted her glass and clinked his bottle. “To slow kisses and everything that they lead to.”

He gave her a slow grin.

They sat close together in silence, listening to the music. Adam put his beer on the wooden coffee table and turned toward her, one knee brushing against hers.

“Em, I’ve been doing a lot of thinking.” His voice was low. “I know you don’t want to rush things, but I would love to take our relationship to the next level.” He let out a slow breath. “Wh-what do you think?”

Emily didn’t answer right away. Instead, she set her wineglass down on the table and turned to face him. Her heart was pounding. YES! *Yes and yes,* she wanted to scream, because this was a milestone for him, but she didn’t want to point it out, make it uncomfortable. But she wanted it for herself too. She was ready to let someone in.

"Adam," she said softly. "I've never been more ready."

He gave a faint smile as his eyes searched hers, as if he needed to be absolutely certain.

She leaned in and brushed her lips lightly over his just once. "I want this. I want you. No more waiting."

That was all it took.

He cupped her jaw, and his lips found hers. Exploring. Teasing. Asking.

She leaned in and gave him everything he was asking for.

The kiss deepened. Hands wandered. She felt his fingers slip under the hem of her sweater, move higher until he gently pulled her bra down. She immediately felt a chill, then he stopped kissing her and pulled her sweater up over her head.

Her breasts were exposed, the nipples tight and dusky pink. He licked his lips and cocked his head.

She nodded.

Then his lips were on one nipple. Sucking. Gently biting.

His hands encircled her back and released her bra. He pulled her onto his lap. She watched him suckle one breast while working the other with his hand.

Finally, he pulled away. "Beautiful breasts," he whispered. "But I want to see all of you."

Emily could only nod.

He gently lifted her off his lap and then offered her his hand. He led her up the stairs to his bedroom. Her pulse quickened with every step. Not from nerves—no sirree. But from knowing there was no going back after this. She had no time to look around before he followed her down onto the bed, kissing her.

When they pulled apart, he stood, unbuckling her pants and pulling them and her underwear off in one swoop. Then he just stared.

"Beautiful," he said. "Sweetheart, scooch over and spread your legs."

Emily did as he asked. She watched him take off his shirt, pants and boxers. She watched him crawl onto the bed and position himself between her legs. She watched his head bob as he sucked her clit and licked her pussy. His hands were busy rubbing her breasts, rubbing her legs.

The sensation was too much. She wanted to tell him to stop so she could reciprocate. She wanted to ...

Scream his name. The orgasm took over her body. She writhed against him, but he never stopped licking and sucking.

When she finally came back to earth, Adam was beside her, grinning like a Cheshire cat. "Beautiful."

"You beast!" she said teasingly. "I wanted to touch you, make you feel good too."

"Oh, you will, sweetheart, just not yet." He chuckled. "I still have more work to do, and then I'm going to make love to you until you come again."

IT WAS hours later and pitch-black when Adam took her again. And then again, early morning when the stars were in their last twinkle. And yet again when the sun was shining brightly through the bedroom window.

"Oh my God," she moaned into the pillow after the last time.

"Just Adam to you, sweetheart," he teased, then he climbed out of bed and smacked her bare rear. "Up you go, lazybones. Take a shower, and I'll start the coffee."

Emily missed his warmth the second he left the bed, but her stomach growled. She got up and showered, slipped on her panties and pants, then realized her bra and sweater were still downstairs. She rifled through his drawer, found a soft worn T-shirt that smelled like him, and put it on.

When she padded into the kitchen, he was standing by the counter in just his jeans—bare chest, bare feet, hair tousled from sleep. Good Lord, Emily thought, there couldn't be a sexier sight. It hit her then how easy it would be to picture mornings like this every day.

"Hi," she said, suddenly shy. Which was ridiculous. The man had just explored every inch of her naked body.

"Morning." He pulled down a mug, filled it and slid it across the counter. "Sit. I've got milk and sugar if you take it."

She shook her head.

"I'm going to take a shower. Be right down." He cocked his head. "Any reason why you have to leave today?"

"Nope."

"Good." His grin was lazy and lethal. "I thought we could grab a beer and lunch at the Beaver Creek Brewery and then ..." He pretended to think, tapping his chin. "And then, if it's all right with you, we'd come back here, make love all afternoon. Eat dinner. Watch a movie. Make love all night."

He stood there trying to look cute and innocent.

He was not innocent.

"Well." She took a sip of coffee. "I do have to leave for work tomorrow, but I'm free until then."

He kissed her on the top of her head. "Be right down."

Emily watched him go, then looked out the window, wrapping both hands around her mug. The morning light spilled through the long windows, ordinary, but everything felt different. She thought about the previous night. About today. About how long it'd been since she had felt this happy —and how much that scared her.

This was what she'd been searching for. A man who could

tease and kiss and make her laugh. A man who knew how to woo a woman and make her feel loved and safe.

She wasn't falling.

No sirree. She'd already fallen.

But somewhere buried deep was the nagging thought that good things sometimes came with shadows. For right now, she refused to acknowledge them. Outside, the wind picked up, rattling bare branches against the windows. Emily shivered, though the mug was hot in her hands. Somewhere in town, the spa sat dark and quiet, and she couldn't shake the thought that quiet didn't always mean safe.

And yet, sitting here in Adam's kitchen, it almost felt like peace was possible. Almost.

Eight

Jennifer lingered in the ladies' room, listening.

The soft spa music had shut off a few minutes ago. The last client had left. Voices faded. The soft click of the front door and front-door lock echoed in the quiet building.

Her pulse was a quiet roar in her ears. She told herself it was just the building settling. But was it just that? She'd been a reporter long enough to know quiet didn't always mean safe.

The moment she'd committed to this insane plan, her stomach had knotted. She wasn't a criminal. She was a reporter. Right now, she was trespassing. But sometimes you had to do that to get to the underbelly of things.

She waited another five minutes perched on the edge of the toilet with her shoes off, her heart beating double-time. She wasn't proud of hiding in the bathroom, but she just had to know.

Was Emily part of the cover-up in Boston or an innocent bystander who got caught up in something she shouldn't have?

She eased the stall door open and peeked out. The spa was

quiet. No voices. No movement. The faint scent of lavender lingered in the air, curling from a ceramic diffuser on the counter. Even empty, the spa felt peaceful, soothing even.

Emily's office door stood just ahead.

She tried the knob.

Locked.

Not a problem. Jennifer pulled a hairpin from her pocket. The cold metal slid between her fingers.

Her breath caught in her throat as she jimmied the lock, a favorite pastime that had come in handy more times than she could count. A bead of sweat slipped down her spine. Her fingers trembled slightly, not so much from nerves but from knowing she was close. She could feel it.

Come on, come on ...

A faint *snick*. The tumblers shifted.

Click.

The door creaked open. Jennifer held her breath and looked around. Safe. She slipped inside, gently closing the door.

But her gut told her this was the calm before the storm. And she trusted her instincts.

Inside, the office was tidy, with clean lines and calm colors. A reflection of who Emily was. Or who she wanted people to believe she was.

But it was the filing cabinet against the back wall that held her interest.

She opened the bottom drawer. People hid things in the bottom drawers, out of sight, inconvenient. Not in the first drawer under *A* for accessible or *L* for look here first.

A thick folder was stuffed at the back, marked with a name she hadn't seen in a year.

Dr. Marcus Vaughn.

Jennifer's breath caught. Could it be that simple?

She flipped it open. There were Boston news clippings

accusing the doctor of malpractice and inappropriate treatments at Evolve MedSpa. There was also a copy of a missing-person report for Shay Richardson. Emily's old roommate. The one who vanished from the Boston spa scene without a trace.

There were notes in the margins. Circled dates. Handwritten questions.

Emily wasn't guilty. She was digging.

She felt a pang of guilt in her chest. She'd pegged the wrong woman. Emily was looking for answers, just as she had been.

Damn. Jennifer's stomach churned. She had it wrong. Emily hadn't been part of the cover-up. She'd been trying to survive it. And she suddenly felt like Emily might be in deeper trouble than she had realized.

A floorboard creaked.

Jennifer froze. *Please be the pipes.* Please be nothing.

She shoved the folder back carefully, shut the drawer and peeked out the door. No one was in the reception area. She closed the door, hearing the lock click. Slipping into the hallway, she moved fast and low toward the back exit.

Ten steps away. Her heart thundered.

Nine.

Eight.

She reached for the handle of the back exit ...

The supply closet door creaked open.

Jennifer spun.

A woman stepped out with a cleaning rag in one hand. Her hair was gray at the temples. Her expression was blank.

They stared at each other for a long minute.

Jennifer's heart dropped. She froze mid-step.

Damn. Not now, when she was so close.

"Oh," she said quickly. "I ... I thought I left my purse. I was just ..."

The woman smiled. Not a smile that inspired confidence but a smile that said danger and made her skin crawl.

Jennifer's blood ran cold.

"Wait. Do I know you?" Jennifer asked, eyes narrowing.

The gray-haired woman smirked. Then Jennifer saw a face she'd never expected to see in Beaver Creek or anywhere for that matter.

"Oh my God, you're Bridget Vaughn!" Jennifer said. The woman thought she could change her name and change her sins.

Dr. Vaughn's widow.

The woman who supposedly covered up her husband's unscrupulous behavior and vanished after the lawsuits were filed and her husband's medical license was revoked. After his body was found in the bathtub. A supposed suicide that left more questions than answers. Not about how he died but about what she knew and why she ran.

Celeste, Bridget, whatever her name was now, smiled, but the smile didn't reach her eyes. "You were always so clever."

Jennifer took a step back, panic surging through her. "They'll figure it out. When they find me ..."

That was all she got out.

She tried to run, but Celeste yanked her arm, yanked hard, sending her off balance and slamming her head into the edge of the doorframe.

Pain exploded behind her eyes. The taste of copper filled her mouth as she bit her tongue.

She staggered, tried to stand, but was dizzy.

Celeste grabbed a heavy ceramic diffuser and swung. The impact knocked the air out of her lungs.

Jennifer gasped and dropped. Her mind screamed, *Tell my sister.* Of the story she wouldn't get to write. Of the truth that would never make it to print.

The second blow was harder.

The last thing she saw was Celeste's eyes. Cold. Empty. And that smile.

CELESTE STOOD OVER HER, chest heaving. Blood pooled beneath Jennifer's head, slow and dark, seeping onto the floor. The heavens were with her when she forgot her tote inside the spa with her prescription medication. She hadn't planned to come back, but fate had given her the perfect chance. Little did she know that the journalist would be hiding out.

"Stupid woman," she muttered. "You should have minded your own damn business."

Oh, she had recognized Jennifer the moment she had come strolling into the spa the other day. Nose in the air like she was some big-shot undercover journalist. Like she wasn't the same nosy reporter who destroyed everything—her reputation, Marcus's career, their entire life.

But Celeste never forgot a face.

The faint scent of lavender still lingered in the air. It was almost ironic. It was meant to calm, yet here it was, clinging to the scene of the crime.

She didn't hesitate as she crouched, tucked a folded towel under Jennifer's shoulders, then wrapped a clean sheet around her head. The blood was mostly contained. Manageable. Just another mess to clean.

She dragged the body toward the supply closet. The spa was silent except for the ticking of the wall clock. Everyone had gone.

It amazed her how easy it was. She hadn't planned to kill tonight, but Jennifer would have thrown a wrench in her plans to ruin Emily. And she couldn't have that.

She locked the supply closet and turned, wiping her hands.

Jennifer hadn't screamed, but then she didn't have a chance.

Her eyes going wide with recognition had hastened her demise.

The damn woman had always been too curious. It was her job, of course. But the woman loved digging into other people's tragedies.

And four years ago, she'd set her sights on theirs.

Marcus had been a brilliant doctor but was misunderstood. His only crime was wanting to help women feel perfect, more confident with their looks. But that wasn't what Jennifer wanted. She wanted the down and dirty. Scandal. Drama. A story that would earn her front-page status.

And she had gotten it.

Her story led to Marcus's board suspension. The loss of his license. The whispers. The lawsuits. Endless scrutiny.

Marcus had come home one night, quiet. He kissed her forehead, said he had a headache and was taking a hot bath.

By the time she found him, the water was cold. So was he.

Jennifer had destroyed him.

And Shay? Emily's missing roommate?

She got too close to the truth.

Shay had snooped around and found the records Marcus kept. Notes from patients no one was supposed to see, orders for treatments that should have gone through channels.

Shay threatened to go to the board. To the press.

And Celeste had begged her not to.

Pleaded even.

Promised her more money than she could imagine.

But had Shay listened? Nooo.

So Celeste made sure she couldn't tell anyone. Ever.

Celeste huffed. No one ever asked what really happened to that girl. They assumed she had just quit. Disappeared.

She grabbed Jennifer's purse and locked the closet door. Flipping through the contents, she pulled out a slim leather notebook and opened it. Page after page of notes, details, passwords.

And there it was. *MacBook: JenJax43.*

God, she made it so easy.

Celeste put the hotel key and the notebook in her pocket. This was going to be so simple. Plant a few clues, delete a few files, and Emily's reputation and maybe even her arrest for murder would be the news.

She walked back to the locker room with the diffuser still spewing its lavender mist. The fragrance clung to her skin. In the locker room, she opened the fifth locker and carefully hung Jennifer's purse inside. Then she moved to the end of the row, slid open another locker, and placed the diffuser on the shelf. Click. The latch clicked shut. Everything was in place.

Tomorrow after she finished at the Green Mountain Lodge, after she had Jennifer's laptop exactly the way she wanted it, the key would be returned to Jennifer's purse, waiting for the sheriff to find it. No one would suspect her. Not when everything looked so neat, so untouched.

She smiled at the locker door, at the neat little time bomb waiting inside.

By the time the police arrived, it wouldn't just be Jennifer's body under suspicion.

It would be Emily.

Emily Harper was going to lose everything.

Just like she had.

And this time, no one would be there to save her.

Nine

Adam stared at the reports he was supposed to process, but his mind kept drifting back to the weekend with Emily.

He didn't know exactly what made him ask her if she wanted to take their relationship further. It wasn't like him. He'd always played the field, kept things light. But that dinner with her Saturday night—laughing, teasing, just being with her—something had shifted. Suddenly he realized he wanted more.

He wanted what Ethan and Dylan had. What a few of the other guys had too. To settle down with a loving woman who called him on his crap, who could make him laugh and love him unconditionally, and who made a home that was more than just four walls and a roof.

And yes, the thought of coming home to all that *plus* mind-blowing sex? That didn't hurt either.

They'd been dating for a few months now, and honestly, he loved everything about Emily. Her work ethic, her laugh, the way she worried about her friends. That tiny lotus tattoo on her ankle. Most of all, he looked forward to being with her.

The weekend had been a blur of food, lazy mornings, and what could only be called a borderline sex-athon. She left this morning right after coffee to get ready for work, and damn, he missed her already.

"Yo, Adam! Those reports ready?" Ethan's voice snapped him out of it.

"On it," Adam called back. God, he really needed to focus. The reports weren't going to process themselves.

The low hum of fluorescent lights buzzed overhead. A stale whiff of burnt coffee lingered from the pot that had been empty since he came in.

He glanced at the clock. Nine a.m. Maybe he'd shoot Emily a quick text just to say hi.

No. Reports first. Focus.

Then maybe a text.

ADAM LOOKED up at the clock. Damn. Eleven fifteen already.

He was halfway through a routine write-up when the radio crackled.

"911?"

"This is 911. What's your emergency?"

"Oh God. Oh God. This is Morgan ... at Serenity Spa. There's a de-de-dead woman in the supply closet. Hurry."

Adam's heart stopped.

He was out of his chair before the dispatcher finished.

"McQueeney!" he shouted, grabbing his radio and keys.

Ethan stepped out of his office. "What is it?"

"Morgan from Serenity Spa called in a dead body."

"Let's go."

They bolted for the cruiser.

Outside, the air was cold. Frost clung to the tree branches. Adam didn't feel the cold. Didn't feel anything except a surge of fear slamming through him.

He drove fast. Too fast. The siren screamed, but all he heard was his heartbeat pounding in his ears. His knuckles were white on the wheel. The spa was only a few blocks away, but it felt like miles.

He prayed that it wasn't Emily. His Emily. Please, God.

They screeched to a stop in front of the spa. The clients and staff huddled on the sidewalk with wide eyes, shoulders hunched against the cold. Some cried openly.

Adam was out of the cruiser before it fully stopped. He and Ethan pushed through the door, guns drawn.

An older woman stood near the front desk, clutching Morgan, who was crying so hard her shoulders shook. She pointed toward the back.

"Emily!" Adam's voice rang out.

She turned. Pale. Eyes wide and glassy. She opened her mouth to say something, but no sound came out.

He reached her in three strides, put his hands on her shoulders, scanning her from head to toe.

"Are you all right? Hurt anywhere? What happened?"

"It's a client," she whispered. "Jennifer. Celeste found her. In the supply closet."

Ethan was already moving down the hall. Adam wrapped his arm around her and guided her toward her office. Someone had turned off the soft spa music. The spa felt cold, foreign.

Flashes of red and blue lights from the arriving EMTs danced across Emily's face. She was shaking. Shock, probably. Her eyes were dry, but he could feel the tension in her muscles.

He held her for a moment longer than protocol allowed. But damn it, this was Emily. His Emily.

The EMT crew rushed past with their gear, heading straight down the hall toward the supply closet. Adam caught a few words—no pulse, obvious signs—before they stepped back, one of them shaking his head toward Ethan. They didn't bring out a stretcher, not for this. They'd wait until the coroner arrived.

Adam gave her shoulders a gentle squeeze. "Stay here. I'm going to find out what happened."

Morgan and Celeste came in behind her as he slipped down the hall.

The smell hit first. Metallic, coppery, tinged with lavender and with a lingering scent of fear.

The woman was lying on her side as if she had fallen asleep there. Except for the dark and matted blood in her hair and a thin trail staining the floor.

Jennifer.

He cocked his head, frowning. He knew her. How? Not the face that was slack and gray under the fluorescent light. There was something about her features that tugged at his memory.

Then it clicked.

Oh, sweet Jesus. It was that woman with the sharp tongue and New York plates. The woman who thought she could take corners around mountains like she was in a damn sports car.

"What've we got?" he asked Ethan, his voice low.

Ethan stood just outside the door, arms crossed.

"I know who she is. Jennifer Bishop," Adam said, rubbing the back of his neck. "I pulled her over last week. I'll grab her info from the office."

Ethan blew out a breath, reached for his radio. "Get Jennings down here. Now."

Within an hour, the coroner would be on site with his own body bag and gurney. A woman was dead, but it was Jennings's job to make it official.

Ethan looked at him for a long moment and then shook his head. "Adam, you're off this one."

Adam blinked. "Excuse me?"

"You heard me."

Adam took a step forward, getting right up into Ethan's face, his voice low but firm. "Emily didn't do anything wrong, Ethan."

"Maybe not. But this investigation's going to have eyes on it. I can't have you in the middle of it. You know that."

Adam clenched his jaw. "Jennifer wasn't just some stranger. When I pulled her over, something didn't sit right. I can't ignore that."

Ethan's expression didn't change. "Which means you had a gut feeling. That's exactly why you're too close. You're involved personally."

"Damn it, Ethan, she was found at Emily's spa. What do you expect me to do, sit behind a desk while someone figures out if my girlfriend's in danger?" Adam was pissed. Not at Ethan but at the whole situation.

"Yes," Ethan replied flatly. "Because if she is in danger, I need you protecting her. Not buried under this case with your judgment compromised. Jennings will do a preliminary tonight. We'll have the official autopsy results in a couple of days, but right now it looks like blunt force trauma."

The words hit him in the gut. Blunt force trauma meant someone had beaten Jennifer, maybe with their hands or worse. It was up close—personal. He clenched his fists, imagining Emily walking in on that scene, inches away from a danger she hadn't even known was there.

Emily had sidled up next to him and flinched. The color drained from her face. She didn't make a sound, but the tension emanating from her body told him enough.

Adam opened his mouth to argue, but Emily's voice cut in.

"I knew her."

Ethan's head snapped around. His pen paused. Adam caught the flicker in his eyes and hated it. He could already feel the shift. The judgment. The suspicion. It meant Emily was already under the microscope.

TEN

Emily stood in the hallway, arms wrapped around herself as if she could hold everything in. Her pulse was racing even though it felt like all the blood had drained from her body.

Her voice sounded steady as she told them she knew Jennifer.

But it wasn't the truth. She knew Jennifer's voice, she knew how tight her muscles were, and she knew how curious, almost nosy, she'd seemed.

"Well, not personally. She came in on Thursday for a massage and made another appointment for Saturday at four. I did both massages."

And now she was dead.

Emily felt Adam's gaze on her before she even looked up. He cocked his head, his eyes searching her face, checking whether she was holding it together or shattering. She was grateful he was here because Ethan had on his serious sheriff's face, and she couldn't read him. But hearing Ethan take Adam off the case made her stomach twist. What did that mean exactly? Had she ruined his career?

Adam stepped closer, lowering his voice. "I need you to stay here for a minute. Ethan's going to have a few questions. Don't go anywhere alone."

She nodded. But her mind couldn't quite grasp why the words unsettled her so much. They echoed in her head louder than the conversation around her.

Don't go anywhere alone.

What was that supposed to mean? Was she in danger? Was her staff?

"Adam," she whispered, uncertain why she was even asking. "You don't think I ..."

His hand tightened lightly on her shoulder. "I think," he cut in gently, "that I'm not taking any chances with you."

Emily's gut clenched. She didn't want to need protection. Who would he even protect her from? She didn't know Jennifer. Her staff didn't know Jennifer. Was this a one-off or something more?

Behind them, the murmur of voices got louder. Ethan was talking to the EMTs and his deputies. The faint metallic scent of blood hung in the air, mingling with the lavender that now made her stomach turn.

It wasn't the idea of death lingering in her workplace that bothered her as much as the knowledge that someone had brought it here. Deliberately.

Someone had chosen her spa. Could it have been one of the staff? It could just as easily have been her.

The big question was, why was Jennifer even here? She'd left at five. Supposedly. Emily wasn't sure since she had rushed out as soon as the massage was over.

She felt Adam's hand on her back, guiding her toward the front. "Let's get you out of here."

Emily wanted to argue. Wanted to say it was her responsibility, her spa. But the idea of getting fresh air even for a minute sounded good.

She glanced back once before they reached the door. Morgan stood pale and shaken as Jennifer's body was slid into a body bag and then onto a gurney.

Celeste wasn't watching the EMTs.

She was watching Emily.

Celeste stood next to Morgan and let her gaze settle on Emily. She wondered what Emily was thinking. Did Emily realize how easily this could have been her?

She almost laughed but swallowed it back. If Emily only knew what was hidden just beyond Jennifer's locker. And a few doors down, Jennifer's purse rested neat and waiting, the phone wiped clean of anything useful, the driver's license and credit cards untouched, the hotel card key carefully placed back inside. One surprise close at hand. One time bomb waiting to go off.

Emily's head turned just then, and for a brief moment their eyes met. Celeste didn't move, didn't blink. Just held the stare.

What was Emily thinking? Did Emily feel she was safe because Adam was close by?

Safety was an illusion.

Celeste had already taken care of the rest. Jennifer's laptop wasn't hard to find in the hotel room. And Celeste knew her way around a computer. A few carefully planted documents and a few files deleted were all it took to point the finger in a new direction—toward Emily. It was enough to make the sheriff wonder if Emily had secrets she'd kill to keep.

The trap was set. All she had to do was wait.

Morgan had finally wandered off toward the reception desk. The sheriff was taking his sweet time talking to one of the deputies. When he finally turned, Celeste took a calming breath and approached him.

"Sheriff?"

Ethan looked her way. "Yes?"

"I'm not sure …" She kept her gaze down, as if reluctant. "I wasn't going to say anything, but … last Thursday after Jennifer's appointment, I overheard Emily at the front desk talking to Morgan about her." She paused for effect. "She said Jennifer gave her a weird vibe. That Jennifer was asking a lot of questions. About the spa. About her too."

Ethan's brow furrowed.

She shrugged lightly. "Emily laughed it off. Said maybe she was a blogger or something."

She looked up with wide, innocent eyes. "But now, I thought you should know."

Ethan studied her, then gave a slow nod.

"Thanks," he said. "We'll follow up."

Celeste dipped her head as she turned and walked away slowly. She didn't need to add more. She'd planted the seed. It was small. Harmless. Perfect.

ETHAN WATCHED Adam usher Emily toward the door.

Celeste drifted down the hallway and stopped to talk to Morgan.

From where Ethan stood, this was turning out to be a mystery as to who Jennifer was and what she was doing in Beaver Creek. More than that, he hoped Jane wouldn't catch wind of it. She was all too eager to spin a good crime story featuring Beaver Creek, and the last thing he needed was her poking her nose into an active case. He'd get Emily's statement soon enough.

He let out a slow breath, flipped open his notebook and headed toward the two women.

"Morgan," he said. "Want to tell me what happened this morning?"

"I opened the spa at eight like I do every weekday. Staff came in, then Emily arrived for her first appointment." Morgan looked at Celeste, then back at Ethan. "Around ten, I was at the front desk when I heard a scream coming from the back."

Celeste clasped her hands together. "I came in at ten to make up some time and was starting my work. When I opened the supply closet, there the poor woman was." A tear dripped down her cheek. "It was horrible."

"I'm sure it was," Ethan replied. "So, neither of you knew her?"

They both shook their heads.

Just then, the EMTs wheeled the gurney past. Morgan covered her mouth, eyes brimming, while Celeste kept her gaze carefully downcast.

"So, Jennifer came in for a massage at four o'clock Saturday night," Ethan asked. "What time did she leave?"

"It would have been at five, since that's when we close," replied Morgan.

"Did you see her leave?"

Morgan shook her head. "No. I was busy putting together receipts in Emily's office."

He turned to Celeste. "How about you?"

"I wasn't here. I had left early that night." Celeste hesitated, then glanced at Morgan.

Ethan studied her carefully. "So, neither of you actually saw Jennifer walk out the door."

They both shook their heads

He shifted his gaze to Morgan. "Did Jennifer come in with a purse?"

"Yes. We have lockers that clients and staff use." She shrugged. "Everyone puts their coats and purse there. Maybe she forgot it."

Celeste kept her eyes lowered as if she were reluctant to say more.

Ethan made a note in his book, though the thought nagged at him.

A forgotten purse. Emily's office. Emily was near the front desk that night.

It was too soon to draw conclusions, but somehow Emily Harper was sliding into the center of this picture. And that unsettled him more than he wanted to admit.

CELESTE CAUGHT the flicker in his eye and the way his pen paused for just a second.

She lowered her gaze and let out a weary sigh. Inside, satisfaction was having a party.

The first seed was planted. Soon the whole thing would unravel, and Emily's perfect life would split wide open. Exactly the way she intended.

ELEVEN

Ethan followed Morgan down the same hallway where Jennifer's body had been found. His deputies were still processing the room.

A couple of doors down, Morgan stopped and opened the door. Inside, the faint smell of eucalyptus and lemon cleaner clung to the air. A row of wooden lockers painted soft white was on one wall. A long bench and a small cubby were in front of each door. Green plants, fake ones judging by the lack of windows, were placed around the room. A full-length mirror stood in the corner, catching just enough light to make the space feel lived in. The wooden floor gleamed underfoot.

He tried one randomly. Locked. Of course, clients don't leave their valuables sitting around.

"Morgan," he called over his shoulder. "You've got the keys, right?"

She hurried over. "Yup, right here. We keep spares in case someone loses one."

Celeste lingered in the doorway, taking it all in. Her face was neutral, but Ethan caught something in her eyes. Like she knew something no one else did. It put him on edge.

"Let's start here and work our way down," he said, stopping in front of the first locker.

Morgan slipped the key into the first lock. With a metallic click, the door swung open.

Ethan leaned in. Nothing. Just a white robe and slippers. Too neat. Most locker rooms he'd seen were cluttered, spare sneakers shoved in, empty lotion bottles rolling around, the remains of snacks.

They went down the row. The next locker was the same, and so were several others.

A pair of shoes, some gum, a headband, someone's sweater. Another locker.

At the fifth locker, they found it. Jennifer's black leather purse hung from a hook.

"I guess this is Jennifer's. She did forget it," Morgan whispered.

Ethan studied the purse for a moment, then pulled on a pair of plastic gloves before easing it free. The clasp opened with a soft snap, and he peered inside—wallet, lipstick, keys. Nothing out of the ordinary. It was incredibly neat, free of loose change, crumpled receipts or any of the other things women had in their purses. Not that he would know personally, except Jane had asked him to retrieve something from her purse once, and it was a jumble of what he considered useless items. He had been told in no uncertain terms that all of it was necessary.

He thumbed open a side pocket and found a plastic hotel key embossed with the Green Mountain Lodge logo tucked beside a referral card to Serenity Spa. His brow furrowed.

Morgan leaned in. "That's part of the lodge's welcome package. They give new guests a spa referral and discount. We've had a few come through."

Ethan turned the card over, eyes narrowing. "So, she didn't just stumble onto Serenity—it was handed to her."

Morgan shrugged. "I guess. But when she came in, it was for a last-minute massage. Never mentioned staying at the lodge."

Unease settled low in his stomach. A clean purse, a neat story, and a convenient referral card leading straight to Emily. It felt too perfect. He didn't believe in coincidences, not when a woman ended dead.

He slipped the purse into an evidence bag, praying that they'd get the killer's fingerprints off something, but his gut told him they weren't finished. It was an old warning he'd learned never to ignore.

"Keep going," he ordered.

Morgan hesitated. "Do you really think ..."

"Keep going," he said.

Another locker was opened. A yoga mat and spare lotion bottles.

"This one is mine," said Morgan as she opened the next one. A change of clothes, some makeup.

There was one last locker. Ethan wasn't feeling optimistic. So far, all they contained were robes, slippers, some personal items, and a hair dryer. Nothing to indicate a crime had been committed.

Click. The last locker was opened. Morgan gasped.

Ethan gently pushed her aside. Inside were a pair of shoes, a jacket, a sweater, one protein bar, and something bloody and smelling of lavender.

"It's Emily's locker," stammered Morgan. "Oh my God. I don't believe this."

Ethan stared at the diffuser. The lingering scent of lavender infused with the metallic scent of blood irritated his nose. His chest clenched. The blood was real enough. But its placement was suspicious

"Oh. Oh." Morgan peeked from beside him. "That's blood, isn't it?"

He didn't answer.

"Are you sure this is Emily's?" he asked.

Morgan nodded. "She always takes this locker."

He shut the locker with a muted clang. "Thank you for helping."

The diffuser's placement nagged at him. Was it too convenient? It was as if someone wanted him to find it. He had a hard time believing Emily would be that stupid. But then again ... the world was filled with people who thought they were smart.

Morgan swallowed hard. "You don't think Emily would do this, do you?"

"That's not for us to decide right now," he replied.

Ethan slipped his notebook into his pocket. "Don't mention this to anyone until I've had a chance to talk to Emily."

Both women nodded and left.

Ethan closed the door to the locker room and motioned for a deputy to come over. Adam had taken Emily to his house, but this conversation couldn't wait forever. When he finally asked her the hard questions, Ethan needed to know if he was looking at an innocent woman or a suspect. And the thought of her being a suspect left him uneasy.

CELESTE FOLLOWED Morgan back to the front. Her pulse was racing with delight. This was far better than she had imagined.

She bit the inside of her cheek to prevent smiling. The trap was set, and Emily was right in the middle of it.

The sheriff was a cautious man. Just because the diffuser was in Emily's locker didn't mean he'd jump to conclusions.

He was the type to weigh all the facts before he made his move. However, she knew better. She'd seen the telltale look in his eyes that something didn't sit right. He had questions. Good. Questions meant he'd dig deeper. The deeper he dug, the more entangled Emily would become.

She had arranged everything with care—the carefully placed diffuser, Jennifer's purse tucked in another locker. She'd straightened and cleaned the room before leaving breadcrumbs that he'd follow.

She knew exactly what he'd find when he went to the hotel. The laptop. The questions. The hint of doubt. She left him a trail he couldn't ignore, and every step led to Emily.

And when he finished his investigation, Emily would be so tangled in evidence that even the sheriff wouldn't be able to untangle her.

Celeste's pulse steadied. This is what she lived for. What she and Marcus lived for. The thrill of manipulation, of turning the truth into something unrecognizable. He was a master of it—how to rewrite reports so the lies read smoother than the facts, how to bury records so deep no one would ever dig them up. Together, they'd crafted realities and silenced anyone foolish enough to question them.

Marcus would be proud. And soon Emily would be exactly where Celeste wanted her, losing everything she had worked for. Alone and utterly defenseless.

Revenge was sweet.

Celeste drew in a long breath. The faint trace of lavender still clung to her skin, mingling with the sharper scent of blood. She let it fill her chest, savoring it. To her, it smelled like victory.

Twelve

Ethan pulled into Adam's drive, turned off the cruiser and sighed heavily. He so didn't want to go in there and question Emily, who he'd always thought kind, especially in front of his best friend. But this was his job, and no one would ever be able to accuse him of sloppy police work. His gut told him this was wrong, but the evidence so far didn't lie.

Adam opened the door before he even knocked. His shoulders filled the frame, jaw tight. His eyes searched Ethan's face, hoping for good news, realizing it wasn't. "She's not your suspect," he said flatly, daring Ethan to disagree.

Ethan rubbed the back of his neck. "I don't want her to be. But we both know I can't ignore facts."

"Someone has to be setting her up," Adam said.

"I hope you're right," said Ethan as he stepped inside. The living room smelled faintly of coffee and woodsmoke. Emily sat curled up on the couch, hands clenched tight. Her face was pale. She looked small, breakable, but her chin lifted as if she was daring him not to believe her. She looked up when Ethan entered, eyes wide and rimmed red. She shook her head as if refusing to believe he'd come here to question her like some stranger or criminal.

"Ethan." Her voice cracked. "You can't believe I would do something like that."

His chest tightened. God, he didn't want to. But the good people of Beaver Creek had entrusted him with a badge, a badge his dad and granddad were proud to wear. He lowered himself into the chair across from her, pen and notebook in hand.

"I don't," he said quietly. "But there are things I have to ask. For the record."

Adam planted himself on the arm of the couch like a sentry. His jaw flexed. He didn't speak.

Ethan drew in a deep breath and forced himself to start. "When was the last time you saw Jennifer?"

"Saturday night around five after her massage."

"Did you see her leave?"

Emily shook her head. "No, I was meeting Adam and in a hurry. But Morgan was there."

"You always use the same locker at the spa?"

"Yes, the one at the end."

Ethan jotted a note, his brows furrowed. "Anyone else ever use it? Or have access to the lockers?"

"Not that I know of. Sometimes delivery people pass through, but they don't have access to the locker room."

Adam shifted his weight on the arm of the couch. "You're wasting time asking her this. She didn't do anything."

Ethan took a deep breath and exhaled. "Adam, you know I have to cover every angle." He turned back to Emily. "Did she mention where she was staying while in town? A hotel? Friends?"

"No," Emily whispered. "She was chatty but asked a lot of questions about the spa, how long I'd been here, did I offer certain procedures, was it hard to run a business here. That kind of thing."

Ethan's pen stilled. Too many questions, too pointed for a casual client. "Let me get this straight. You never met Jennifer before Thursday, when she showed up for the first time out of the blue. You don't know where she was staying or why she was in town. And you can't explain how she ended up at your spa of all places?"

"That's right."

Ethan hesitated. "There's something else you need to know," he said quietly. "When we searched the spa, we found what appears to be the murder weapon in the locker room."

Emily blinked. "What murder weapon?"

"The diffuser," Ethan said. "It was in your locker, Emily." He swallowed hard. "And it had blood on it. Most likely Jennifer's."

Adam surged to his feet. "Jesus, Ethan..."

Ethan held up a hand before he could finish. "I'm not saying she put it there. But someone did. And they wanted it to point straight at her."

Emily's hands trembled in her lap. "Do you ... do you think I'm lying?"

He froze at the raw ache in her voice, then shook his head firmly. "No. But someone's not telling the truth, and I have to find out who."

Adam pushed away from the couch, jaw clenched. "Then look at everyone else, not her."

Their gazes locked. The air between them was taut with tension. Friendship versus duty. Ethan's heart was heavy, but duty came first. Always.

Finally, he nodded. "I'll be in touch."

He turned toward the door, feeling Adam's glare burning into his back the whole way.

As he stepped out onto the porch, the chilly evening air was a welcome respite from Adam's simmering fury.

The door shut behind him, muffling the low murmur of Adam and Emily's voices.

Sliding behind the wheel, he sat for a minute staring through the windshield. His gut said Emily was innocent, but the facts weren't lining up.

Damn. It wasn't just Adam standing in her corner. His own wife, Jane, thought the world of her. Savannah loved Emily, and Leah, Tanner's girlfriend, called her one of the best friends she'd ever had. The women in his own family, the women he trusted most, all loved Emily.

And here he was digging through her life as if she were a stranger on the wrong side of the law.

His badge demanded answers. But his gut whispered that if Emily was guilty, then half the people he cared about were blind to it. And that didn't sit right.

He started the engine. First stop, the spa again. Check in with his deputies, retrace every detail, every locker. Then he'd head out to Green Mountain Lodge.

Something about this case didn't add up. He didn't like it. The evidence lined up too neatly. Emily had the means. She had opportunity. But no damn motive. Until he found more, all he had were suspicions that didn't line up with the facts. And Ethan McQueeney wasn't about to let Emily Harper take the fall if she wasn't guilty.

EMILY SAGGED against Adam the moment the door shut. Her pulse thundered in her ears. *How could this be happening? A body in my spa? Did I run from the problems in Boston just to wind up in this situation?*

Adam wrapped his arms around her, holding her tight. "Hey, sweetheart, look at me."

She turned toward him.

"I believe you. I know you're not capable of anything like this."

Tears burned at the back of her eyes. "But Ethan doesn't. He looked at me like—like I was a criminal." She pulled back, shaking her head. "What if nobody believes me?"

"They will," Adam said with certainty. "And if they don't, I'll make them." He tipped her chin up. "You're not alone, Emily. I've got you."

The air stilled around her. She tried to breathe, tried to let his words steady her. But Jennifer's voice kept echoing in her head. The casual questions about Botox, fillers, procedures. They'd been too specific, too familiar, just like Boston all over again.

Why would someone want to frame her this badly? What did Jennifer know or suspect that made her dangerous? How far would they go to destroy everything she built? And what would be next?

Thirteen

His badge demanded he follow the evidence. But his gut ... his gut told him the evidence was lying. And somewhere between those two truths stood Emily Harper, waiting for him to figure out which one was real.

Ethan's thoughts were heavy as he headed to the lodge. The dead woman, the blood, the diffuser tucked into Emily's locker. It felt too neat, almost as if it had been planted there. But why?

He hated taking Adam off the case, but it was the only prudent thing to do. Adam was in love with Emily. He had his suspicions about that, but Jane told him outright, and he trusted her opinion. He wondered how Emily's friends were going to react to this latest development. Emily was well-liked in town. Regardless, small towns lived for gossip.

Before continuing to the lodge, he swung by the spa for a minute to check on his deputies, who were still processing the crime scene—photographing and swabbing. The coroner had arrived just as he was pulling out of the lot, black bag in hand. Ezra Jennings never hurried, never wasted words. But Ethan needed something, anything, before he walked into Green Mountain Lodge.

The phone buzzed, knocking him out of his thoughts. He didn't need to look at the caller ID.

"McQueeney."

The coroner's voice came through steady, clinical. "Female, mid-thirties. I'll have more when I get her back. Rigor suggests she's been gone at least thirty, maybe forty hours. Lividity's fixed along her back and thighs."

Ethan frowned and gripped the wheel tighter. "But she was found on her side."

"Yup. She wasn't lying that way when she was killed. The body's been moved."

Ethan stared out at Crescent Street—traffic moving, people walking, talking, laughing. No one interested in one dead woman. Not right now. Not until this got out, and then the town would take sides. Emily's or the law.

"Time of death?"

Ezra paused, papers shifting. "Preliminary estimate? Between 5 and 11 p.m. Saturday evening, pending post-mortem confirmation."

Ethan's grip on the wheel tightened. Emily had been at the spa then. She swore she'd left around five to meet Adam, and he confirmed she'd met him at the Log & Lantern.

But that still left a few minutes unaccounted for. It would be easy for her to detour to the back where nobody was and kill Jennifer. He'd have to go back and talk to Morgan. See who was still there at five. And double-check Celeste's version. The woman was a little too eager to give him information.

"Cause of death?"

"Well, I'll confirm with the autopsy, but it looks like blunt force trauma."

Ethan let out a long breath. Means. Opportunity. But there was no motive.

"Appreciate the update." He ended the call.

Silence pressed in as he drove. His mind drifted back to the purse, to the hotel key and to the Serenity Spa referral card. Morgan had called it a lodge perk, part of their wellness welcome package. Maybe Jennifer had just pocketed it the way travelers do and never thought twice about it.

But the timing bothered him. She hadn't wandered into Beaver Creek blind. She had known about Serenity. And now she was dead, her body staged in the very place the card pointed to.

Coincidence? Maybe. But he didn't believe in those.

The case just didn't add up, and until it did, he wasn't about to let Emily take the fall. He'd follow the evidence. Jennifer Bishop had been curious, asking questions. Maybe her room at the Green Mountain Lodge held the answers. Ethan prayed the truth wouldn't destroy Emily in the process.

THE GREEN MOUNTAIN LODGE was outside town, nestled in a valley surrounded by green pine trees interspersed with bare-branched maples and oaks. It was beautiful for most of the year, but right now, after the leaves had fallen and before snow fell, it looked forlorn. The fields surrounding it were flat and brown, the gardens cut back to stubble, and the bare branches gave it an abandoned look.

He turned down the long driveway, the crunch of gravel loud under his tires. The lodge came into view. Weathered green shutters framed the windows, and a wide wraparound porch was lined with rocking chairs. Pots of late-season mums added splashes of gold and rust. The lodge had clearly been added onto over the years, branching out at odd angles, giving the place a lived-in charm.

A faint curl of woodsmoke rose from one of the chimneys. He pulled into the half-full lot and cut the engine. Sure, he could have rolled up to the front door, lights flashing, siren blaring, but there was no reason to announce his arrival or send the guests into a panic.

It wasn't leaf-peeping season anymore, and the nearest ski resort was owned by the college, twenty miles in the opposite direction. Still, the lodge kept busy with its farm-to-table dinners, beer fests, wagon rides if the weather permitted it, and sleigh rides in the winter, but Ethan wasn't here for any of that. He was here for answers.

He stepped inside, noticing the fire crackling and spitting in the huge fieldstone fireplace. Leather armchairs and a comfy sofa surrounded it, and several guests sat around with glasses of wine, their laughter low and easy. Chairs and small tables were scattered around the polished wood floor. Above, an antler chandelier cast a golden glow. The beams overhead were heavy timber, dark with age. On the floor, handwoven rugs added color and warmth.

This part of the lodge was over a hundred years old, and he could feel the history in his bones. The scent of roasted meat and fresh bread drifted out from the dining room and mingled with the sharper tang of hops from the bar. Ethan's stomach growled. He had missed lunch but had no time to stop to eat.

He tugged his jacket tighter against the chill. His gaze landed on the front desk, where a young woman looked over at him with curiosity, wondering if he was a guest or trouble.

He certainly wasn't a guest. And he hoped this wouldn't turn into trouble. To Ethan, this wasn't just a cozy mountain lodge, it was a crime scene waiting to unfold. And Jennifer's room was the next piece of the puzzle. Ethan only hoped the answers inside wouldn't raise more questions. But he knew better—crime had a mind of its own.

The young woman straightened as she followed his footsteps to the desk. "Sheriff."

Ethan stepped up to the front desk and placed his badge on the counter. "A Jennifer Bishop is registered here in room 205. I need access to her room."

The woman froze, her eyes darting from the badge to Ethan's face. "I'm not supposed to give out guest keys without ..."

Ethan mentally rolled his eyes. Civilians.

"She's dead," he said flatly. "This is an active investigation. Either hand me a key or walk me up yourself."

The woman swallowed hard, the color draining from her cheeks. She hesitated for a moment, then nodded and reached under the counter.

The card encoder clicked. She slid the new keycard across the counter.

Ethan picked up his badge and the key. He leaned in slightly. "What day did she check in?"

She typed quickly on the keyboard, pulling up the record. "She checked in Monday afternoon."

Ethan rapped the counter once. "Room 205?"

She pointed down the hall. "It's in our newer addition, just down the hall and to your right, second floor."

He nodded and set off.

Room 205 was at the end of the hallway. Ethan slid the key card into the lock. The light blinked green, and he pushed the door open. He stood there for a moment, his senses on high alert.

The room was neat. Almost too neat.

The walls were painted a warm cream, with nature prints spaced evenly around the room. There was a large double window overlooking a lake, letting in lots of natural light. A king-size bed was placed under the eaves, covered in a cream coverlet with two accent pillows embroidered with subtle deer antlers. It looked soft and inviting, but he wasn't here to judge the quality of the mattress.

He stepped in farther and took in the plant by the window, a small desk and chair, and a television on a dresser in one corner. It was a well-appointed room, and it should be for four hundred bucks a night.

What was missing were signs of an actual guest. A tossed bag, a water bottle, shoes, anything.

It looked clean and cozy on the surface. But to Ethan, it was something else. Something that made his neck prickle. This was more than just a maid coming in to clean. It felt staged.

He closed the door behind him and took another slow sweep of the room. Bed. Nightstand. Desk.

Ethan snapped on a pair of gloves and tugged the desk drawer open. Empty. No laptop. Everyone seemed to travel with one these days, so it had to be here.

He checked under the chair cushion. Under the pillows on the bed. Then he crouched at the foot of the bed. A sliver of black caught his eye.

"Gotcha," he muttered.

He reached down carefully and pulled the laptop out. Carrying it to the desk, he pressed the power button, half expecting it to be dead. The screen flickered, then lit. A password prompt appeared.

Ethan pulled out the notes he had copied from Jennifer's notebook. He typed in the password.

The laptop unlocked.

His gut tightened as he leaned back in the chair. Whatever got her killed was waiting for him on this screen.

He pressed enter—and instantly wished he hadn't.

A single folder labeled INVESTIGATION—BEAVER CREEK sat in the middle of the desktop.

Ethan's pulse raced. He didn't want to know what was

inside. Every instinct told him it wasn't going to look good for Emily. But the cop in him wouldn't let it go. He clicked it open.

Dozens of files popped up. He clicked on BostonSpa_Fallout_Timeline.

These weren't the kinds of files someone kept for personal curiosity. Jennifer had come chasing something bigger. A story.

Questions Jennifer had written to herself: *Fired or pushed out? New identity? Reputation rebuilt? Timelines. Connected to the Boston cover-up. What did Shay find? Where is she now?*

Ethan frowned. He was no computer expert, but some of the questions seemed like accusations. *Money for Spa suspicious? Harper—key to cover-up? Roommate vanished.*

And one line underlined twice: *hotel, Daniel Cross. Did he follow me?*

Ethan stared at the screen until the words blurred. The name meant nothing to him, but Jennifer marked it as if it mattered.

His chest tightened. He fought the urge to slam the lid shut and walk away.

Emily. Every damn question pointed at her.

The cop inside him ticked off how the pieces were starting to line up. Emily had the means. She ran the spa, knew every quiet corner where someone could vanish.

She had been there the night Jennifer died. So, opportunity.

If Jennifer was digging into a cover-up in Boston, and Emily was hiding secrets, then yeah, she might have a motive, if she were guilty of something.

But the man, the friend, wanted to pretend he hadn't seen a thing. He sighed. This was Emily. The woman who calmed people with lavender and hot stones, not a conniving schemer with blood on her hands. Who smiled at Adam as if he were her safe place. She wasn't a killer.

Ethan shoved back from the desk. Evidence pointed one way. His instincts another. And notes like these? Sometimes they twisted the truth. He'd seen it too many times. Scribbles passed off as gospel, theories dressed up as fact.

Still ... Jennifer had been chasing Emily. And now Jennifer was dead. The question was: How did she find Emily?

He snapped the laptop shut. If he mentioned this to Adam, it would break his friend in half. If he didn't, he wouldn't have done his job.

Ethan stood, sliding the laptop into an evidence bag. One way or another, this investigation was about to rip apart the lives of people he cared about.

And he had no idea if he'd be able to patch them back together.

He left the room and made his way back through the lodge. At the front desk, a stack of Serenity Spa referral cards caught his eye. How had he missed that the first time?

No matter.

The clerk looked over as he paused. "That's part of our welcome package," she said. "Guests get a discount at the spa. We fax over a list of names so Serenity knows who qualified."

Ethan's brows lifted. "A list?"

She nodded. "Yes. Should have gone out Monday when Ms. Bishop checked in."

His jaw clenched. No one at Serenity had mentioned it.

Ethan left the lodge with the laptop tucked under his arm. Every step toward his cruiser felt heavier. He'd come looking for answers, but all he'd found were more questions, more reason to doubt.

And always circling back to Emily.

By the time he got back to the office, his jaw ached from

clenching it. He dropped the bag on Deputy Kyle Mercer's cluttered desk.

Mercer looked up from his monitor, one eyebrow arched. "What'd you drag in this time, Sheriff? Evidence or just more headaches?"

Ethan gave him a tight nod. "Jennifer Bishop. Bagged it myself. I need a full workup—mirror the drive, preserve every log, every time stamp. Don't touch the original. You know the drill."

Mercer smirked as he slipped on gloves, already pulling the laptop free. "Headaches it is. It'll take time. Imaging alone takes a few hours, and that's before I even start digging. You want the timeline exact?"

"Yes. No speculation."

Mercer's grin faded into something more serious. "Got it. If it's there, we'll find it."

Ethan walked back to his office, glad he found it in the budget to hire Kyle, a self-taught computer whiz who built his first PC at age twelve. He enjoyed hacking, legal or not. Ethan never asked. He was easygoing, sarcastic, sharp and reliable and the kind of deputy you wanted in your corner when the trail was digital. Otherwise, he'd have to send the laptop to the State Police Computer Crimes Unit, which could take a while.

He checked in with Nora Foster, his receptionist. No new messages. No new crimes demanding his attention.

But his mind wasn't still. Not with Jennifer's notes rattling around in his head, pointing straight at Emily.

He drove back to the spa to check in with his deputies and Morgan, if she was still there. After that? The visit he didn't want to make—Adam's house and a talk to Emily.

The spa looked deserted. He parked and stepped inside. The spa felt wrong. No lavender drifting through the air, no soft music. Just heavy silence. Yellow crime scene tape stretched across the hall where the supply closet was.

In the lobby, Morgan sat behind the reception desk staring at the computer. Celeste was sitting on one of the lobby chairs, legs crossed, eyes tracking Ethan as he walked in.

"Sheriff," Morgan said quickly.

Ethan stopped at the desk. "The Green Mountain Lodge faxed over a list of names of people who signed up for the discounted massage. Can I see it?"

"List?" She tilted her head, frowning. "I haven't seen a list. I know they send one over when guests register for a massage. But I haven't received one in a while."

"Are you sure you never received it?"

She shook her head. "Sheriff, I check every day. We never got it."

"So, it just disappeared?"

Morgan's brows furrowed. "Maybe they never sent it over or the machine jammed. Things happen."

He didn't like the answer, but faxing was unreliable at best. God only knew how many times his office didn't receive something that was definitely sent. Probably still floating around in some big void. Even so, something didn't sit right.

"Jennifer circled a name. Daniel Cross. Ring a bell?"

"No, should it?"

"Not to me, either." Ethan exhaled slowly. "Follow up anyway. Maybe the lodge still has it."

Morgan nodded. "On it."

"Good. Then you two should go home. Check with Emily about tomorrow." He slapped the counter lightly and turned toward the door.

Outside, the cool air hit his face but did nothing to clear his thoughts. Celeste's silence, the missing fax and Daniel Cross's name settled heavy in his gut. A stranger. A name that meant nothing to him at the moment. But Jennifer had thought he mattered.

Fourteen

Adam handed Emily a hot cup of tea with strict instructions to drink it. God, she wanted to. She inhaled the faint scent of chamomile, which normally was enough to settle her nerves. But tonight, her stomach was rebelling against the idea of swallowing anything. All she could do was cradle the mug and let the warmth soak into her hands.

He'd already mentioned that Ethan would probably be back. To question her. The word "accuse" lingered, although he hadn't said it aloud. Accuse her of what? Murder? She didn't want to think about that.

What she did know was that she had never met Jennifer before, and she most certainly didn't kill her.

But Jennifer had sought her out. Asked her weird questions like she knew or thought she knew something about Emily. And someone had put that bloody diffuser in her locker. It wasn't an accident. Someone wanted to frame her. But why? And how far were they willing to go?

What was going to happen to her spa? Once the news spread, the town would choose sides. People always did. Some would believe her. Others wouldn't. What about her employees? Those that were left, anyway? Would they jump ship? What about her friends? Oh God, she couldn't lose them too. Without them, she'd have nothing.

Adam sat down next to her, his hand resting gently on her thigh. Emily felt bad that Adam was off the case. He should have been at work, chasing leads. She understood why Ethan took him off the case, but being a part of the sheriff's department and protecting people was all he'd ever wanted. But he was still here. By her side. For now.

Her chest tightened. How long would he stay if Ethan built a case against her? Would that tear Adam's relationship with his boyhood friend apart? Could love survive that kind of doubt or guilt?

Damn, the waiting was killing her. In the silence, the ticking of the clock felt like a countdown to her doom. When would Ethan get here? Maybe if she wished hard enough, he'd tell her this was all a mistake. A nightmare she could wake up from.

The crunch of gravel and the sweep of headlights across the windows were all the warning they got. Emily set the untouched tea on the coffee table, her fingers trembling as she did. Was this the moment he told her she had the right to remain silent? Would he take her out in cuffs? The thought made her stomach cramp.

Adam rose to open the door, his jaw tight, but not before leaning down and kissing her on top of her head.

"Everything is going to work out," he murmured.

She almost laughed. A promise, even if he couldn't know for sure. But one she desperately wanted to believe.

Then he crossed to the door and opened it before Ethan even got out of the cruiser.

Ethan stepped out of the cruiser and faced the man he'd known all his life. The man whose face was set in stone.

"Adam ..."

"Don't." Adam put his hands up.

Ethan nodded. "I'll be brief. For now."

He found Emily sitting on the sofa, her hand wrapped around her middle.

"Emily ..." Ethan lowered himself into the chair across from her. The faint smell of some herb he couldn't identify was in the air, but beneath it was a sour, vinegary smell he recognized all too well. Fear.

"I just need to clear a few things up. First off, I'm sorry this is happening to you, and I promise to get to the bottom of this quickly."

"Just ask me your questions, Ethan," she said quietly.

Adam walked over and sat next to her and reached for her hand.

Ethan exhaled. God, this was harder than he thought. How do you accuse your friend's lover of murder? He pulled out his notebook. "Okay. You said you left the spa around five on Saturday."

"I did," Emily replied.

"Sometimes people forget things," Ethan countered. "Keys. Purse. Phone. You ever pop back in?"

Emily blinked. "I ... no. At least I don't remember going back in." She glanced over at Adam. "I was looking forward to our date."

Ethan sat there quietly, letting Emily try to remember Saturday night. The silence was broken only by the ticking of the clock. Sometimes people tried to fill in the silence.

Emily's neck flushed red. "I left Morgan at the desk to

finish up. I don't know how long that took her. Sometimes half an hour, sometimes more. She mentioned Celeste had left earlier. She left before me, but … I didn't actually see her walk out.

"I didn't even know Jennifer was still there," Emily continued, her voice rising. "Do you really think I would've walked out, waited until everyone left and then come back and kill her? In my own spa? For what reason?"

Ethan took a deep breath. "People do desperate things."

"Goddamn it, Ethan," Adam bellowed. "You can't believe Emily killed that woman."

Emily laid her hand over his, her voice soft. "It's okay, Adam, he has to ask."

"Adam," Ethan replied, keeping his tone firm. "You're a deputy sheriff. You know I have to ask hard questions to get to the bottom of this. I'm doing it the right way so no one can ever say I showed favoritism. Or that I looked the other way because of who was involved."

A growl was all Ethan got in reply.

"Okay, so Jennifer asked you a lot of questions, Emily. Like what? Did she ever confront you about anything?"

Emily shook her head. "She was curious as to how long I had owned the spa. Would I ever offer Botox or fillers? Was I upset about the new spa? Things like that."

Ethan wrote it down, though none of it sounded right. The notes he saw on Jennifer's computer told a different story. All of it circled back to Emily.

"What about Boston?"

Emily's head snapped up. "Boston?"

"Jennifer was digging into a Boston cover-up." He watched her carefully. "Why would she connect your name to that?"

Emily's fingers tightened around Adam's hand. Her throat bobbed up and down.

"I ..." she started, swallowed hard. "She didn't have the whole story."

Ethan leaned back, his eyes narrowing. "Then tell me what it was."

She opened her mouth, but no words came out.

Adam cocked his head and stared at her. Waiting.

The silence stretched.

Ethan's pen hovered above his notebook, but he didn't write. He just watched Emily. Every instinct told him she was hiding something. If she talked, maybe he'd get the answers he needed. If she didn't ... well, the suspicion only grew heavier.

Fifteen

Emily's mouth opened, but no words came out. The silence was overwhelming except for the pounding of her heart. Ethan waited expectantly. Adam looked at her curiously.

She took a steadying breath. "It wasn't what Jennifer made it out to be."

The memory washed over her as if it were yesterday. The scent of eucalyptus, the bustle of the spa, the music playing overhead. It had been her safe spot, her happy spot. Until it wasn't.

She blew out her breath. "I worked at a place called Evolve MedSpa, a high-end spa in Back Bay," she whispered. "On the surface, it was all about health and beauty. We offered state-of-the-art treatments, exclusive memberships." She looked over at Ethan. "It was the kind of place people paid too much money to be seen at, hoping for perfection.

"But—" Her voice dropped as if Boston could hear her. "Underneath, there were whispers of offering injections they weren't licensed for. Fillers. Botox done off the books in treatment rooms. There were rumors of women who had complications, but nothing ever reached the papers. It was all brushed under the rug."

Ethan and Adam were staring at her, mesmerized by her statement.

She twisted her fingers together. Adam reached over to hold her hand, giving her comfort. She gave him a small smile. "I never saw it directly. But something wasn't right." Emily sighed. "You have to understand, the business was divided into two sections. The massage therapists worked on one side; the treatments were on the other. So, while there was a break room in between where we could congregate, one side really didn't know what the other was doing.

"I left because I wanted no part of that mess." Her eyes flicked toward Adam and then Ethan. "I couldn't stand by and pretend nothing was happening while rumors swirled about people getting hurt. That's not who I am." She swallowed hard. "Jennifer must have thought I was involved or knew more than I did. I walked away from that before it could swallow me, before I became just another person looking the other way."

Ethan leaned back. "You're saying there were rumors that women were harmed. And that's why you left."

Emily nodded. "Yes."

His eyes narrowed. "Why wouldn't you have reported that to the police?"

The question landed like a punch. Her chest constricted. Why indeed? She should have. Any decent person would have. But she remembered the whispers that died when management walked into the break room, the subtle threats at staff meetings, the way people who asked too many questions disappeared from the schedule.

"I ..." She bit her lip. "I didn't have proof. Just rumors." She closed her eyes, then opened them again. "People who asked questions didn't last long at Evolve. I wasn't brave enough to take them on. So, I did the only thing I could do. I got out. Came here for a new start."

Ethan didn't look convinced. "So instead of doing the right thing, you walked away. And now someone who's investigating Evolve ends up dead in your spa, and I'm supposed to believe you had nothing to do with it?"

Emily flinched. The bile rose in her throat, sour and acidic.

Before she could reply, Adam jumped up. "Enough." His eyes were blazing. "You don't get to come into my home and treat her like a suspect. She told you the truth. If you want to chase ghosts in Boston, fine, but don't you dare throw this on Emily."

For a moment, the two men stared at each other. Boyhood friends standing on opposite sides of a line neither wanted to cross.

Ethan's jaw flexed. Then he exhaled and leaned back into the chair. "Fine. I'll back off for now."

He snapped his notebook shut. "But we're not done here. I need to hear from Ezra, and my IT guy is still digging through Jennifer's laptop. I have no idea what he'll find, but if her notes point back to Boston and you, Emily, you'll have to give me more than rumors."

Emily pressed her lips together.

Adam's hand closed over hers. "Then wait until you have the facts, Ethan. Don't come in here and make accusations until you do."

Ethan rose. "Fair enough. I'll be in touch."

He closed the door softly behind him.

Emily sagged against the cushions. Her pulse was racing in her ears. She hadn't been handcuffed, but nothing had been resolved.

ETHAN SLIPPED out the front door. His last vision was of Emily looking pale, wrung out, and Adam gathering her in his arms.

On the surface, what Emily said made sense. It sounded like the kind of thing he'd expect from Emily. Still, the cop in him heard the pause, the way her eyes darted toward Adam before she spoke.

She was telling the truth, just not all of it, and he wondered what was missing.

He took a deep cleansing breath, inhaling the brisk, cold air. It burned his lungs but steadied him. This was the first time in his career that he had felt torn.

Inside the house was his boyhood friend. The friend who stood by him all through the years. Stood by him when his ex-fiancée, Corrine, left him for greener pastures, when he'd nearly lost his badge on that domestic call years ago. Adam had always been there backing him up.

He could still see that incident as clear as day. A rundown trailer surrounded by junk, the smell of booze and anger thick in the air. The call had spiraled out of control fast. The husband was drunk and swinging; the wife was screaming, and the little kids were crying.

Ethan had drawn his weapon, shouting commands, his pulse hammering through his body. The man chose that moment to lunge at Ethan, stumbling along the way. He quickly holstered his gun and reached for his Taser instead—less lethal, safer with kids nearby. He fired. The prongs hit. The man jerked and went down hard, slipping off the edge of the trailer on the way. The sound of his head hitting still made Ethan's stomach twist.

When the dust settled, Internal Affairs had questions. The

photos, the statements, the body-cam footage, all said the same thing. Justified, but barely. His dad, who was sheriff at the time, couldn't get involved, and now Ethan understood exactly how Adam must feel, caught between loyalty and duty.

Back then, Adam stood by him, defending his judgment when no one else would. If not for Adam, Ethan wasn't sure he'd still be wearing the badge.

And now that relationship might be fractured.

He shoved his hands into his pockets. Adam knew, hell, he had to know that he couldn't ignore the evidence, give Emily a free pass. It was his job to dig until he found the truth, no matter how much it hurt.

But he also knew that when love was involved, it bent the rules. It changed the way a man saw things. Adam wasn't just defending Emily because she was scared, he was defending her because his heart was on the line.

And for a moment Ethan wondered if doing the right thing might cost him the one friendship he thought he could always count on.

The drive to his house was quiet except for the low hum of the engine. He couldn't turn off his thoughts. Boston. Cover-ups. Unsanctioned procedures.

What a fucking mess. One journalist dead, Emily's name tied to Boston, Adam caught in the middle. The Boston police would have to clear that up, but if Emily was involved in any nefarious activity, Adam would be devastated.

He drove past Tanner's place. The lights were still on. Tanner and Leah were probably having dinner. He drove a little farther. The porch light on the farmhouse glowed as he pulled into the drive. Jane's silhouette peered out the window. By now, she had to have heard what happened. Emily was her friend.

The door opened as he stepped onto the wraparound porch. "Ethan," she murmured as she pulled him in for a kiss.

The scent of roast beef and freshly baked bread made his stomach growl.

"Do you want to eat or talk about it?" she asked.

Ethan sighed. He took off his jacket and hung it up. "My stomach can't handle food right now."

"Then sit. I'll get you a beer." She looked over at him. "Maybe a double scotch and you can tell me what happened."

He sat and stared at the fire Jane had started. He was home, yet it felt alien.

"Here you go," she said, handing him a glass, then placed a cup of tea for herself on the table and sat next to him on the couch. "What happened? I heard there was a death at the spa."

"Yeah." Ethan rubbed a hand over his jaw, took a long swallow of his drink and set the glass on the coffee table. "A journalist was murdered investigating a cover-up in Boston. And everything points to Emily being the killer."

Jane arched a brow. "Emily? Come on, Ethan. You can't believe that. It doesn't fit."

He tilted his head back. "Doesn't matter. The evidence is lining up, and her name is in the middle of it."

"Boston?" Jane asked, her voice tight with curiosity. "What kind of evidence?"

"Rumors," Ethan replied, hating to even talk about it. "Emily claims the spa she worked at, Evolve MedSpa, was offering treatments under the table and some women had complications. Supposedly it was all hush-hush, whispers but nothing official." He blew out his breath. "I found notes on the journalist, Jennifer Bishop's computer pointing toward Emily."

Jane took a sip of the tea. "Evolve MedSpa? I worked crime stories for years, talked to half the precinct and never heard of them." She shook her head thoughtfully. "But then again, hush money can make a lot of noise disappear."

She leaned forward. "If you want, I can reach out to a few old contacts. See what they know."

"No." Ethan's jaw tightened. "Stay out of it, Jane."

She blinked. "Excuse me?"

Damn. Now he had done it. Jane was like a dog with a bone when it came to mysteries and crime. "Sweetheart," he said, his voice low. "I know you want to help, but this time you might do more harm than good."

She leaned back on the couch, her lips tight. "So, I'm just supposed to sit back while you try to either clear my friend's name or condemn her? Oh, I can't even imagine how Adam feels about this."

"Adam." Ethan scrubbed a hand over his face. "God, I felt like I was betraying them just by asking."

"They're your friends."

"Exactly." He stared at the floor. "Adam's been there for me so many times. Back when Corrine left, back when IA had me under a microscope after a domestic call. He's always had my back. But tonight, it felt like I was driving a wedge between us with every question."

She reached for his hand. "You weren't. It's your job." Her gaze softened. "But I know what it's like when people look at you and see guilt instead of truth."

Ethan looked at her. She rarely brought it up, but he knew where she was going.

Her voice lowered. "When Mike died, the police thought it was because of one of my stories. That someone thought that they'd get back at me by killing him. For months I believed it too. The police pointed fingers at me." Her voice caught. "It wasn't true. It was an accident, but the guilt nearly broke me."

Ethan's chest ached. He squeezed her hand. "That was never your fault, Jane."

"I know that now, but at the time?" She shook her head. "I

would've given anything for someone, anyone, to look me in the eye and say they believed me. So, if you believe Emily isn't lying, she needs you to stand steady even if the evidence says otherwise because suspicion alone can ruin a person faster than any bullet."

Her words sank deep. He didn't believe Emily was guilty of murder, but she was definitely hiding something.

Jane shifted then. "She's lucky. She's got Adam and friends who will stand by her side."

"You're right." Ethan let out a long breath. "But I need you to trust that I'll do my job. I know how my best friend feels, but I have to find out the truth. Promise me you'll stay out of this."

The silence stretched between them. Then Jane nodded slowly. "Fine. I promise. For now. But don't ask me to sit by while Emily drowns under suspicion. She has friends here. We'll make sure she doesn't get isolated."

He reached over and pulled her into his arms. "Just let me handle this the right way."

Ethan kissed the top of her head, knowing that Jane might promise to stay out of it, but trouble had a way of finding her. He sighed. This was going to be a long investigation. However, if his IT guy and Ezra turned up something different, then friendship and loyalty might not be enough.

Sixteen

The station smelled of burnt coffee and something sweet—doughnuts! It was Tuesday. Doughnut Tuesday! A tradition Nora kept alive as long as Adam could remember, going back to Ethan's dad when he was sheriff. How did it all begin? He had no clue.

The box sat open on the break-room counter. Several doughnuts were missing, and he got a glimpse of a chocolate glaze, his favorite, before looking away. His stomach roiled, unsettled from too little sleep and too much worry.

Adam walked to his desk, avoiding the stares of the couple of deputies who were working. Thankfully, it was a slow morning, and only a few people were here today. Still, he felt the unspoken curiosity lingering in the air.

He hated leaving Emily. He'd nearly called in for a personal day, but she insisted he go to work. That was what she was going to do. Do normal things, she said. Although nothing about this case was normal.

He shrugged his jacket off, hung it on the back of his chair and dropped into his seat. The paperwork was neatly stacked on one side—incident reports, traffic citations, last night's arrest report and several noise complaints. It was never-ending. Paperwork never took a holiday or time off for sickness, tragedy or the heartache of real life. Although the sight of it grounded him. Emily was right. There was comfort in routine, in normal, but it didn't silence the chaos in his head.

However, his mind wasn't on any of it. All he could think about was Emily. How pale she'd gotten when Ethan pressed her. How scared and yet brave when she said she had to walk away from Boston. She'd been alone, and God only knew what could happen to those who blew the whistle. He wanted to believe every word out of her mouth. God help him, he did believe her. But ... the badge on his chest whispered caution.

He'd already read Olivia Metcalfe's piece in the *Beaver Creek News*. Olivia had been careful in reporting Jennifer's death without pointing fingers at Emily. Adam only hoped Emily wouldn't see it. The thought of her reading it made his chest ache.

Across the room, Ethan's office door was shut. Adam could see his shadow pacing, chasing answers. He knew his best friend wouldn't rest until he had them.

Adam leaned back in his chair, staring at the ceiling. He always thought of himself as the kind of man who never wavered between right and wrong. But right now, the lines were blurred to hell and back. Ethan was right to take him off the case because the woman he'd fallen for was the same woman his badge said to question.

THE STAIRWELL CREAKED as Emily came down from her apartment. She'd showered and changed, hoping to wash the nightmares, fear and lingering scent of lavender off her skin. Normally, the faint scents of lavender and eucalyptus calmed her. But not this morning. In fact, she was going to change out the lavender for something else. Something that didn't carry memories of blood and death. Maybe chamomile, which was also calming, with a touch of sandalwood for warmth. Yes! That would work.

The yellow crime scene tape was still strung across the locker room and supply closet. She forced herself not to stare and walked toward her office. Her palms were damp, and each step sounded too loud in the quiet hallway. She wondered whether anyone would be in today. Hopefully, Morgan and Celeste and whoever else was scheduled would show up. Coming here today was a huge step for her, but Emily was determined not to let this get her down. She'd worked and sacrificed too much to give in.

Her office door was ajar. That wasn't how she had left it. Although yesterday was a blur, so maybe she had.

She stepped in. It looked the same, but sitting dead center was a folded copy of the *Beaver Creek News*.

Her chest went tight.

Emily pulled out her chair and picked up the paper. Time to get this over with. The front-page article had Olivia's byline above the story of Jennifer's death.

Suspicious Death Under Investigation at Serenity Spa

By Olivia Metcalfe, Staff Reporter

The Beaver Creek community was shaken when the sheriff's department responded to a call at Serenity Spa on Firehouse Road. A woman was discovered deceased in the building late Monday morning.

Authorities have identified her as Jennifer Bishop, 32,

> of Falls Village, New York. Bishop was visiting the area at the time of her death. Law enforcement officials have confirmed the case is being investigated as suspicious, although no further details have been released.
>
> Sheriff Ethan McQueeney said in a statement, "We are pursuing all leads at this time. We ask for the public's patience as we work to determine the circumstances surrounding this tragedy."
>
> Serenity Spa remains open to clients, though certain areas of the facility will remain closed during the investigation.
>
> The sheriff's department encourages anyone with information to contact the office directly.

Well, that could have gone worse, she thought. At least her name wasn't there in black and white and bold lettering. Olivia had been careful. But this was a small town. Everyone knew she owned the spa. Everyone would read between the lines and draw their own conclusions. And the irony wasn't lost on her. Rumors in Boston. Rumors in Beaver Creek. She ran from one once. She wasn't running again.

What bothered Emily the most wasn't the article itself but the way it landed on her desk. It was the fact that someone had gone out of their way to make sure she saw it.

Why?

Her stomach tightened. Whoever it was wanted her rattled. Shaken. And the worst part was, it was working.

She sat at her desk and shoved the paper to one side. There was no time for self-pity. No time to fall apart. She needed to get the spa back on an even footing. This was all she had right now. It paid the bills. If she lost clients, staff or, God forbid, the building, what then? Where the hell could she go?

Sure, she could always move back with her parents in Cambridge. They'd welcome her. But damn it, she was a grown-ass woman. Plus, whatever was going on, whatever trouble she was in, she didn't want to bring it to her parents' doorstep.

At least she had Adam behind her. For now, anyway. Later, when she sat across from her friends, she wondered what they would say. Jane had called this morning and said she believed her, but what about the others? The thought that they might suspect her made her stomach knot. She couldn't lose them, not now. She'd already lost one friend, her roommate Shay, who'd warned her to watch out but never said why. Then Shay disappeared, and Emily was left with only questions she couldn't answer.

And then there was Adam. She knew how much he loved being a deputy. How much the job meant to him. How he valued his friendship with Ethan, who was like a brother to him. The thought flashed through her mind that if standing by her put that friendship in jeopardy, she'd have to let him go. The idea was so painful, she shoved it aside, tossing good vibes into the universe that this would all be resolved before it came to that.

The bell tinkled, and she heard voices and footsteps. Morgan peered around the corner.

"Oh goody, you're here. I wasn't sure you would come in this morning."

Emily forced a smile. "Of course I came in. This place doesn't run itself."

Behind Morgan, Celeste gave her a small smile. "I wasn't sure if you read the paper this morning. The reporter was kind, just laying out the facts. Although when I stopped for coffee this morning, I heard someone say maybe the spa wasn't as safe as they thought."

A hot flush crept up Emily's neck, but she lifted her chin. "I read it." She let out a long breath. "Clients expect us to show up, and that's exactly what we'll do. I have faith that the sheriff will find the truth in what happened."

Morgan clapped her hands together. "That's the spirit. We've got a full book today. No time to dwell on the press."

Celeste tilted her head, her voice warm. "I'm sure this will all blow over soon. People just talk when they don't know the full story."

Morgan huffed. "That's right, Emily. It's just rumors. It's a small town, and people live for this."

Celeste's smile lingered. "Of course. Rumors fade fast. People forget once the next shiny story comes along."

Emily nodded. "Then we'll just keep doing our jobs." Still, a chill crept over her skin, raising goosebumps along her arms. If the rumors faded, what would take their place? How much worse could this get? Damn. Not going there today. She took a deep breath. One step at a time.

By noon, Emily was ready to get out of there. She grabbed her purse and headed out. The phone started ringing before she even made it to the front door. Morgan picked up, her voice cheerful. Emily stopped. Morgan's smile dropped a moment later, and all she heard was a lot of uh-huhs and thanks for calling.

"That's the second cancellation this morning," Morgan murmured. "Your two o'clock can't make it."

Before Emily could respond, Sharon, one of the yoga instructors, walked in. "Tell me you saw my texts. Almost half the class dropped out. Do you want me to reschedule or ..."

"Run the class for whoever shows," Emily said quickly. "Consistency matters."

Her stomach twisted as she stepped outside. Clients

canceling. Classes thinning. The phone was still ringing as the door shut behind her. At this rate, she wouldn't be able to afford staff, let alone keep the spa open. And now, lunch loomed ahead. Emily couldn't shake the fear that it would bring more bad news. Then she would find out which of her friends still believed and trusted her and which ones were stepping away.

She thought of Adam, still steady at her side. For now, that had to be enough.

IT WAS a short walk to the Harvest Moon Diner, and Emily was grateful for the crisp, cool day and blue sky. The birds were chirping; there was activity on the street. Normal people doing normal things. Not worrying about being accused of murder.

Inside, the scent of grilled meat and fried onions hit her, and her stomach growled. She'd had been too upset this morning to eat breakfast. Emily spied her friends at a large corner booth and made her way over, pretending not to notice people looking up and away or pointing at her, thinking she couldn't see them.

"Hi," she said breathlessly, sitting next to Jane. She looked around the table and almost cried. Savannah, Piper, Claire, Ivy, Leah and Lily were there.

"Oh my. You all came."

Jane patted her hand. "Of course we did. I hope you didn't think something like a little murder would keep your friends from supporting you."

"Oh, lordy." Savannah sighed. "Leave it to the mystery writer to think a death in Beaver Creek is the next thing to bestseller material."

"Shush." Jane smiled. "We're here for Emily."

"I can't thank you all enough," Emily began. She bit her lip and wiped a tear from her eye.

"No one thinks you are guilty," said Piper. "I was over at the paper this morning. Olivia wanted to come, but she had another story she was working on."

Relief swept through Emily. But doubt still twisted in her gut. Her friends believed her. But how long before the whispers seeped in? And how long before suspicion found its way to them?

"Stop," exclaimed Piper, cutting through her thoughts.

"What?" asked Emily.

"Stop thinking what you're thinking. This is going to be resolved. I just feel it," replied Piper. "Tell us what happened and what is being done."

The server came over just then to tell them the specials and take their drink orders. Emily thought she stared a little too long at her, but it was probably her imagination. Was this how it was going to be? Second-guessing herself, imagining people staring at her? Wondering whether she was a killer or not?

"Emily?" Jane gently poked her in the side. "Can you tell us? Ethan hasn't mentioned a thing, so I have no idea other than what I read in the paper about what happened."

Emily let out a shaky breath. Ethan had never mentioned that she couldn't talk about it, and God, she needed to. "They found her in the supply closet. I didn't really know the woman. She came in for two massages, asking lots of questions. Then, when Ethan came, he found ..." Her voice faltered. "He found her purse in a locker and the diffuser with blood on it in mine."

A shocked silence fell over the table before Savannah spoke. "That's insane. Anyone could have planted those things."

"Exactly," Leah agreed. "The lockers are open for people

to use. Whoever's doing this is setting you up, plain and simple."

Piper shook her head. "I can't believe people believe that. After everything you've done for this town. All the baskets for the shelter fundraiser. The money you raised. It makes me sick."

Ivy reached across the table and touched Emily's wrist. "Ethan's smart and a good sheriff. He'll figure it out. You've got Adam in your corner and us. You're not alone."

Emily wanted to cry. These were her friends, and they were standing by her.

Jane leaned forward. "Details matter," she murmured. "The placement of the purse, the diffuser with blood on it ... that's not random. Someone wanted it to look deliberate." She frowned. "It's almost too deliberate."

Emily blinked at her. "What are you saying?"

"I'm saying I've written enough crime stories and mysteries to know when something feels staged. And this does. Which means there were a few things the killer overlooked. But I promised Ethan I wouldn't poke around, so I'll keep my theories to myself."

She squeezed Emily's hand. "Just know this. Things aren't always what they look like, and the truth has a way of coming out."

Emily swallowed hard. A flicker of hope warmed her chest. For the first time all morning—no, since yesterday—it didn't feel like the ground was slipping out from under her.

Seventeen

Emily dreaded what the afternoon might bring—whether she still had clients, let alone staff. Thank God, Morgan and Celeste had shown up this morning along with Sharon. If they hadn't, she would have lost it.

After hugging the girls goodbye after lunch and promising to keep them updated, she walked back to the spa, enjoying the day a little more. It felt good to have people at her back, even though the whispers and sideways glances at the diner still disturbed her.

She wondered how Adam was faring. It had upset him that he was off her case, but she hoped other work would take his mind off it—maybe a bank robbery or some high-stakes drama would help. Gah, now she was being silly. He was a grown man; this was not the end of the world. She decided to call him when she got to her office.

Cars whizzed by her even on this short walk. Then she heard a police siren, and her heart dropped. Were they after her? Would Ethan stop, get out of the cruiser and handcuff her, right here on the sidewalk? Emily froze, rooted to the spot.

She had the silly thought that she was sure making it easy for the sheriff. Maybe she should make a run for it? Hide—where? The town was too small. Besides, everyone knew where she lived.

Before she could make up her mind what to do, the cruiser passed her and continued on, red lights flashing, siren wailing as it headed out of town. Whew. She let out a shaky breath and shook her head. Now she knew for certain—yep, a life of crime wasn't for her.

Before she realized it, she was standing at the front door of Serenity Spa. A few cars were parked on the street, and she hoped they were clients. She had massages scheduled for most of the afternoon.

Looking at her watch, Emily saw she had a few minutes before calling Adam. She'd check in on him, see how he was doing and maybe suggest he stay with her tonight.

He'd never been in her apartment. Somehow, she'd never thought of inviting him. They either met at a restaurant or she stayed over at his place. But tonight, she wanted the comfort and familiarity of her own place, such as it was.

The spa was quiet when she stepped inside. Morgan glanced up, gave a shrug and went back to whatever she was doing. A yoga class was in session, and several women's voices drifted from the small kitchenette she'd installed for the staff and clients. Water and snacks were available for the taking.

Emily opened her office door, stepped in and closed it behind her. She glanced around. Good. No more surprises. The newspaper she had read this morning was neatly folded at the corner of her desk where she had left it.

Sitting down, she pulled out her phone, took a deep breath and punched in Adam's phone number. After three rings, he picked up.

"Sweetheart. How're you doing? Everything okay? Do you need anything?"

Emily giggled. "I'm fine. Everything is okay, and no, I don't need anything."

"Okay, then. Just called to check on me, huh?"

She smiled, shaking her head, before realizing Adam couldn't see her. "Any chance you could come for dinner and stay overnight at my place?"

Silence.

Emily's eyes scanned the room. Was he going to turn her down?

"I would love to," he replied. "I get off at six. Can I bring anything?"

Hmm. Emily thought for a moment, mentally running through what she had in the fridge. Wine. Check. Beer. Check. Cheese and crackers. Check. Oh! She had a homemade lasagna in the freezer that she could take out.

"No, I have everything. If you want to pick up dessert, that would be great."

"Humph." His voice dropped. "Well now. I will, but I can think of a different kind of dessert that I'd like."

"Men!" Emily chuckled, shaking her head. "I'll see you soon then."

They hung up, and Emily got up to check in with Morgan. "What's the afternoon look like?"

Morgan sighed. "Surprisingly, after a strange morning, we've had only one cancellation, and that was because the woman was sick." She glanced at the schedule. "You have massages at two and four."

"Okay, good." Emily frowned, biting her lip. "Was Celeste able to put together a makeshift changing room in the back? I'm not sure how long the sheriff's going to keep the crime tape up."

"We repurposed one of the facial rooms," she replied. "Looks pretty good."

"Good, it won't be for long." Emily tapped the counter. "Thank you. For everything."

Morgan pressed her lips together. "Emily, you don't have to thank me. This was an unfortunate accident that has nothing to do with you."

"Well, I hope this gets resolved soon."

Emily ran upstairs and took the lasagna out of the freezer and spent the rest of the afternoon tending to business in between massages. Thankfully, the two women she worked on didn't ask any questions. They were regulars, and she would have hated losing their business. She saw Celeste cleaning the mats and doing laundry and exchanged a few words with her. The woman actually brought her a cup of hot coffee late in the afternoon. Emily smiled her thanks, though part of her wondered why it felt odd to accept comfort from someone she barely knew.

"Sure has been a couple of days," Celeste said. "I'm glad to see you back at work."

"Thanks. I'm hoping we'll be back in business in a day or so." Emily stood. "Do you need help with anything before I go upstairs?"

"Nah, I'm all set. I'll finish cleaning and leave."

Emily stepped out of her office behind Celeste. "Thank you again for coming through for me."

Celeste turned. "Oh, it's my pleasure, sweetie. I'm only glad I can help."

EMILY LEFT Morgan at the front desk to close. Celeste had her own key and would leave when she finished.

She climbed the back stairs to her apartment, unlocked the door, and stepped in. She inhaled the fresh scent of vanilla. No more lavender for her. She picked up a pair of shoes and a top she hadn't had time to put away. Then turned on the shower.

She threw her clothes in the hamper and stepped under the spray, letting the hot water sluice over her body. The pipes rattled a little before settling into a steady stream. There was nothing like a hot shower to get the kinks out and ease the tension. That was the irony of being a masseuse—you had to book an appointment with one just like everyone else. She was past due.

Emily reached for the new vanilla and amber soap she had bought from North Hollow Soap Works, inhaling the warm, rich scent as it filled the steamy air. It was comforting and undeniably sensual. It was perfect, she thought. For Adam.

Laurel Ames had bought the converted carriage house just outside town a while ago, and Emily immediately signed her up to sell her products in the spa. Laurel was an interesting woman. Very calm and grounded except when there was a full moon. She laughingly told Emily and Jane when they visited that she turned into a night owl, rearranging furniture, alphabetizing her spice rack and baking sourdough bread. That led to a long conversation with Jane about how to keep a starter alive and dough hydrated. And while it was more detailed than Emily ever wanted to know, she was the lucky recipient of Jane's sourdough bread, so she couldn't complain.

Emily smiled at the memory as she rinsed off. The soap's scent lingered on her skin, and she couldn't help but wonder if he'd notice. The idea made her stomach flutter like a teenager's. She wanted tonight to feel normal. Well, as normal as living in a house where a murder occurred and being the number one suspect of said murder could be.

She wrapped herself in a towel and padded into her bedroom. The wooden floor was cool under her feet. Opening a drawer, she chose a soft pink sweater and leggings and moved into the kitchen. She slid the lasagna into the oven and set the timer. The warm smell of garlic and tomato already filled her small apartment with comfort.

The wine was chilling; the beer was already cold. She pulled out a log of goat cheese with herbs from Goats R Us, a sharp cheddar from Burlingham Cheesery, and a wedge of Shepsog cheese from Grafton Village Cheese. She placed the crackers around the cheese, and she added a small bowl of olives and another with nuts. Perfect.

Looking around the small apartment, Emily decided she needed candles for atmosphere. She pulled out some from the cupboard, setting a pair on the table, a couple on the coffee table and last, but most importantly, several on her bedroom dresser. She stepped back and glanced around.

Now it was perfect.

ADAM GLANCED AT HIS WATCH. Five forty-five. Fifteen minutes and he could call it a day. Reports sat half-finished in front of him, the words making no sense.

All he could think of was Emily.

Not the case—well, not just the case—but Emily and her apartment. After all this time, he realized he had no idea what it looked like. He could picture the spa, the various rooms, the folded towels, but her apartment? No idea.

He shoved the thought aside, leaning back in his chair. Ethan hadn't said much today. No updates from Ezra or Kyle, the IT guy. He wondered whether Ethan would clue him in when he had information or shut him out.

No, he wouldn't shut him out, but he'd definitely keep the lines clear. Adam was off the case, and Ethan played things by the book. Still, it gnawed at him. He hated to be on the sidelines, especially while Emily was a person of interest.

The station hummed with the usual background noise—phones ringing, the distant chatter of deputies, a drunk yelling from the cell in the back—but Adam's thoughts were on Emily.

He lasted about five seconds before saying, "The hell with it." He grabbed his keys and got into his truck. First stop, Crumb and Co.

A few minutes later, a white bakery box sat on the seat beside him, the scent of chocolate and raspberry filling the cruiser. He drove across town, his thoughts blocks ahead.

When he pulled into the lot behind Serenity Spa, he cut the engine, staring up at the second-floor windows. The past few days, he'd spent more time than he ever had at the crime scene, but he'd never been upstairs.

He walked around to the front door, the bakery box tucked under one arm. Said hello to Morgan, who was working at the counter, and made a detour to the taped-off hallway. Ethan told him he was off the case but never said anything about visiting the scene of the crime. Oh, who was he kidding? It was implied, but still. This was Emily's place. The yellow tape was still there. He figured they'd take it down in the next couple of days.

He walked to the back hall. Celeste was vacuuming and didn't notice him. The vacuum's low roar echoed off the walls. He didn't stop and say hi. She made him uneasy for some reason. Always staring but not saying anything. Weird.

As he climbed the stairs two at a time, his nerves buzzed low in his gut, which was ridiculous. His hand brushed near his hip out of habit as he listened for anything out of place. He'd faced down armed men, walked into situations that could have gotten him killed. But somehow, standing on the landing outside Emily's door with a bakery box tucked under his arm felt more dangerous.

He knocked once, and the door opened. Emily stood there

in a pink sweater and leggings, her hair still damp, and that smile—God, he'd dreamt of that smile. It was like walking out of a storm into the sunlight. He leaned in to kiss her and caught the faintest trace of something warm and sweet in the air clinging to her skin. Vanilla and something else. Soap? He resisted the urge to sniff her.

"Hi," she said softly, stepping aside to let him in.

He hesitated in the doorway. The apartment wasn't large, but it was cozy, scented with candles and the aroma of tomato and cheese. Lasagna—his favorite. The ceilings were low and sloped in the corners, beams cutting shadows across the room. A bookshelf filled with books and knickknacks lined one wall. The furniture reminded him of his own place, mismatched but comfortable. A window seat was tucked under the dormer. There was a small watercolor on the wall of Boston that looked like something Savannah would paint.

The kitchen was not much larger than a walk-in closet. A small table was squeezed into the corner with two chairs already set with plates, real napkins, and wineglasses. She'd already set out cheese and crackers, little bowls of olives and nuts. Candlelight gleamed off the glassware, turning the humble spread into something elegant. It was warm, not at all pretentious and all Emily. His throat tightened. He wasn't used to being welcomed like this.

"Ohhh, you brought something from Crumb & Co."

"Yep. Vanessa had chocolate mousse tarts and raspberry-almond bars. I couldn't make up my mind, so I got some of each." He smirked. "Although I did promise another kind of dessert."

She rolled her eyes, but her cheeks flushed, giving her away.

She took the box from his hand and set it on the counter. "Well, come on in." Emily glanced around as if trying to see the space through his eyes. “It isn’t much, but it’s all mine and doesn’t cost me anything.”

“It’s nice.” He walked over to the window. “You can see the whole town from here.”

She followed his gaze. “Yeah. Not much to look at, but I like it.”

“I do too,” he said quietly. He turned to look at her standing in the soft light of her kitchen. For the first time in days, the weight slid off his shoulders. All that was left was her.

He opened his arms. “C’mere, Em.”

Eighteen

Emily woke with the early morning sun streaming through her window. She didn't need to reach over to know Adam had left. He'd mentioned over dinner that he had to get to the station early. She had heard the shower running, felt him kissing her cheek, then whisper all the things he wanted to do to her that night.

Oh lordy. She was most certainly on board for that. Last night had been different. Not just because he stayed at her place for the first time but because of the quiet moments that struck her. The slow dance in the living room while the lasagna cooled, the way his eyes softened when the candlelight flickered across her face. It was easy and comfortable.

She stretched under the covers, savoring the tenderness of her body. They'd spent most of the night making love. Emily yawned. Adam had to be tired. She certainly was. What she wanted to do was stay in and sleep for a few hours. Hide from reality just a bit longer, wrapped in the lingering warmth of his arms. Unfortunately, there was a business to run, people who depended on her, and then there were her clients. Without them, there would be no business.

Ugh. Emily sat up. On the nightstand was a note propped against the light. *See you tonight. Love you.* There was a tiny smudge where his pen hesitated. They had never said the *L* word. Her chest tightened. He was the one who wanted them to be exclusive, the one who insisted they belonged together. And yet, was it a "love you" tossed out the way people said "love ya" at the end of a phone call? Or a "love you" like he really did?

She knew how she felt. She loved him deep down. But they never sat down and discussed what came next. No future plans, no big declarations. Just moments.

She smiled to herself and threw all those thoughts out to the universe to sort out. For now, she had a shower to take and a business to keep alive.

The morning passed quickly. The good news was the yellow crime tape was taken down. Celeste had already gone in and cleaned. Sharon and the other yoga instructors were already leading classes, and the massage rooms were booked. Emily had a free moment and ducked into her office to grab more brochures. The newspaper, which she had folded and placed on the corner of her desk, was open. Not just open but turned to a new page entirely.

Emily frowned. A bold headline read: "Aspire Day Spa expands community programs: Taryn Keene to speak at the Beaver Creek Chamber of Commerce."

Of all the pages to land on, why that one? And how had she missed that yesterday? Oh yeah, because Olivia's front-page exposé about Jennifer's death was all she read. She never looked further.

"Everything okay?" Morgan asked from the hallway.

Emily held up the paper. "Yeah, just noticed Aspire Day Spa is growing. Guess we'll hear all about it at the Chamber meeting."

Morgan smiled, unconcerned, before walking back to the front desk.

Emily leaned back in her chair, the newspaper resting where she left it. If Morgan hadn't touched it, had Celeste? She did point out Olivia's article yesterday. But why would she leave the paper open to the article about Aspire Day Spa?

She shook her head and sighed. Was she looking at things that didn't matter? Or was she finally learning that every small thing could matter? In this town, secrets hid in plain sight, and even a turned newspaper felt like a warning. But the other thought was someone was sitting at her desk, sifting through her space. Why? Who?

Emily tucked the newspaper away, but the headline still nagged at her. Why was Taryn Keene coming to town to speak to the Chamber? Did she have plans to really put Emily out of business? God, between stealing employees and the murder rap hanging over Emily's head, it wouldn't take much.

Gah. Not going there. She carried the brochures to the front desk and arranged them on the side.

"Thanks," Morgan said, glancing up from the computer. "I forgot to do that."

Emily's gaze drifted over toward Celeste, who was hovering around the front desk.

"Good turnout this morning," Celeste said smoothly. "People need to see we're moving on."

Moving on. Emily swallowed. Easy for her to say. How do you move on from blood and a dead woman in the supply closet and the whole town watching your every move?

Her phone buzzed in her pocket. A text from Adam. *Working late, will talk tonight*.

No smiley face. No *love you*. Just business. Her chest tightened. She slipped the phone back into her pocket. Perhaps she was reading too much in his earlier note.

The front doorbell chimed. She turned with a smile on her face, but it slipped when she saw Ethan stride in.

"Ladies," he said.

Celeste looked up immediately and gave him a big smile. "Sheriff."

Ethan gave her a polite nod, but he was already looking at Emily. "Can we talk?"

Nineteen

Oh God. Oh God. Was Ethan here to arrest her? Emily's heart plummeted. Could things get any worse?

"Sure, Sheriff. Step into my office." The smile froze on her face. Her throat felt tight. Was her voice trembling? Were her hands? She looked over at Morgan, whose brow was furrowed, and Celeste, who looked ... a little too curious.

"Emily?"

"Right, come on in." She stepped aside and let Ethan go first, then closed the door and sat behind her desk.

Ethan took the seat opposite her. "I have a few more questions for you."

"Shoot."

Had she really said that? Oh God, shut up, Emily. What the hell was wrong with her today?

Ethan cocked his head. The sides of his mouth almost ticked upward before flattening again. "Emily, I'm not here to make things worse. I'm trying to get to the bottom of this murder."

"I know," she said, sighing.

"Okay." He pulled out the small notebook she was beginning to hate, clicked his pen. "Tell me about Daniel Cross."

Emily racked her brain and frowned. "Daniel who? I don't know any Daniel."

"Cross," Ethan repeated. "His name was on Jennifer's laptop. He's a journalist. You want to tell me why there was a connection?"

She shook her head slowly. "Still don't know him. I've never met him. I don't know why she'd put my name next to his."

Ethan blew out his breath. "What can you tell me about Shay Richardson? Your roommate in Boston. Care to explain that one?"

Shay! Sweet, innocent Shay. Emily closed and opened her eyes. She could still hear her roommate's voice. "*Be careful, Em. You don't know who you're messing with.*" Then nothing. Silence. Gone.

"I don't know where Shay went," Emily whispered. "One day she was there. The next, she wasn't. But ..." she hesitated. "I always thought something happened to her. She would never just walk away and not tell me."

Ethan's brow tightened. "Anyone report her as missing?"

"She was an only child, and her parents had passed away." Emily swallowed hard. "There wasn't anyone else to look for her."

Ethan leaned forward. "If you were her friend and roommate, why didn't you report a missing person?"

Her stomach knotted. *Good question, Ethan.* No matter what she said, Ethan was going to think she was covering something up. Damn. The truth sounded thin even in her own ears. But it was the truth. At least the truth she had at the time.

"I almost did," she said softly. "But the morning after she

vanished, I got an email from her. Saying she needed space and was chasing the next adventure."

Emily shook her head, her eyes burning. "She was always taking off for a weekend or a new idea. I wanted to believe she was okay."

Her voice dropped to a whisper. "But something about the email felt off. It didn't sound like her. And when days passed, and she didn't call, I knew something was wrong. I was scared." She lifted her gaze to his. "Scared that if I told the police, whoever scared her off would come for me next."

The silence stretched. Ethan stared at her, waiting for answers. Emily stared at her hands, praying she could disappear.

Finally, Ethan straightened, jaw tight. "If you're telling the truth, we'll find out. But if you're holding back ..." He left the rest unsaid.

He lowered his voice. "Emily, I'm trying here. I'm trying to be impartial, even though my best friend is involved with you. Even though my wife and our friends love you. But my duty is to the good folks of Beaver Creek."

Ethan stood, walked over to the door, and turned before leaving. "If you think of anything else, let me know."

When the door clicked shut behind him, Emily sagged against her desk. Her hands trembled. Her heart was racing. She didn't know Daniel Cross. She didn't know what had happened to Shay. But now the sheriff was looking at her like she held the key to both.

ETHAN NODDED at Morgan and Celeste, who were feigning interest in the computer. He strode out of the spa, letting the door swing shut behind him. The crisp mountain air hit his face, sharp and clean, but it didn't do a damn thing to relieve the heaviness in his chest.

He wanted to believe Emily. Always had. She was kind, hardworking, someone who'd taken the broken-down Victorian and turned it into something to be proud of. Adam loved her, that much was clear. And he wasn't lying when he told Emily that Jane and her friends were behind her. They didn't believe she was capable of the crime. But he couldn't ignore the fact that a woman was dead, and Emily's name kept coming up.

Her answers replayed in his head. *"I don't know him. I don't know why Shay disappeared."* She hadn't lied about Shay, practically admitted she suspected foul play but had no proof.

He walked to his cruiser, shoved his hands in his jacket pockets and blew out a long breath. Adam was curious but, thankfully, had not overstepped the boundaries of their friendship to ask about Emily. But as he told Emily, he wouldn't let his friendship cloud his judgment. Not when there was a dead woman on a slab and more questions than answers.

Sliding into the driver's seat, he pulled out his phone. "Mercer, it's McQueeney," he said when his IT guy picked up. "I need you to go through the laptop with a fine-tooth comb and flag anything on a Daniel Cross, Shay Richardson and Emily Harper. I don't care how small, just connect the dots."

"On it," Mercer replied. "I have some preliminary information whenever you're ready. But let me go through again, see what else is on the laptop and do it all at once."

Ethan's phone buzzed with another incoming call. Ezra. He frowned and clicked it on. "Talk to me."

"Prelim only," Ezra said. "Cause of death lines up with asphyxia and compression using an object which fits your diffuser. Bishop's blood is confirmed. I'll have a full write-up on your desk soon."

"Appreciate it," Ethan said.

He ended the call and stared out the windshield. His fingers drummed once against the wheel before curling into a fist. Daniel Cross, Shay Richardson, Boston. Emily's name kept coming up.

He shoved the cruiser into gear and pulled out onto the winding road. If Daniel Cross was in Beaver Creek following Jennifer, he'd bet he was holed up at the Green Mountain Lodge. And Ethan damn well intended to find him.

SHADOWS STRETCHED across the wide porch at the Green Mountain Lodge, making the place look more foreboding than welcoming. Although that could just be his frame of mind. Smoke drifted and swirled in the cold air from the chimney.

Ethan pushed through the door, his boots loud on the wooden floor. The clerk stiffened behind the desk, her smile nervous. "Sheriff."

"I need to speak to one of your guests. Daniel Cross."

She glanced at the keyboard and then looked up at him. "Room 314. I don't know if he's here." She picked up the phone. "I can call and find out."

"No, that's okay."

The clerk put the phone down. Ethan took the stairs two at a time. He could have taken the elevator, but he'd had little exercise today, and his gut told him speed mattered.

On the third floor, he found the room and knocked.

The door cracked open a few inches. A man in his late thirties peered out, hair mussed like he'd been dragging his hands through it, eyes sharp behind wire-rimmed glasses, shoulders tense.

"Daniel Cross?"

The man's eyes flicked to the badge on Ethan's chest, then back to his face. "That's me. Sheriff, right?"

"Yes. We need to talk."

Daniel sighed, stepped back, and opened the door wide. The room behind him was the opposite of Jennifer's. Where hers had been tidy, almost sterile, his looked like a storm had torn through it. The room smelled of stale coffee and BO. It was cluttered with open notebooks, a half-drained cup of coffee, and a laptop opened on the desk.

"You were following Jennifer Bishop before she died, following a story she was digging into," Ethan said. "She's dead, and your name is on her computer. Care to explain?"

Daniel pursed his lips and started pacing the room. He didn't pace as much as prowl—shoulders hunched, head jerking toward Ethan every few steps. "She and I were chasing the same lead. Boston, Beaver Creek, Evolve MedSpa. The cover-ups. And then she winds up dead. There's a story here, and I'm going to print it."

Ethan stepped into the room, closing the door behind him. "Not if it gets someone else killed first."

Daniel stopped pacing and jabbed a finger at him. "All roads lead back to Emily Harper. She lived in Boston and worked at Evolve MedSpa. Her roommate vanishes without a trace. Shay was digging. She's gone. Jennifer thought Emily might know more than she admitted. You can't tell me she doesn't know more than she's letting on."

Ethan studied him. "And what do you think?"

Daniel's voice lowered. "I think Emily is neck-deep in something dangerous. Either she's running from it, or she's smack dab in the middle of it. I want to make sure Jennifer's death wasn't for nothing."

Ethan's jaw clenches. "Emily's name comes up, yeah. But names don't prove guilt."

Daniel gave a short, humorless laugh. "That's the thing about small towns, isn't it? Everybody circles the wagons. Protects their own. Everyone wants to believe she's sweet as pie. Convenient cover."

Ethan's spine stiffened. No, he couldn't clock this asshole. He took a deep breath. "You don't know this town."

Daniel tilted his head, eyes narrowing behind the glasses. "No, but I know stories. And stories with missing pieces always come back to haunt people who think they're safe."

Ethan stepped closer to Daniel. "Cross, if you've got information, hand it over. Otherwise, stay out of my investigation."

Daniel's jaw flexed. "The truth doesn't stay buried. Sooner or later, it comes out. With or without your badge."

He snatched a notebook from the desk and quickly wrote something only he could read. Ethan's gaze snagged on the movement—left-handed, fast, angry. Daniel slashed an underline beneath whatever he'd written, the stroke so heavy the pen almost ripped the page in two.

The room went quiet. Ethan exhaled slowly. Cross had just lit a fire under Emily, and Ethan wasn't sure whether it would burn her down or burn him if he ignored it.

And that made Daniel Cross a problem.

Twenty

Ethan left the lodge and slid behind the wheel of his cruiser. He blew out his breath. This case had more twists and turns than a back road in mud season. Cross definitely knew more than he was saying, but short of torturing him, which wasn't exactly in the sheriff's handbook, Ethan couldn't make him talk. And thanks to the Vermont Shield Law, reporters like Cross had a layer of protection. Ethan believed in and respected the law. But right now, it felt like a brick wall between him and the truth. Every hour wasted gave the killer more time to run.

His mind kept circling back to Emily. He didn't want to believe she was a murderer, but until he had proof otherwise, he wouldn't, couldn't rule her out.

By the time he got back to the station, his head was pounding. He nodded at Nora, who was on the phone, and walked toward his office. Thankfully, it was quiet. Most of the deputies were out, including Adam. Ethan didn't think he could face Adam right now knowing he had no answers. He desperately wanted to clear Emily or, if he couldn't clear her, at least have enough evidence to book her. This in-between was killing him.

He sat at his desk and closed his eyes. What a clusterfuck. He needed just a little bit, damn, he'd take a minuscule bit of good luck. His fingers drummed against the armrest; it was hard to sit still.

"Ethan!"

Kyle strode in, laptop tucked under his arm. "Finally pulled more from Jennifer's hard drive. You won't believe this."

Ethan straightened. His chair creaked as he leaned forward, bracing his forearms on the desk. "What've you got?"

"First, some of the entries focusing on Emily are time-stamped after Jennifer's murder."

"Damn." Ethan's hand curled into a fist on the desk. That changed the whole investigation. Ethan mentally crossed his fingers that Emily would be cleared.

"Not only that, but Jennifer also mentions Shay was about to blow the whistle on the Boston spa scandal and thought somebody had wanted her gone for good. She flagged Emily's name to get her perspective, but whoever silenced Shay, if she was killed, thinks she maybe confided in Emily."

"That would make Emily the next loose end." Ethan let out a long breath.

Emily wasn't the killer. He dragged a hand over his face, relief loosening his shoulders. "What about Daniel Cross?"

Kyle shrugged. "It looks like professional jealousy. Jennifer was hoping to crack this case and win a Pulitzer, but Daniel was dodging her the whole time, hoping for the same thing."

He hesitated, glancing at his screen. "One more thing. I tried tracing the IP address that accessed those modified files. The signal bounced from the Green Mountain Lodge where Jennifer was staying, so it doesn't tell us much. But someone used her laptop after she died."

Before Ethan could process all the information, his phone buzzed. Ezra.

"Just to update you, Ethan. Based on the wound patterns, the killer was left-handed. There's no question about it."

Ethan's pulse kicked. Left-handed. That ruled Emily out. Relief surged through him. But then the names started flashing through his mind.

Who was left-handed? Morgan. He could still picture her jotting notes with her left hand. Who else?

He drew in a slow breath.

Daniel. He remembered that factoid this morning when Daniel flipped open his notebook and began writing.

Ethan pulled in another steady breath, forcing his mind to keep turning. There was someone else. Not a deputy. Not a reporter. Someone closer to Emily. Yoga instructor? No. Someone else. Then it hit him. Coffee. At the spa. Celeste had handed him a steaming cup, her left hand curled around the handle.

"Thanks, Kyle, that was great work."

Kyle nodded and disappeared down the hall.

Ethan sat in his chair, the silence pressing in, and reviewed his list of potential suspects. The hum of the overhead light competed with the thud of his heart.

Celeste: had access to the spa, especially later at night, too friendly for first meeting her.
Morgan: always there, always watching, computer skills.
Daniel: a reporter with secrets, computer skills.

Three suspects. One killer hiding among them. Or not. It could be someone else entirely.

Ethan leaned back. The chair groaned under his weight as he exhaled. For the first time in days, Emily was off the list. The weight of suspicion he'd been carrying eased but left a sense of urgency. Whoever had killed Jennifer was still out there, and they weren't finished, and it all tied back to the Boston spa scandal.

He'd keep this case close, investigate quietly. Watch the three suspects.

However, there was one thing he had to do first. Emily deserved to hear from him. Adam, too. He shoved away from the desk, grabbed his hat and headed for the door. Time to tell Emily the truth. But until he could cross off the other names one by one, no one in Beaver Creek was safe.

EMILY FINISHED her last massage and drifted into the reception area, rearranging space just to keep herself busy. She adjusted a vase, shifted a stack of brochures, nudged a plant three times before deciding it still looked wrong. Anything to keep busy.

Ethan had left a couple of hours ago, but she still felt his presence and accusations hanging over her. Her chest tightened every time she replayed his questions. She hated how rattled she felt, how it made her stomach knot.

"Everything okay?" Celeste's voice was soft, sympathetic. She leaned against the counter, holding a bucket and brush as if she just happened by. "What did Sheriff McQueeney want with you?"

Emily forced a smile even though her pulse jumped. "Just follow-up questions."

Morgan looked over from the computer, brow furrowed. "He seemed pretty serious. Everything all right?"

Emily swallowed hard. Her palms were clammy, and she rubbed them down the sides of her pants. She didn't like being in the spotlight. Was it concern or curiosity on their part?

Maybe both. She moved the plant again, though the leaves shook slightly in her hand.

"I'm fine," she said, forcing her voice to be light. "Really. Just part of the investigation."

She felt a hand on her arm. Celeste was closer than Emily realized, smiling that all-too-patient smile. "You know you can talk to us if you need to."

Emily nodded. What else could she do? But her mind wasn't on them. It was spinning on Shay. Her roommate. Her friend. Was she dead? Silenced before she could talk? Or had Shay just disappeared, terrified for her life? Either way, if Shay was gone because she knew too much, what did that mean for Emily?

A chill raced through her. She wrapped her arms around herself, suddenly cold. Would she have to disappear too? Was someone already out to get her for reasons she didn't even understand? She never created waves at the spa, never asked questions, always kept her head down.

Ethan's doubt hurt. She knew he was doing his job, knew he wanted more than anything to catch Jennifer's killer. She just didn't want fingers to be pointed in her direction.

All she had now were questions circling around her like vultures, and she wasn't sure whom she could trust anymore. Her throat tightened, and she blinked hard, refusing to let the tears come.

Twenty-One

The day was almost gone, the sky darkening early, as Ethan swung into the Harvest Moon Diner to grab a burger. He'd forgotten about lunch, and his stomach was letting him know. The smell of grilled meat hit him as soon as he stepped inside. The low hum of conversation and the clink of dishes in the background made the place feel alive, a sharp contrast to the heaviness in his chest. He spent a few minutes talking to Leah as she bagged everything up for him. He'd eat in the car on the way to Adam's house.

Adam had left the office a short time ago, mentioning he was going to meet Emily at his house. Perfect. He could talk to the two of them together.

He steered his cruiser down Adam's gravel drive. The glow of lights shone through the windows, a welcome sight after the day he'd had. How many times over the years had he come down this driveway, with the smell of a bonfire and the sound of their friends' laughter hanging in the air? Back then, he never thought he'd have to put on his sheriff's hat and tell his best friend to step back from a case and maybe even fracture their relationship.

He hadn't given Adam any updates, so he hoped this would be good news. It also meant that Adam could be involved in the case again, something he knew his friend desperately wanted, as did he.

Ethan turned off the engine and sat there for a moment, the burger sitting heavy in his gut. After all this, he hoped he hadn't ruined a lifelong friendship. He knew they'd be happy, but was it enough? Would they blame him for letting it go this far? He'd worn the badge long enough to know the job always took something. He just prayed it hadn't taken Adam's trust. The silence in the cruiser was suffocating until he shoved the door open and stepped into the cold night air.

Damn. Time to get this party going.

Ethan knocked twice on the door. Adam opened it, holding a beer in one hand, frowning, and cocked his head. "Ethan."

"Can I come in?"

Adam stepped aside, allowing Ethan to enter. Emily was at the kitchen island chopping vegetables, and the scent of garlic and onions filled the air. The cozy domestic scene should have been comforting, but normalcy and murder didn't belong in the same room. Yet here they were.

Emily glanced over at him, offering a polite smile, but the tension lingered in her shoulders. "Sheriff."

Not Ethan but Sheriff, and boy did that hurt.

Adam had come to stand beside Emily. The three of them stood there, silent. Staring at each other.

Adam broke it first. "You look like a man with something on his mind."

Ethan cleared his throat. "Long day." He nodded toward the cutting board. "Smells good in here."

Adam took a long pull from his bottle, then set it down with a thunk. His eyes narrowed.

"Cut the crap, Ethan. You didn't come here just to compliment dinner. What's going on?"

Ethan blew out his breath. "Yeah," he said, his gaze shifting between the two of them. "It's about the case. And you both need to hear it."

Emily's knife stilled mid-slice. She looked at him wide-eyed. Adam put his arm around her as she placed the knife carefully on the board.

Ethan rubbed the back of his neck. "The coroner said the blow came from a left-handed person. There were no prints on the diffuser, but the blood was all Jennifer's. As far as the department is concerned, you're cleared."

She took a deep breath and pressed her hands flat onto the counter. "Cleared?"

"Cleared," Ethan confirmed.

Adam smiled. He bent his head toward Emily. "Told you," he said quietly. "Didn't I tell you?"

Ethan cleared his throat. "Before you start celebrating, there's more. The evidence does point somewhere, but I'm not ready to share details yet. What matters is that the killer's still out there. And Emily ..." He glanced at her. "You're not out of danger. I think you're being targeted."

The relief in the room evaporated. Emily's breath hitched. Adam pulled her closer, his arm tightening around her protectively, and looked at Ethan.

"Then we make sure she's not alone," Adam said.

Ethan gave a short nod as he turned toward the door. "I'll see you tomorrow."

They didn't need him lingering. They needed each other and time to process what this all meant.

EMILY MOVED TO THE COUCH, watching as Adam shut the door and locked it behind Ethan. What a day this had been. She was up, then down, now up again. Cleared. She could almost breathe. But Ethan's words echoed in her mind.

You're not out of danger.

What did that even mean? In danger from whom?

She'd thought the worst part was being a suspect. Now she wasn't so sure. The shadows outside the window seemed darker. The old house creaked. Every sound felt amplified. Fear prickled her skin. Would she have to look over her shoulder forever, wondering who would want to harm her? And why?

Adam came and sat beside her, his arm sliding around her waist. She leaned into him, grateful for his warmth and strength.

"You're not carrying this alone," Adam murmured, pressing a kiss to her temple. "We'll figure this out."

Emily nodded. God, she really wanted to believe him, to pretend none of this was happening. But deep down, she knew better. A killer was out there. And if Ethan was right, she was in their crosshairs.

Adam pulled her tighter against his chest, his hand slowly rubbing her arm. She let herself sink into him. For tonight, she wasn't alone.

Tonight, she would let herself rest in his arms. Tomorrow? Who knew what tomorrow would bring?

BY THE TIME Ethan eased into his own driveway, the burger sat heavy like a brick in his stomach. Although giving good news to Emily lifted some of the weight in his chest, it was offset by the warning. His headlights washed over the house, and for the first time in hours, he was grateful to be home.

He stepped into the quiet house, shrugging off his jacket. Jane was curled on the sofa in front of a crackling fire, a book in her hand. She looked up with a smile, then her expression shifted.

"Tough night?"

"You could say that." He sat beside her, letting out a long sigh. "Emily's cleared." He rubbed his hands over his face. "But it's not a win yet. I'm worried that she has a target painted on her back."

Jane set the book down and laid her hand over his. "Then we keep watch. You've done everything you can tonight."

For the first time all day, the knot in his gut loosened a fraction. He leaned back, letting her warmth soak in. Jane shifted closer, tucking herself to his side, steadying him. He let his arm fall around her, pulling her in. For a few moments, he let himself forget about the case and just feel the quiet, the fire and her.

For now, the world was simple. Safe. He closed his eyes for a moment, relishing the warmth of her tucked against his side. But he knew it couldn't last. Tomorrow would bring the weight of the case all over again.

Twenty-Two

By the next morning, Emily forced herself back into her routine. She'd spent the night cuddling with Adam, not exactly celebrating but breathing a sigh of relief that she was no longer under suspicion and yet terrified that someone was gunning for her. She was sure it had to do with Boston, but who? Why?

It was a bright, beautiful day. The birds were singing. The sky was blue with puffy white clouds except for that very dark one hanging low over the mountains. Emily sighed. That was her life right now. Sunshine all around but always a storm waiting to break.

Morgan was at the front desk when she arrived. "You look like the weight of the world slipped off your shoulders. Everything okay?"

Emily exhaled. "Ethan said I'm cleared of Jennifer's death."

Morgan let out a whoop. "Thank God. I knew they'd figure out you're not a killer."

"Yeah," Emily murmured. "It feels good to breathe again."

"So do you and Deputy McDreamy have plans to celebrate?"

Emily rolled her eyes. Before she could answer, Celeste sidled up to the desk. "Is it true? You're in the clear?"

"Yes," Emily replied. "Finally."

"Well then, that's cause for celebration," said Celeste. She looked over at Morgan. "We should do something."

Morgan grinned. "Yes!"

Emily shook her head quickly. "No. No parties. No celebrations. Not yet. I just ..." She exhaled. "I just need normal for a while."

Morgan's grin faltered, but she nodded. "Oh, of course. Normal is good."

Celeste tilted her head, still holding a rag in her hand. "Of course. Whatever is best for you."

Emily tapped the desk. "I appreciate your concerns. I'm fine. This will be fine." Her gaze shifted toward the hallway. "And I noticed Mrs. Klein is here for her massage." She offered a small smile before adding, "I appreciate you both hanging on and supporting me."

NORMAL? Supporting her? Emily was delusional if she thought that. As if being cleared erased Boston, erased guilt, erased whispers. As if it erased Marcus's death and the destruction of her life.

Foolish girl. Celeste pressed harder onto the table she was dusting as Emily's footsteps faded toward the back hallway. The citrusy-clean scent of polish filled her nose, sharp and stinging.

The front door chimed. Celeste straightened. A man

stepped inside: tall, slender, brown hair, glasses perched on his nose. His eyes swept the spa like he was cataloging every detail. Celeste didn't recognize him.

Morgan gave him a bright smile. "Welcome to Serenity Spa. Looking for a gift or a treatment?"

The man gave a polite smile. "I was thinking of surprising my wife."

Morgan stepped around the desk, brochure in hand. "Perfect. We have great packages. Massages, facials, yoga classes, you name it. Would you like a tour?"

"Yes, that would be great."

As Morgan pointed toward the massage rooms, his questions started. Not about prices. *How many staff work here? Was the murder connected to the spa? Is it safe after what happened?*

That was the one thing about being a cleaning woman—you blended into the background. Invisible. People talked freely as if you weren't there. Her rag moved in small circles, but her ears caught every word.

Morgan told him how many staff worked there. "We're completely safe. The sheriff himself comes here, you know. Everyone's been cleared. It was just a terrible thing." She moved on quickly, turning down the other hall toward the yoga classes and locker room.

Celeste laughed. The sheriff certainly did come here. Not to get spa'd but to investigate. She wiped the table harder, listening. A little too curious, this "husband." He tucked the brochure under his arm. "Good to know. I'll call when I decide what I want."

"Okay, Mr. ..." Morgan started.

"Mr. Jacobs."

No phone number. No credit card. No wife's name. Just a quick look around and he was out.

Morgan let out a breath, shaking her head. "Weird guy. But hey, if he buys a package, who cares?" She shrugged and sat back at the computer.

Celeste twisted the rag. Stupid girl. Mr. Jacob wasn't a husband. He was a journalist looking for dirt. She knew the type. Just like Jennifer, who thought she could dig up secrets.

She wondered what his angle was. Was it the murder? Was it Jennifer or Boston? The thought sent a chill down her spine, but she forced it away. Whatever "Mr. Jacobs" wanted wasn't her problem.

Celeste's rag twisted in her hands, her anger fixed squarely on Emily.

OUTSIDE, "MR. JACOBS" drew his first real breath, adrenaline coursing through his veins.

Wow, that had been intense. The thrill of being undercover never got old. His heart was pumping, and he wanted to jump for joy. There was a story there for sure.

The spa's door shut behind him, cutting off the soft music and scent of eucalyptus. Daniel blinked in the brightness of late morning, then headed for his rental car down the street.

Inside, he sat for a moment, carefully folded the glossy brochure into thirds, his left hand working automatically while his right stayed on the steering wheel. The receptionist had been too eager to show him around, eager to insist the spa was safe and eager to distance Emily Harper from the murder. He'd learned some of what he needed. People were nervous but happy to pretend everything was normal.

And that cleaning woman pretending to dust the same area repeatedly. She hadn't said a word, but he could feel her looking at him with sharp eyes, almost as if she knew what he was doing there. It was unsettling. She didn't match any of the faces from Boston. Just another worker in the background, he convinced himself.

His focus returned to Emily. He hadn't seen her today. Not yet. But he would. He had to look her in the eye and decide for himself if she was guilty of the cover-up or not.

Daniel tapped his fingers against the steering wheel. "Mr. Jacobs." The alias slipped easily off his tongue. They hadn't questioned it. No one ever did when you smiled just right and looked harmless. He wasn't here to be harmless.

Boston had left too many loose ends. There were too many buried stories. Jennifer thought she was chasing one, and now she was dead. That wasn't a coincidence. Just like Shay Richards disappearing.

He still remembered the last email Jennifer had sent him, probing, trying to see if he knew more than she did. He'd learned the hard way not to give up any information. She gutted one of his biggest stories, twisted it and slapped her own byline on it. He hated her for that. Still did.

So, no, he wasn't sorry she was dead. Nope. Not at all.

But even through his anger, one thing was clear. There was a story here. A big one. He just didn't know the angle yet. But he would. He wasn't leaving Beaver Creek until he found it.

Movement caught his eye. A marked cruiser pulled up to the front door. Daniel's pulse jumped. Sheriff? He ducked low. If it were the sheriff, that could blow everything up.

But when the door opened, the man looked different. A deputy.

Daniel leaned back, exhaling slowly. Why was the deputy there? Did the sheriff send him? Or was this someone closer to Emily? He squinted through the windshield.

A moment later, Emily appeared. The man rested his hand lightly on her back, guiding her out. Protective. Possessive. He opened the cruiser door for her like it was second nature.

Daniel's thumb traced the folded edge of the brochure. Hmm. With a deputy at her side, acting like a boyfriend. That wasn't nothing. It meant Emily Harper wasn't just under suspicion, she was under protection.

That was interesting. Very interesting.

Twenty-Three

Emily slipped out of Adam's place early Sunday morning, the cold air welcome following the hot and heavy sexcapades last night. The girls were gathering at Savannah and Dylan's house to fill baskets for the annual fundraiser for Harbor Haven, a women's shelter in town that Serenity Spa sponsored.

Was it only a year ago that she and Savannah were doing the same thing when everything shattered? When they were kidnapped? The memory had the power to twist her gut. She and Savannah had come so far from that day.

But today wasn't about fear or bad memories. Today was about hope, giving other women a new lease on life and a safe place to land.

Jane and Savannah were in charge of acquiring the baskets and getting them ready. Piper, Leah, and Lily would be there to help fill them. Also, Skye Penrose, the whirlwind behind Rustic Revival.

The drive to Dylan's was a good twenty minutes from Adam's place. The sky was cloudy, maybe rain or snow. She crossed over the Callahan Bridge, the river running dark beneath it, and pulled in beside Jane's car. Laughter drifted from the house.

Savannah answered the door when she knocked.

"Oh, goody. You're here!" exclaimed Savannah. "Leah was just about to make her famous Bloody Marys."

Emily groaned. "Shoot. I forgot the cheese bread I was going to bring."

Savannah tugged her inside with a laugh. "Trust me, there's enough food for ten more people."

The air smelled of cinnamon, coffee and garlic. The familiar voices were comforting. Emily let herself sink into it, the normalcy she'd been craving.

She passed through the living room with its floor-to-ceiling windows letting in light and saw about fifty baskets stacked neatly off to the side, ready to fill. The house itself was a converted barn with an open-concept design. The girls were laughing and gathered around the massive island. Emily took in the deep-forest-green cabinets and butcher block countertops with brightly colored pots filled with herbs. It was calming, earthy and definitely an artist's kitchen.

"Where's Moose?" asked Emily, already bracing for a lot of loving from the giant pup.

"Oh, Dylan is getting together with Tanner and Ethan. He took him so we could relax," replied Savannah.

Jane laughed. "I just hope the house is still in one piece when I get home."

"Hmm, Moose has been going for dog training." Savannah's brow furrowed, though she tried to sound confident. "I'm sure everything will be okay."

"I'm only kidding," Jane replied quickly, waving a hand. "He's a sweetheart."

Emily turned her attention to the food spread on the island. "Oh, Leah, you brought your mini ham and cheese quiches and those yummy cinnamon rolls."

"Yup." Leah pointed to another basket. "Skye brought sourdough bread, croissants and cranberry nut bread and assorted jams."

"Bread is my love language," Skye said with a wink.

"Piper made the lemon poppy seed bread," Lily chimed in. "And I made the seasonal fruit salad with a honey-lime drizzle and the veggie frittata."

"And I brought the tomato juice, vodka, shrimp and pickled green beans for our Bloody Marys," Piper announced, holding up a jar of green beans. "I pickled them myself."

Emily gazed at the silky fish, soft cream cheese coated in chives, pickled red onions, capers, dill, and a tower of sliced bagels. "Who put together this beautiful smoked salmon platter?"

"Savannah and I," Jane said. "We thought it would be a perfect brunch centerpiece."

Piper leaned in, lowering her voice. "Honestly, having Dylan take Moose with him was smart. He would have had a field day with this spread."

Everyone burst out laughing. Emily took a moment to let herself feel normal. The food, the laughter and this group of women who had her back.

Savannah clapped her hands. "Okay, everyone grab a Bloody Mary and load your plates. After we eat, we'll fill the baskets."

It didn't take long to fill plates and sit at the long dining room table that Savannah said was handmade with wood cut on the property by a friend of theirs, James Monroe. And it was beautiful. Eight-foot-long boards of pine polished to a golden sheen and grains telling their own story.

The conversation was lively as lunch was devoured, then the dishes picked up and put in the dishwasher.

Savannah clapped her hands, and the chatter died down. "Okay, ladies, time to get serious. We have about fifty baskets to fill, and it seems like half the town donated goodies this year."

The group brought the baskets to the table, and boxes of donations were spread out on the island.

Jane slid a piece of paper from her pocket. "I've got the list. We should fill each basket as we go through the donation boxes. First up is Rose Delaney from the Scented Nook. She sent over hand-poured botanical candles."

"Oh my," exclaimed Piper as she pulled out and smelled each one. "Smells like heaven." They all had different names printed onto their labels. *Hope. Dream. Courage. Second Chance*. Each in pastel colors and herbal scents.

"Next up is honey from Honey Hollow Apiary," Jane said. "Maisie Bellamy makes the best honey."

"Oh, Wild Bean Roasters came through big," said Piper, lifting a bundle of envelopes. "Gift certificates because coffee makes life better."

A box of books for both women and kids drew their attention. "Oh, this is from Mary," said Jane. "She donated books for women and kids. I have to make a trip to see her at the BookNook and thank her."

Skye reached for a box. "Laurel Ames sent soap from her shop, North Hollow Soap Works. Almost too pretty to use."

The group chatted and laughed as they filled the baskets. But the baskets weren't just pretty arrangements of food and gifts. They were lifelines. A reminder to the women and children in the shelter that they mattered, that people cared. The baskets would be auctioned off at the fundraiser, and Emily would deliver the baskets herself to the shelter.

But that wouldn't be the end of it. The proceeds from the fundraiser funded programs at Heartwood Community Center for classes, supplies and even small grants to help women take their next steps forward. One basket meant comfort today and an opportunity tomorrow.

It was a win-win-win in Emily's book. The town got together to donate to the baskets. The fundraiser raised funds to give back to the shelter, and the recipients—the women and children—got a new lease on life.

It was the kind of work that Emily loved. Hope wrapped in ribbons and generosity that stretched farther than the eye could see.

"Dylan and I donated paintings for the live auction," said Savannah.

"Oh, I have gift certificates to Wild Fern. Nothing like a new outfit to make someone feel fabulous," said Jane.

There was one box left, and Lily opened it. "Girls, look at what Cecelia Whitcomb sent over. She uses vintage fabric to make quilts." She pulled out small heart-shaped pouches and a tag that read Memory Pouches. "Look at these fabrics."

The girls gathered around the box. Emily's fingers brushed over the textures. Cecelia hadn't used just rich brocades or calico. The pouches were pieced from scraps that had carried another woman's life. A strip of linen, a square of feed-sack cotton, a corner of velvet, silk, lace and denim.

Emily's throat tightened. These weren't just pieces of fabric, they were stories—Sunday dresses, work shirts, wedding gowns, aprons. Pieces that had seen joy and sorrow were now sewn together to make something new. Something whole. Just like these baskets, she hoped they would bring comfort and a second chance to women starting over.

Each piece carried a message stitched in pale thread—*Believe. Home. Strength. Heal. Loved.*—with tiny motifs like keys, stars, hearts, gentle reminders that every woman was worth it and had the power and courage to begin again.

Emily blinked hard, swallowing the lump in her throat. She hadn't realized the others had gone quiet until Savannah's arm slipped around her shoulders. Lily touched her hand, and Savannah gave a firm nod.

They didn't say anything. They didn't have to. The simple act of standing close, sharing her quiet ache and unspoken hope, said more than words ever could.

Then, Jane cleared her throat and held up one of the pouches. "Well, if Cecelia made one that says *Don't Eat My House*, I'm stitching it to Moose's collar. Either that or one that says *No Drooling Over Food*."

The girls burst into laughter. The sound filled the kitchen, and Emily found herself smiling through her tears. The sadness hadn't vanished, but it shifted, loosened. For the first time in days, she felt the weight in her chest ease. Not gone. But shared. And that was enough.

AT THE BOTTOM-UP, Adam slid into the empty chair at the battered table, the wood scarred from decades of spilled beer and the occasional bar fight.

"'Bout time," grumbled Nic, sliding over a basket of wings. "We thought you ditched us for your woman."

Adam raised a brow. "She's with the girls filling fundraiser baskets. I'm not into glitter and ribbon. Besides, I wasn't invited."

"Better than smelling like beer and buffalo sauce," Reed shot back. He tossed a bone onto the plate in the middle of the table, licking sauce from his fingers.

Charlie leaned back in his chair, arms crossed. "Hey, don't knock glitter. Makes it hard for the bad guys to sneak up on you. They sparkle in the dark."

"How would you know?" asked Nic.

Charlie shook his head. "Experience, fucker."

"Man, I'd pay money to see Adam walk into the station covered in glitter. The whole place, hell, the town, would call you Deputy Sparkle," said Levi, picking up his beer glass.

Adam gave him the finger. The guys erupted in laughter. He took a long swallow of beer. He knew his friends were just trying to defuse a bad situation.

"So, how is the case going? Is Emily okay?" asked Nic. "She still a suspect?"

Adam hesitated, not sure how much he wanted to tell them. But these were his friends. They would want to look out for Emily. "She's been cleared, but we think she's a target."

"From who?" asked Levi.

Adam shook his head. "No idea. She's acting brave, trying to do normal stuff, being with friends. But ..."

"But you don't feel good about it," Reed finished.

Adam sighed. "No. I'm just waiting for the other shoe to drop."

"So, what's the plan?" Levi asked. "You two moving in together?"

Adam's jaw tightened. "No. She spends some nights at my place. I spend some at hers."

"And the gaps?" Levi pressed. "What about the in-between hours when you're not there?"

Adam scrubbed his hand over his face. He didn't answer right away. He stared at the froth in his beer, heard the clack of pool balls in the background, the low murmur of voices. Normal noise. And yet. "That's what keeps me up at night. I can't chain her to my side. She deserves a life of her own. But I can't be there every second."

Reed leaned forward. "Doesn't take more than a minute for things to go bad."

"And you can't exactly post a deputy outside the spa door without drawing more attention and turning people away," said Charlie.

Adam grunted. "Business is already down just over the

murder. I don't want her living like she's under guard, but I'm not naive either. One misstep, one gap in coverage. That's all it would take."

"Doesn't have to be," Levi said, leaning in. "You know I install security cameras on the side. Let me cover the entrances and hallways. Not her apartment upstairs. It'll give her some space and privacy. But if anyone so much as breathes down there, you'll know."

"She won't like it."

"She'll like being alive better," Levi countered. "I've got the gear, and I'm discreet. They won't affect the vibe of the place. She doesn't have to worry about my putting the cameras in any private place. Not a perv."

Nic whistled. "You'd be stupid not to, Adam."

"Shit." He rubbed his hand through his hair. "She's gonna fight me on this. Claim it's bad for business. But I'd rather have her mad at me than laying flowers at her grave."

Charlie drummed his fingers on the table. "Yeah, women have a way of making things complicated. Speaking of which, anyone heard if Ivy's back? I haven't seen her in a while."

Nic smirked. "Are you asking for business or pleasure?"

Charlie's ears turned red. He didn't answer, just took a long pull from his glass.

Adam smirked. Charlie might not be saying much. And he probably didn't know that all his friends knew he was sweet on Ivy. Had been forever. But something had happened way back when, and Ivy had been avoiding him for years.

"Anyhow," Charlie continued, choosing to ignore Nic, "half the town would go to bat for her. We've all got eyes. You're not alone, Adam."

"Damn straight," Nic said, lifting his beer. "Family."

Adam's chest tightened. This ... this right here was a small town standing with some of its own. It was the reason he never moved away. His friends had his back and now Emily's. He raised his glass, clinked it against theirs.

The guys sat back and ordered another beer. Conversations about Charlie's garage, Nic's latest disaster date, the fire that turned out to be kids roasting marshmallows in a trash can. Adam only half listened. All he could think about was Emily. Laughing with her friends, feeling safe at home. Living a life she deserved, not one filled with dangers.

But danger was already moving in the shadows. He could feel it. Adam gripped his beer tight. Decision made. Levi would get those cameras up this week. And if Emily didn't like it, too damn bad.

Because Adam wasn't going to lose her. Not ever.

Twenty-Four

The spa was just stirring when Emily walked downstairs, the faint scent of eucalyptus still clinging to the air. Morgan's laughter drifted from the front desk, mingling with the scent of freshly brewed coffee and the soft shuffle of papers, but Emily's mind was elsewhere.

She talked to Adam last night while he was with his friends at the Bottom-Up, before he said good night. He wanted to come over, but she was exhausted and needed time to herself. The afternoon had been spent laughing and talking with her friends, and she just wanted to wallow in the comfort of their companionship and warmth one more night before facing reality again.

Today was the meeting of the Chamber of Commerce. She never scheduled massages during that time. It was important for them to know that her business wasn't just her livelihood but a part of the community.

Then she remembered Taryn Keene was on the agenda.

She paused on the bottom step. An influencer with a national following, Taryn had been invited to speak about "Self-Care Trends and Small-Town Opportunities."

Aspire Day Spa was more about beauty and lifestyle branding that drew attention. It wasn't wrong, just different. Serenity Spa was about comfort and care. Aspire was about glow and glamor. Still, knowing some of her former staff were working there didn't make the sting any less sharp.

The Chamber wanted Taryn's insight, not hers. For a moment, she let the little green monster of envy on her shoulder tell her she was just small potatoes. Then she thought, the less attention paid to her, the less people would remember the murder, the investigation, the suspicions. And going further back, Boston. The city and its rumors never left her. She didn't need to reopen those wounds.

What was Taryn's endgame? Was she testing the waters for Aspire Day Spa? Or planning on taking all of Emily's staff and clientele until Serenity Spa was nothing more than a memory?

From the front desk, Morgan called out, "Coffee's hot if you need it. You might want something stronger, though. Half the town's buzzing about today." The worry in her eyes didn't match the smile on her lips.

Emily exhaled slowly. She might not know what Taryn was up to, but she wasn't about to roll over and let anyone take away what she'd built.

Not without a fight.

THE OLD BRICK Chamber of Commerce building was already buzzing with the low murmur of conversations, occasional laughter and the scrape of chairs on the hardwood floors when Emily walked in. She greeted several members of the community and slipped into a seat along the side, hoping to blend in.

A few minutes later, the president of the Chamber

stepped up to the podium, cleared his throat and launched into the usual updates—budget, tourism initiatives and downtown improvements. Emily tried to focus, but her mind kept circling back to the real reason she was here.

When Taryn Keene stepped up to the podium, the energy in the room shifted. Phones came out, and people focused on her. The woman was tall, poised, with chestnut-brown hair that fell in sleek waves over her shoulders, warm brown eyes and flawless makeup. She wore a tailored cream blazer over slim pants, and her heels clicked against the hardwood floor.

"Thank you for inviting me," Taryn said in a smooth voice. "Aspire Day Spa was a dream of mine when I first became a beauty influencer. It was never about the money or the spotlight. It was about how a little self-care can change the way someone sees themselves."

She clicked to the first slide on the screen behind her, filled with glossy photos of farmers' markets, yoga retreats, cozy inns and farm-to-table dinners featuring organic food. "That's what self-care looks like beyond the spa," she said. "Small towns like Beaver Creek have an opportunity. People are craving authentic experiences, things that help them slow down and feel restored. They don't just want to visit. They want to feel connected, taken care of and part of something genuine. You already have so much of that here."

Emily blinked. That didn't sound like someone swooping in to take over. That sounded supportive. Things she was already doing.

Taryn went on to talk about partnerships, many of which Beaver Creek already had. Stores offering locally sourced products, businesses teaming up to create weekend getaways.

Emily's spa packages were already paired with hotels and B&Bs, and those collaborations brought in new clients most weeks. But still she couldn't help wondering if the Chamber saw her spa packages and local partnerships as small potatoes compared with Taryn's glossy presentation. Part of her ached to be included in that bigger vision, to matter more in the scheme of things.

Still, the way Taryn painted it, creating a style and self-care trail, a digital guide highlighting each town's uniqueness, made it sound bigger, more cohesive. As if Beaver Creek could market itself as an actual destination for people who wanted to feel renewed and not just relaxed.

When she finished her presentation, the crowd stood and clapped. Emily's mind was working overtime with thoughts of how much more was possible if the town pulled together. The Chamber had the means and budget to do that if they liked the idea. She looked around the room and noticed one woman's eyes linger on her, then she turned and whispered to her neighbor. Emily's stomach tightened. Her palms dampened, and she smoothed them over her pants. Not the kind of attention she wanted.

She was just getting ready to leave when Taryn targeted her.

When she reached Emily, Taryn smiled. Not the smile of a professional or competitor but one that felt almost personal.

"Emily Harper, right? I'm so glad to finally meet you," she said, extending a hand.

Emily shook it, offering a polite smile of her own. "Likewise."

Taryn hesitated and then lowered her voice. "It's come to my attention that an overambitious regional manager thought it would be a clever recruitment idea to offer bonuses. It's just something we offer everywhere. I never thought about the impact on local businesses. By the time I found out, it had already caused waves. I never meant for it to affect places like Serenity Spa or any of the others."

Emily's gut twisted. An apology? She never thought she'd

hear that today. "I understand. These things happen," she murmured.

Taryn shook her head. "I hate that it hurt you, though. You've built something beautiful here. I hope we can work together to make it more meaningful and profitable for everyone."

"Fingers crossed," Emily replied.

Taryn gave her arm a quick squeeze before returning to the waiting circle of Chamber members.

Emily stood there for a moment longer. Taryn hadn't meant harm. But intent didn't erase losing staff members or the fear of losing her business.

The bell over the door chimed as Emily stepped back into the spa. The familiar scent of eucalyptus soothed some of the tightness in her chest. Morgan looked up from the front desk.

"So? How was the meeting? Did Taryn sparkle everyone into submission?"

Emily gave her a small smile and dropped her bag on the counter. "She did sparkle. But she was ... nicer than I expected. Even apologized."

Morgan blinked. "Apologized? For what?"

"For Aspire offering signing bonuses. Said she didn't know about it. One of her managers pushed it." Emily sighed. "She seemed genuine. Like she didn't realize how much it hurt us here. I wanted to be mad at her but just couldn't."

Morgan crossed her arms. "That doesn't change the fact that you've been running this place shorthanded ever since."

"True," Emily replied, pressing her fingers to her temples. "But she wasn't gloating, even said we built something beautiful here."

From the product shelves, Celeste's voice cut in. "So, she just admitted all of this to you? In front of everyone?"

"No, not in front of everyone. She pulled me aside."

Celeste arched a brow. "And you believed her? Seems to me influencers know exactly what to say. Image is everything in their world. And they don't care who they hurt."

"Celeste!" Morgan reached across the counter and gave Emily's hand a squeeze. "Don't listen to her. You've kept this place alive when most people would have folded. That's what matters."

"It's okay," Emily said quietly. "She seemed sincere."

Celeste shrugged. "Maybe. Or maybe she was just playing you." She returned to the shelves, restacking bottles that were already straight, her movements just a little too sharp, too precise.

Emily exhaled. Taryn hadn't felt like a threat. But now with Celeste's words lingering in the air, she wasn't so sure of anything.

Twenty-Five

Emily was in her office going over the day's schedule when she heard faint scratching outside. She got up and opened the front door, half expecting to see if a delivery had come early and the driver was leaving it by the door.

Instead, Adam stood on the porch with two other men, staring at the spa.

"Adam?" She stepped out and shivered as the crisp morning air bit through her sweater. Damn, the air was cold. "What are you doing here?"

The three men exchanged glances, silent long enough for her to suspect something was up. Finally, Adam cleared his throat.

"We're going to install cameras inside."

"Excuse me?" Emily blinked, then narrowed her eyes. "Did you say cameras?"

"Um, yeah."

Her jaw tightened. She crooked her finger at him. "Can I see you for a moment?"

Adam turned to the men and held up a *just a minute* finger before following her inside.

"What on God's green earth are you talking about? I can't afford cameras."

"Em, Levi is going to install them free of charge. Just downstairs by the back door and front door."

"Who the hell is Levi?"

"Levi Barrett is an old buddy of mine. Used to be in the military police before he got out. Charlie Anderson runs the garage in town," he said. "And he's sweet on Ivy."

Emily blinked at him. "What does Ivy have to do with my front door?"

"Nothing," he admitted, giving her a cheeky grin. "I just figured you'd rather hear about Charlie's crush than how bad I think the security is here."

"Why?" she pressed, still not convinced.

Adam caught her hands, his touch warm and steady. "Because I worry about you when I'm not here. Because I want to keep you safe." He leaned in and brushed a kiss against her nose, his breath carrying the faint scent of coffee and mint. "Because I care. Please don't fight me on this."

Emily's first instinct was to argue. To tell him she wasn't a helpless damsel in distress. She survived the Boston fallout and an almost-murder charge. She damn well was not going to let fear dictate her life.

He gave her a moment to think it through. This wasn't about control. It was about her. About him. Keeping her safe when he wasn't around.

She shook her head. "You drive me crazy, you know that?" she muttered.

Adam grinned. "Yeah, but you like me anyway."

And God help her, she did.

"So, give me a kiss and come meet the guys," Adam said, taking her by the hand and leading her outdoors.

The two men stood awkwardly on the porch like kids caught in the act.

"Em, meet Levi, a man of all trades. Former military cop, bartender, firearms instructor, halfway decent mechanic ..."

"Hey," Levi cut in. "I'm a fantastic mechanic."

Levi was in his early thirties, tall and broad through the shoulders with close-cropped blond hair and an easy grin. His eyes were a sharp, clear blue, which suggested he didn't miss much, probably why he had been a military cop.

"Small engines," Charlie muttered under his breath.

Adam smirked. "Fine. Fantastic small-engine mechanic, firearms instructor and now security expert."

Emily gave a small finger wave. *God, this wasn't awkward. Nope, not at all.*

"And over here"—Adam waved his arm—"we have Charlie Anderson, mechanic extraordinaire and undercover romantic."

"Jesus, Adam," Charlie sputtered, his neck turning red. "What the hell?"

"What?" Adam smirked. "Just telling it like it is."

Charlie looked a couple of years younger than Levi, early thirties as well, tall, muscular with dark hair that flopped a little over his forehead, already touched with streaks of gray. Scruff shadowed his jaw, giving him a rugged look, though the blush climbing his neck ruined the tough-guy act.

Levi stepped forward and held out his hand to Emily. "Everything Adam said about me is true."

Emily shook his hand, his grip firm and confident.

Charlie sighed and scrubbed a hand over the back of his neck. "Don't believe half of what he says about me. I fix cars and trucks with big engines." He glared at Adam. "Not hearts."

Levi smirked. Emily bit back a smile, and Adam's grin widened.

"Uh-huh," she said. "Well, anyone who's willing to help keep this place safe is welcome. Big engines, small engines, romantic or not."

Charlie's ears turned an even darker shade of red, and Levi made a noise that was half snort, half laugh.

"Okay then. Back to business," Adam said. "We came over early before clients came in to install the cameras. They'll only be downstairs and not by the changing room or treatment rooms."

"Well, I'll let you get to it. Let me know when you're finished." She turned to step inside.

Levi and Charlie brushed past Adam, lugging toolboxes and a coil of wire. Levi whistled low as he took in the lobby. "Nice place. Smells good too."

"Anything smells better than stale beer," Charlie muttered.

Emily smiled at the exchange, but her humor was short-lived. The clatter of tools hitting the floor broke the peaceful quiet she tried to cultivate.

Adam squeezed her hand. "They'll be quick. By the time your first client walks in, you won't even know the cameras are there."

Maybe not, she thought, but she'd feel them. A reminder that someone out there wanted her scared, looking over her shoulder.

From across the room, Levi called. "Adam, you want the first one by the back door?"

"Yeah," he replied and then turned to Emily. "Trust me on this."

Emily swallowed hard. Trusting him was easy. Trusting that danger wouldn't find a way in, cameras or no cameras, was something else.

The front door chimed, and Morgan breezed in, phone tucked under her chin and purse in one hand. She stopped mid-step, eyes widening at the sight of toolboxes and wires spread across the floor. "Okay, what fresh chaos is this?"

She looked at Emily. "Did I just walk into a secret mission?"

"Installing cameras," Emily replied.

Morgan's gaze landed on Levi, who was by the front desk. She grinned. "And who might this be? Please tell me he's single, Em."

Emily closed her mouth, which had been hanging open. Morgan never ceased to surprise her. And now apparently Levi, who glanced up, startled by Morgan's declaration, then grinned. "Depends. You looking for a fantastic"—he smirked at Charlie—"small-engine mechanic, firearms instructor or bartender?"

Morgan laughed. "Triple threat. I like it."

Adam groaned. "Don't encourage him."

"Let's get this shitshow on the road," grumbled Charlie. "I have some really big engines to work on."

The guys laughed. Morgan looked confused, and Emily shook her head. Men.

The door chimed again, and Celeste breezed in with a cardboard tray of coffees.

"Morning. I thought I'd come in early and catch up on inventory before clients arrived." She glanced at the men, her curiosity obvious. "Looks like I picked the right day for excitement."

Emily frowned. What was going on this morning? She had hoped to get a quiet start to her day, but instead her lobby was filling up like Grand Central Station. First, Adam's surprise. Then Morgan *and* Celeste coming in early?

But then she told herself she was reading too much into it. Morgan sometimes came in early just to gab, and Celeste had every right to come in early and catch up. Besides, she brought caffeine with her, so Emily couldn't complain.

Morgan eyed the tray with a grin. "Bribing us with coffee? Smart move."

Celeste laughed, sliding one of the cups toward her. "Never hurts to sweeten the deal."

Emily accepted hers with a small smile. Maybe this morning wasn't turning out so bad after all.

WHEN CELESTE PUSHED through the door with the tray of coffees, she hadn't expected to find Adam and his friends here, but her smile didn't falter.

So much for slipping in unnoticed.

The inventory lie rolled off her tongue like butter. People rarely questioned someone bearing caffeine.

As she passed a cup to Morgan, she let her gaze wander. The men were busy with wires and small black boxes. Cameras.

Now that was interesting.

Celeste shifted her weight, sipping her coffee, while listening to Morgan ramble on about something. She tracked each spot where they mounted a camera. Thorough, yes, but not flawless. The staircase to Emily's apartment wasn't touched.

A slow ripple of satisfaction spread through her chest. She might not have accomplished what she'd come for this morning. But she gained something better—knowledge.

Emily thought she was safe. But safety was an illusion. And sooner or later, Emily would learn that.

Twenty-Six

Ethan stepped out of his cruiser into a damp, gray day. The temperature wasn't cold enough for snow yet, but later if it dipped below freezing, it definitely would be. Then the roads would have black ice, and the station would be busy with accidents. Yuck. People were so careless about the weather. He wished he could just tell everyone to stay inside, but—he shrugged—can't fix stupid.

He nodded to Nora, who held out several messages, and walked through the bullpen, chatting with a couple of deputies on his way to his office. The familiar hum of phones ringing and murmurs of voices should've felt comforting. Instead, his brain refused to let go of the murder case.

After settling in, he stared at the old photos on the wall. His dad, grandpa, great-grandpa and the brothers. Generations of sheriffs vowed to serve and protect. Sometimes he wondered if it was a legacy or a curse.

Sunday afternoon had been fun catching up with Tanner and Dylan while Moose was on a mission to explore every inch of the farmhouse. He shook his head and grinned. The special treat was that his older brother, Sean, who ran Champlain

Security Solutions in Burlingham, and Dylan's twin, Kane, a mountain guide in Stowe, were able to make the trip. It'd been a while since they had seen Kane, but Sean had been down to install cameras at Savannah's house when she was dealing with her stalker. Family together again, even if briefly. He missed them.

Thankfully, Jane and Savannah were with Emily. The two women had a crush on "tall, dark and sexy," as they called Sean —a factoid Ethan wasn't sharing with him, since his ego was already too big. Plus, the women would have made plans to crash the brothers' get-together. The thought almost made him laugh out loud. Almost. Sean didn't need more admirers, and Ethan sure as hell didn't need the chaos of Jane and Savannah barging in.

He made a few phone calls, then noticed Adam walking in. The sight of his best friend brought him straight back to reality, the weight of the badge weighing heavy on his shoulders. He knew Adam was still hurt and furious, even though he knew Ethan had to take him off the case. He hoped with time that their friendship would mend, smoothing over the cracks. But right now, that was wishful thinking. This was business.

It was time. Ethan had cleared Emily of suspicion of murder, warned her and Adam that she was in danger. Adam was no longer off the case, and it was time to update him. Ethan's gut tightened. Adam wasn't going to like what he had to say. But better an angry friend than a dead woman.

"Adam," he yelled from the doorway. "Come here."

"What's up?" Adam stepped into his office.

"Sit." Ethan dropped into his chair, rubbing a hand over his jaw. "I wanted to bring you up to date on Jennifer's case."

Adam narrowed his eyes. "So, I'm on the case now?"

"Damn it, Adam. You know I had to do that."

Adam rolled his eyes. "I know. But I'm still pissed."

"Be pissed, but it was the right call." Ethan pulled out his notebook. "I have a couple of suspects. Ezra said that a left-handed person struck Jennifer. I have three people in mind." He flipped through his notes. "First is a Daniel Cross."

Adam frowned. "Never heard of him."

"He's a reporter from Boston, mostly tailing Jennifer before she died. He's staying at the Green Mountain Lodge. Said he was out of town that night. Maybe you could interview him again, get his alibi, if he has one.

"Then there's Morgan."

"Morgan? You can't be serious."

"I'm as serious as a heart attack. She's left-handed, computer-savvy. She was there the night Jennifer was killed." Ethan took a deep breath and exhaled. "Then I have Celeste. No tech skills that I've seen, but she's too curious, too polished. Came out of nowhere to work there. People like that don't just blow into Beaver Creek without a reason."

"Damn," Adam muttered. "Emily really could be in danger."

Ethan leaned back. "Jennifer's death wasn't random. She was at the spa for a reason, and someone wanted to silence her. Emily may not know what Shay knew, but someone thinks she does."

"I'm not letting her out of my sight," Adam said.

"Good. I was thinking that Sean could install cameras at Emily's place. He did that for Jane and Savannah."

Adam shook his head. "Already handled. Levi installed cameras at the spa yesterday. Coverage is solid, entry points, common rooms. Nothing in private spaces. She's protected when she's there."

A flicker of surprise crossed Ethan's face before he nodded. "Smart. Levi's solid. I can live with that."

Adam stood. "I'll start with Cross. Want me to talk to Morgan?"

"Nah, I'll handle Morgan. She'll see you coming a mile away."

Adam paused at the door. "And Celeste?"

Ethan scraped a hand over his jaw. "For now, she goes on the back burner. I don't have enough to pin her down. I'll keep an eye on her, but Cross and Morgan are hotter leads."

Adam left, clicking the door behind him. The office seemed too quiet except for the tick of the wall clock.

Ethan leaned back in his chair, the notebook opened in front of him. Three names. That was it. Three people he could point a finger at, but none fit cleanly.

He'd already pulled their basic info. Nothing deep, just the standard run every cop did before interviewing a potential suspect. Morgan's history was straightforward. Daniel's had a few gaps tied to his reporting years. And Celeste ... well, she had almost no footprint before moving to Vermont. Not illegal. Not even uncommon these days. It was thin, but he wasn't jumping to conclusions. People had their reasons for their quiet lives. Until he talked to each of them, the list stayed open.

Cross was shady, but reporters chased stories and were not open to sharing information. Following Jennifer didn't make him a killer unless there was another reason. Morgan was loyal to Emily and dependable. She'd been there since the spa opened. He hated himself for even writing her name down. And then there was Celeste. She was polished, but there was no solid motive, no evidence, nothing that screamed murder.

He'd gone over every angle, but nothing fit together long enough to make sense. The truth was that the case was hanging by a thread. Threads that could snap at any minute.

He pressed his palms against his eyes, trying to block out the noise in his own head. What if he were wrong? What if the real killer wasn't even on his list? Jennifer was a reporter with secrets. She could've dragged someone else's secrets with her to Beaver Creek. Someone who'd kill to keep them buried.

His gut twisted. His gaze went to his father's photo. Legacy. Duty.

Don't screw it up. He wondered if his dad ever dealt with false leads, half-truths?

Ethan lowered his hands and squared his shoulders. He'd follow the leads, but he'd also keep his eyes open. Because if there was someone out there, hiding in plain sight, Emily's life depended upon them finding out who it was before it was too late.

TWENTY-SEVEN

Emily left the spa at six, leaving Morgan to close and Celeste to do laundry. It had been a busy day with a couple of new clients and the yoga classes filling up.

People didn't seem to notice the cameras, although Morgan kept looking over at them and smiling. Emily guessed she thought Levi, her new crush, was monitoring them. She didn't have the heart to tell Morgan that only she had access to the cameras.

She pulled her jacket tighter as she stepped into the brisk cold air. The air smelled faintly of woodsmoke, and the distant mountains were a dusty pink that made her smile. She hated to admit it, but the cameras did make her feel safer, although she couldn't get rid of the nagging thought that danger might be just one step behind her. Tonight, she wanted to believe in normal.

Jane's farmhouse was lit up like a beacon as she passed the McQueeney farm. Gravel crunched underneath her tires as she headed down the drive. Familiar cars parked single file off to one side. She pulled her car in, turned off the engine, grabbed the wine bag and stepped outside. Laughter spilled out into the night. Emily walked around to the kitchen and opened the door.

The kitchen was crowded with her friends. A huge platter of sliders was nestled between a green salad and a pasta salad. A bowl of chips and a tray filled with hummus and cut-up vegetables were on either side.

Jane spotted her and hurried over. “Finally. We were beginning to think you weren’t coming.”

“Never. I wouldn’t miss this for the world.” It was their once-a-month girls’ night dinner. Tonight, it was at Jane’s house, next month at someone else’s, and other women would join in.

She held up the bag of wine, and everyone cheered. Then there were hugs all around.

“I’ll take those,” said Olivia. She looked at the bottles. “Yum. Someone went to Fallen Timbers Winery.”

“It was a hard chore, but someone had to do it,” quipped Emily. “I got two reds, Wandering Stag and Lost Lantern Red, and two whites: Golden Birch and Willow Creek White.”

“Oh, I’ve had their Lost Lantern Red.” Olivia smacked her lips. “Yum, hints of cherry, black currant, smoked oak and vanilla. I love it.”

The women poured glasses of wine, helped themselves to food and sat around the large wooden kitchen table.

Emily ran her hands over the polished wood. “This table is beautiful. Did someone make it?”

Jane looked over at her. “Clarence. He’s a terrific woodworker.”

Clarence worked on Jane’s farm, renovating the old farmhouse. “I haven’t seen him for ages,” said Savannah.

“Oh, he moved away. Wanted to be closer to his daughter and grandkids.”

“Well, at least he left you something lasting.”

Jane clinked her glass when everyone was settled at the

table. She raised the glass. "To good friends, good food and good memories."

"Hear! Hear!" The women clinked their wineglasses.

Conversation was lively, and Emily learned about Moose's new trick of hiding a piece of Dylan's clothing. Olivia gave them an update on Beaver Creek gossip. Leah mentioned a new pie flavor she was testing at the diner—maple pecan with chocolate drizzle—and she brought a pie with her.

"I was out at Maisie's place photographing her beehives and honey for this month's *Beaver Creek Gazette*," said Piper. "That woman! She's a pistol, and she sure loves bees. I almost felt like she's named them. Thankfully, the hive isn't busy in late fall. I can't imagine bees swarming around me. But the honey is delicious."

"So, when is the next issue of the *Gazette*?" asked Emily.

"Oh, it's monthly," Piper replied. "It'll be after the fundraiser. I should get some great pictures there."

Finally, dinner was finished, dishes placed in the dishwasher, and dessert brought out. Jane put coffee on and told everyone to grab a plate and dessert, and she'd bring the cups and coffee in when it was finished.

The women traipsed into the living room, where Jane had lit a fire. After Jane brought out the coffee, Emily settled back on the couch.

"So, Emily, what's going on with your case?" asked Lily. "Has Ethan said anything to you?"

Emily hesitated. She wondered how much to tell them, but she needed her friends to have her back. "Humph, the good news is that I'm not under suspicion of murder anymore.

"Well," Savannah said with a smirk. "If you need a guard dog, I know one. You only have to pay him in snacks."

Emily laughed. "I have a feeling I'd be protecting Moose."

"Ethan didn't have any more information?" asked Olivia.

"He said the blow that killed her was from a left-handed person," Emily replied, then cocked her head. "Adam's friend Levi came over and installed cameras yesterday. That's all I know. Oh, Ethan did mention a name. Cross. Daniel Cross. His name was on Jennifer's computer."

Olivia paused with her fork halfway to her mouth. "Cross?" she repeated, then gave a little shrug. "Never heard of him."

Jane lifted her glass. "Honestly, secrets, cameras, left-handed killers? You can't make this stuff up."

"I hope this isn't fodder for one of your crime-fiction books featuring Eddie McDermott and his sidekick, Aaron Stone," teased Savannah.

"No promises," said Jane with a sly grin. "I told Ethan I wouldn't get involved, and I won't."

"Uh-huh," Olivia said, arching a brow. "That's exactly what no author ever said just before they based a book on their friends and changed the names just enough to deny it."

Laughter rippled around the table, and Ethan's name was quickly drowned in jokes about Jane's fictional sheriff and deputy. Emily smiled into her wineglass, enveloped in the warmth of her friends, even as a thread of unease slid down her spine.

An hour later, coats and hugs were exchanged at the door as people left. Savannah pulled Emily aside and jingled her keys. "I'll follow you back, just in case. Don't argue with me, Em."

Emily rolled her eyes but didn't fight it. Truth was, she was grateful.

The drive back into town was quiet. Her headlights cut through the darkness. Savannah stayed in her rearview all the way until Emily parked in the spa's lot. The building looked still and ordinary, but the glow of the upstairs lamp in her apartment was comforting.

Savannah pulled in behind her and lowered her window. "Text me once you're locked in."

"I will. Thanks."

Savannah gave her a pointed look. "No skipping. I want proof."

Emily smiled, waving as Savannah pulled away, taillights disappearing into the night. The silence was oppressive. She slipped inside, keyed in the code and locked the door behind her.

Alone again, Emily unlocked the door to her apartment and drew in a slow breath. The house was quiet, the cameras were watching, and she was safe.

For now.

NOW THAT ADAM HAD EMILY, he hated working nights, but that was part of the job, so he sucked up the disappointment. She'd told him she was going to Jane's for their once-a-month girls' get-together.

She didn't know he had asked Savannah to follow her home. He couldn't shake the thought that someone might be waiting in the dark. Cameras were a deterrent but wouldn't stop someone who was determined.

It was dusk. The sky had deepened into a soft purple that made the mountains look like silhouettes. With nothing pressing at the station, Adam decided it was a good time to take a trip to the Green Mountain Lodge and do a face-to-face with this Cross fellow. Ethan hadn't given him much except that Cross was following a lead tied to the Evolve MedSpa mess.

Now that Ezra said the fatal blow came from a left-handed

person, Cross was in the crosshairs. Adam snorted. Crosshairs. Real funny.

The left-handed detail had narrowed things down but not nearly enough. Cross wasn't the only one who fit.

He turned down the long gravel driveway, following the flickering lights in the windows. The familiar wraparound porch came into view. The only splash of color came from pots of gold and rust mums. God, how long had it been since he was out here? Years. The lodge didn't have problems with guests.

Adam parked the cruiser out front and stepped out into the brisk, cold air smelling faintly of woodsmoke. He could hear a jazz quartet coming from—he had to stop and think—right, the dining room.

He opened the front door, and the warmth of a crackling fire in the fieldstone fireplace surrounded him. Guests lounged in the reception area. The scent of grilled meats and other mouthwatering smells from the dining room hit him, and his stomach grumbled. He hadn't eaten dinner yet. But he wasn't here to eat, and besides, the dining room was a little too pricey for a quick meal. He'd wait until he headed back to town to grab a burger.

Adam had Cross's room number, so he took the elevator to the third floor and knocked on room 314.

He stepped back and cocked his ear. Silence. Was Cross in? Maybe he should've called first. No, no sense in giving a suspect a heads-up.

He knocked again.

He heard footsteps. The door opened. A man in his late thirties, with brown hair and glasses, blinked at him with a satchel slung across his shoulders. Was he going out? Or coming in?

"Daniel Cross?"

"Yeah."

"Can we talk?"

Cross blew out a breath as if Adam had just ruined his evening. He stepped aside to let Adam in. Inside, the room smelled faintly of coffee and wood polish. Paper littered the desk, his laptop open.

"So, what's going on that the Beaver Creek police have to disturb me twice?" Cross's tone was clipped. His hand flexed against his thigh. "I told the sheriff everything I could."

Adam huffed. Too defensive. Too fast. His eyes didn't quite meet Adam's. "Maybe not all. I need to know where you were the evening Jennifer Bishop was killed."

Cross hesitated, then dropped his bag on the chair and pushed his glasses higher. "I was in Burlingham, interviewing a source at the university library. I signed in at the desk when I came in—guest researcher access. The log will show it. And if that's not enough, the cameras above the circulation desk caught me walking in. You can check."

"All night?"

"From about five until closing. Didn't leave until nearly eleven." Cross folded his arms across his waist. "I don't know anything about Jennifer's murder. I'm not your guy."

"Who was the source?"

Cross shook his head. "I can't tell you that. Confidentiality matters. You'll just have to verify the log."

Adam waited, letting the silence stretch. Most people filled it in fast, tripping over themselves to explain. Cross didn't. His fingers twitched against his arm. Every instinct he had was shouting that Cross was holding something back. Maybe not about the murder but something else.

"You sure that's all you want to tell me?" Adam asked quietly.

Cross sighed. "Look, I didn't kill her," he snapped, then shoved a hand through his hair. "She was digging into Evolve

MedSpa. I was hoping to collaborate with her, so I followed her here."

"Followed her?" Adam repeated. Could Cross make it any easier? A left-handed journalist tailing a woman who is writing the same story and somehow ends up dead. Adam didn't believe in coincidences.

Cross lifted both hands. "Don't make it sound like stalking. I was trying to get a story. I'm a pain in the ass, but I'm not violent. You can ask anyone."

Adam's voice dropped. "Call it what you want, but sneaking around after a woman never looks good, especially if she ends up dead."

Adam noticed Daniel's eyes darting from side to side as he rubbed his hands on his pants. Was Cross nervous? Guilty? Or finally realizing this didn't look good?

"I'll check out your alibi," Adam said. "But if you're lying ..." He didn't finish the sentence.

Cross's jaw clenched. "Then check. Library staff will back me up."

Adam held his gaze for a long moment and then turned toward the door.

Twenty-Eight

Thursday morning Adam crossed the university quad in Burlingham, his breath fogging in the cool air. Students streamed past in jackets and hoodies, earbuds in, coffee cups clutched in their hands. The scent of roasted beans and fresh pastries drifted from the café just inside the lobby of the library entrance. A few students were sitting around small round tables outside, staring at their phones and drinking coffee.

He pushed through the library's heavy doors. Inside it was warm and quiet except for the low murmurs of conversation. At the front desk, a student worker glanced up.

"Hey," Adam said, flashing his badge. "Looking for guest sign-ins from the night of October twenty-fifth."

The kid's expression shifted from curious to worried. "Uh, you'll need Ms. Patel for that. Procedures, you know."

Ms. Patel arrived a minute later holding several books. She placed them on the counter as the student told her what Adam wanted. "Oh dear. That's not possible. We log visitors on a tablet after 5 p.m., but it crashed that night."

"Crashed?" Adam said.

"Unfortunately, it auto-updates during off-peak," she replied. "Off-peak was apparently seven fifteen. We lost about two hours of entries."

Of course they did. Adam pinched the bridge of his nose. Every delay, every missing scrap of proof stretched the case thinner. And the thinner it got, the more exposed Emily became.

"Cameras?"

She winced. "Facilities swapped the hallway camera by the entrance last week. The new unit's recording, but the archive didn't complete." She shrugged. "IT says 'by the end of the day.'"

Adam stared at her for a moment. He could already hear Ethan sigh. "Anybody on staff who might've seen this man?" He showed her Cross's picture.

Ms. Patel looked closely at the picture. "I don't recognize him, but Mark and Elena, who are usually on the night desk, might. Mark will be here at noon. Elena has class until two."

"Great." Adam looked around the library, wishing he'd chosen another profession. Today was not his day. He thanked Ms. Patel, who'd already turned toward the desk, and then he took a slow lap around the library. He walked past glassed-in study rooms, the silent reading room, and a row of computers with students sitting at them.

At noon, a lanky student with a man-bun wearing a sweatshirt that read "Question Everything" in bright yellow letters strode past the desk, earbuds in, mouthing along to lyrics. Adam stared at the shirt for half a second. Damn straight. The problem was that every answer Cross gave him only raised more questions.

Adam walked over to the desk, asked if Mark had seen Cross the night of the twenty-fifth, and slid a photo over. Mark frowned.

"Glasses guy?" Mark said. "If I remember correctly, we had two that night. One asked about reserving a study room."

"Time?"

Mark stared up at the ceiling. "Uh ... around six, I think, but certainly before the eight-thirty rush. He had a messenger bag slung over his shoulder."

"Did he sign in?"

"Tablet was acting wonky. I waved him through while I rebooted." He grimaced. "Sorry."

"Did you see him leave?"

Mark shook his head. "We got slammed with printer problems. Elena and I were knee-deep in paper jams."

"Was he with anyone?"

A pause. "Not when I saw him."

"Thanks." Adam slapped the desk and walked out. *Not when I saw him* wasn't the same as *no.* Cross's alibi was almost credible but still riddled with holes. Adam hated the uncertainty. Hated that he couldn't rule anyone out. And Emily deserved answers.

On his way out, Adam checked the café. The hiss of the espresso machine cut through the low murmur of students. Cups clattered, chairs scraped on the wooden floor, and the scent of burnt coffee irritated his nose. He scanned the room, sliding Cross's photo across to the barista, but the kid just shook his head.

Adam got into his cruiser and pulled out of the university lot. They were no closer to finding Jennifer's killer than they were before he came up here. He wondered whether Ethan had had any luck with Morgan.

The drive through Burlingham's South End was gray and blustery. The air carried the scent of hops from the brewery district. Old warehouses were painted with bold murals of the mountains, forest animals, and half-finished abstract shapes. But he barely noticed any of it. His head kept circling back to

Emily. She was strong but, thankfully, not alone. He was right there by her side. He prayed they would resolve this case soon before the killer found another way to strike and she might be the one in the crosshairs.

He slowed at the corner lot, where a tall fence enclosed several black SUVs. The Champlain Security Solutions logo stood out against the weathered brick. Sean McQueeney's base.

A figure stepped out of Ironwood Brewing next door, coffee cup in hand. Sean.

Adam pulled his truck over and got out. The men did a man hug with a slap on the back.

"Didn't expect to see you up here," Sean said. "Beaver Creek doesn't keep you busy enough?"

Adam shivered and pulled his jacket tighter against the wind. It whipped down the side streets, carrying the damp bite of the lake. "It does. Came to check on a suspect's alibi."

Sean tilted his chin. "Ethan mentioned the case. Said the woman was a journalist and murdered in Emily's spa, right?"

"Yeah. She was killed by a left-handed person. We have three suspects, none of whom seem likely."

"Well, Ethan thinks this one plans ahead. Not impulsive. The case is not going to be easy to crack. Just keep an eye on Emily, make sure she's covered." Sean took a swallow of coffee. "She need any security cameras?"

"Nah. You remember my friend Levi Barrett. He's installing them now as a business and did Emily's place."

Sean huffed. "Levi! I've been trying to get him to work for me, but he claims he likes the small-town vibe of Beaver Creek."

Adam looked at his watch. His stomach growled, reminding him he hadn't eaten since dawn. "I've got to get back. Good seeing you."

"Same. Come up sometime and I'll show you the facility."

Adam nodded. "But then you'd have to kill me, right?"

"Fuck, Adam. You've been watching too many late-night cop shows," Sean said, grinning. "We only have a special room in the basement we use."

"Ass." Adam laughed and shook hands with Sean. He climbed back into the cruiser and drove south, wondering what Ethan had uncovered.

Twenty-Nine

Ethan pulled in front of Serenity Spa early Thursday morning. He stepped out of his cruiser and took a deep breath of the crisp, cold air. Frost clung to the corners of the porch steps, twinkling like diamonds. This was the part of his job he hated most—walking into quiet places, into ordinary mornings, interviewing seemingly innocent people and trying to get them to confess.

Adam was in Burlingham chasing down Cross's alibi. Now it was his turn to check Morgan's story. He wanted to talk to her before the spa got busy. Best to corner people before they had time to rehearse or line up excuses.

He stepped onto the porch. Pots of russet and gold mums flanked the door, and bundles of dried corn swayed in the breeze. The scent of eucalyptus was faint, but he'd never forget that smell. Every time it hit him, he thought of Emily and wondered if danger was pressing closer.

The bell tinkled when he opened the door. Morgan looked up from behind the front desk computer.

"'Morning, Sheriff," she said with a bright smile. "What brings you here?"

Ethan scanned the reception area—empty, though he heard a murmur of voices coming from one of the massage rooms. She was alone. Good. Fewer eyes meant fewer distractions.

"I need to ask you a few questions."

Her smile faltered. "Okaaay. But I told you everything I know about Jennifer."

He exhaled slowly. "I'm trying to establish time. You said you were here after five. Anyone else here when you closed?"

Morgan shook her head. "No, Emily had already left, and Celeste left even earlier."

Ethan's brows pulled together. "Earlier? What time?"

"About four. I saw her walk out. She had her purse and said she'd come in early Monday morning to finish her work. After that, it was just me and Emily until she left at about ten minutes to five after Jennifer's massage."

He made a mental note. If Morgan really saw Celeste leave, that gave her cover. Except Celeste had keys to the building. She could have slipped back in without anyone knowing.

"What were you doing here at that time?"

Morgan hesitated, her fingers tightening around a pen. "Are you asking me for an alibi?" Her voice got shrill. "You think I murdered that woman?"

Ethan leaned forward, keeping his voice calm. "I'm not thinking anything at this time. I'm just looking at all the angles."

Her shoulders sagged. "I left a little after five when I finished wrapping up for the day."

"Can anyone verify that?" Ethan asked, saying a mental prayer Morgan wasn't involved. That left her plenty of time to kill Jennifer.

Morgan blurted, "My friend picked me up to grab dinner and a movie."

"What friend?"

"Dana Simmons," Morgan said quickly. "She swung by out front. You can ask her."

Ethan's pulse quickened. Jennifer had been killed between early evening and eleven. Morgan slipping out at five gave her both time and freedom to do it.

"Did you come back here for your car?"

She shook her head. "No. I stayed overnight at Dana's house."

Ethan gave a short nod and then turned to leave. He remembered he had a picture in his pocket. He pulled it out and slid it across the counter. "Do you recognize this man?"

"Hmm, he looks familiar." Morgan picked it up, studying the face. Her brows drew together, then her eyes brightened. "Oh, I know. That's Mr. Jacobs. He came in maybe a week ago."

"What did he want?"

"He said he was looking for services for his wife. I gave him a tour, explained our packages, but he didn't book anything, just thanked me and left." She cocked her head and held out the picture to him. "Why? Who is he?"

Ethan took the picture back, tucking it into his pocket. "Nobody. Just curious."

He gave her a polite nod and stepped toward the door. He didn't have much to go on. Morgan had given him Dana's information. Her alibi was thin at best. Dinner, a movie and an overnight? Almost too convenient.

But sometimes the truth sounded like a lie and lies sounded like the truth. Damn. He'd track Dana down and see if the story lined up. If it did, maybe all Morgan was guilty of was being left-handed. If it didn't ... then he had a whole new problem.

As for Cross, why did he give a fake name? Was he watching Emily for some reason? Every answer led to more questions, and Emily was the thread tying them together.

Ethan tightened his jaw. He hated turning friends and neighbors into suspects. But if it kept Emily safe, he'd burn through every alibi in town.

DOWN THE HALL, tucked in the shadows of a massage room, Celeste smiled. She had come in early, hoping maybe to catch Emily alone, but instead she'd been gifted with something better.

Again.

The sheriff had questions. He suspected Morgan. And if Morgan was in his sights, that meant she wasn't. Perfect.

She slipped out silently, her pulse racing as she crept toward the back hall. All she needed to do was adjust her timing, but the game was still on.

LATER THAT MORNING, Ethan tracked down Dana Simmons at the One-Stop General Store where she worked. He pushed open the heavy wooden door. A bell jingled overhead, and the warm smell of coffee, maple syrup and fresh apples mixed with the faint scent of fertilizer drifting up from the back. He nodded to Mabel Johnson, the petite woman who owned the place.

"Sheriff," she called out from behind the counter. Barely five feet tall, she was stacking candy jars in neat rows. "What can I do for you today?"

"Mabel." Ethan tipped his hat. His gaze skimmed the rows of shelves as he stepped inside. On one side of the store were neat stacks of canned goods and homemade jams; baskets of fresh apples and squash sat near the door. A peg rack displayed hand-knit scarves and mittens. By the back wall, a small cooler was filled with milk, eggs and butter. On the other side were shelves of rope, duct tape, and seed packets. A rack of fishing poles leaned against the far wall.

It really was one-stop shopping. But it was places like this in a small town that kept it alive.

"I'm looking for Dana Simmons. Is she here?"

Mabel's brows knit. "Dana? Is she in trouble?"

"No," Ethan replied. "I have a couple of questions to ask her."

"She's in the back doing inventory." Mabel jerked her thumb toward the swinging door at the back.

Ethan nodded and headed for the stockroom. He pushed through the swinging door. Boxes of paper towels and flats of soda were stacked high, and a young woman in a faded flannel shirt and jeans stood on a stepstool, clipboard in hand. She looked up as Ethan entered.

"Dana Simmons?" he asked.

"Yup, that's me." She stared at him for a second. "Is something wrong?"

"Not wrong," he replied. "I just need to confirm a few details. You were with Morgan Tate a week and a half ago, Saturday night."

Dana blinked. "Saturday night? Oh yeah, I picked her up around five fifteen to head into town."

"What did you do?"

"We grabbed a bite to eat at the Harvest Moon Diner. Then we went to the eight o'clock showing of that new superhero movie at the Marquis. It didn't get out until after eleven." She smiled faintly. "I can give you a rundown of the plot if you don't believe me."

Ethan gave a small smile. "No need. Did she stay the night with you?"

"Sure did. She didn't want to drive back. Crashed on my couch. My roommate was there too." Dana's expression tightened. Her eyes clouded with worry. "Is Morgan in trouble?"

Ethan shook his head. "Just routine questions."

Dana let out a breath. "Well, I can promise you, she was with me the whole night. You can ask the waitress at the Harvest Moon or the kid selling popcorn at the Marquis."

Ethan nodded, some of the tension leaving his body. The timeline checked out, but in his line of work, even airtight alibis could spring leaks. And until he knew who was circling Emily, every name stayed on his list.

Thirty

It was late afternoon when Ethan pushed open the wooden doors to the station. The place smelled faintly of burnt coffee. Voices were muted in the background along with the usual ringing of phones.

Adam was already sitting at his desk. He stood as Ethan passed, following him into his office.

"Give me some good news," Ethan said as he slid into his chair, the leather creaking under his weight.

Adam dropped into the chair across from Ethan's desk and rubbed a hand over his face. "Cross has an alibi. Sort of."

"Sort of doesn't help the case."

"The library logs crashed a little after 6 p.m. that night."

Ethan shook his head. "Of course they did. Anything else?"

"Humph." Adam leaned back in the chair and let out a short, humorless laugh. "The cameras were swapped out, and the archiving didn't finish."

"So, what do we have besides a giant clusterfuck?"

"The good news is a student worker remembered seeing Cross around six. Messenger bag, glasses, recognized him from the photo. Cross reserved a study room. There was no record of when he left or that he stayed the whole time."

"Which means he could have slipped out, killed Jennifer and got back before anyone noticed."

"Yeah," Adam admitted. "Except the timing is crazy, and he doesn't feel like our guy. Defensive, sure, but more like a reporter protecting a source." He shrugged. "Not seeing someone leave is normal, but Burlingham is an hour away each way. Long shot at best."

This case was falling apart faster than they could tie the ends together. Ethan drummed his fingers on the desk. "I agree, but I'm not clearing him yet."

"What happened when you interviewed Morgan?"

Ethan gave him the rundown about interviewing Dana Simmons.

"So, Morgan is off our list," Adam said. "Who's left? Celeste?"

Ethan rubbed a hand over his jaw. "That's the problem. Morgan swears she saw Celeste leave around four. Said she walked out with her purse. Emily left a little before five, Morgan at five fifteen when Dana picked her up. After that, the place should've been empty."

Adam frowned. "So, if Morgan actually saw her leave at four, why's she still on the list?"

"Because she's got keys," Ethan said grimly. "She could've come back any time after Morgan locked up. No cameras at the time, no logs, nobody watching.

"That keeps her back in play. What are you going to do? Want me to interview her?"

Ethan tapped his fingers on the desk. This whole scenario sucked. His gut told him they were getting closer. They had all the edges of the puzzle but were still missing the all-important center. Not knowing gave the killer more room to breathe.

"No, I'll call her into the station. Maybe that'll put the fear of God in her and she'll confess. If she's guilty." He sighed. "If not ... I don't know who else to look at. We might have to get a list of all Emily's employees and clients and investigate them."

Adam's jaw clenched. "That'll ruin Emily's business. You know damn well people won't forget if we drag her clients into this."

Ethan's head came up, meeting his friend's glare. He got it. Hell, he'd be fierce too if it were his woman under fire. But he had a duty to the town first.

"I don't have the luxury of protecting reputations," Ethan said calmly. "Our job is to keep Emily alive."

Adam blew out a breath and ran his fingers through his hair. "I know. I don't disagree, but I just ... hope it doesn't come to that."

Me too, Adam. Me too. Ethan's chest tightened. The ache in his chest was sharp and unrelenting.

He wanted to give Adam the reassurance he needed, but he couldn't. Not when every lead they chased dead-ended with nothing but question marks.

Ethan called Celeste into the station early the next morning. The bullpen still smelled faintly of floor polish and burnt coffee. The building was quiet. Sunlight streamed through the blinds, striping his desk like bars.

Before heading in, he skimmed her file again. Celeste Miller had the thinnest digital footprint he'd ever seen—no tax records before Vermont, no social media, no previous employer he could verify. Not illegal. Not even rare. But it made the hair on the back of his neck stand up. Most people left at least a breadcrumb somewhere. She hadn't. And that alone made his instincts twitch.

She arrived with her purse and tote bag clutched tight, dressed neatly in a sweater and slacks, her gray hair tucked into a bun.

"Sheriff," she said with a polite smile. "You wanted to see me?"

He gestured toward the chair opposite his desk. "Thanks for coming in. I just wanted to clear up a couple of details regarding the unfortunate incident at the spa."

She sat, placed her belongings on the floor next to her, and looked at him. "Of course. Anything I can add to help solve this horrible murder."

"Before we get into the timeline," Ethan said, flipping his notebook open, "mind if I ask you something? Your background's pretty thin. Nothing wrong with that but it stood out. You move around a lot before Vermont?"

Celeste smiled. "Not really. I just never believed in putting my life all over the internet. I live simply. Pay cash when I can. People track too much these days. Privacy feels safer."

Ethan nodded, though his gut tightened. People who didn't want to be found made the same choices.

"Fair enough. Now you told me that you left around four."

Celeste blinked once. She folded her hands in her lap. "Yes, I had errands to run before the shops closed."

Ethan leaned back in his chair, watching her carefully. Her voice was steady, her eyes clear, but it was that pause that hooked him. It was a beat too long, as if she flipped through her replies before answering. She was good, no doubt about it.

"Anyone see you leave?" he asked casually.

Her eyes widened slightly, and she shrugged. "No one that I can think of. Maybe Morgan, but she was busy at the desk."

Ethan jotted down a note. "And you didn't return later?"

Celeste shook her head firmly. "No, Sheriff. I went straight home. I don't go out after dark much these days." She gave him a small smile. "Safer that way."

Ethan studied her. Every word fit. Every detail answered, and yet it seemed too smooth. His instincts were prickling. He'd learned long ago that the neatest stories were usually the ones hiding the biggest mess.

"So, let's go back to that Thursday," he said. "You mentioned then that Emily said Jennifer gave her bad vibes, that she was asking a lot of questions."

For a second, something flickered across Celeste's face. Then she narrowed her eyes, thinking. "Yes, I heard her mention it to Morgan after Jennifer left. Emily said Jennifer kept asking if it cost a lot of money to run the spa. It felt odd."

Ethan leaned back in his chair and steepled his hands. That was very specific. Emily had said Jennifer was nosy but not in exact wording like that. "You remember that clearly?"

Celeste lifted a shoulder. "It stood out because Emily doesn't usually talk that way about clients." She paused. "Honestly, it made me wonder if something was bothering her."

"Hmmm. You've been here, what ... a few months?"

"Not long," she replied. "I moved from Boston. Needed a change."

"What kind of change?"

Her smile was thin. "The usual kind. New town, fresh start." She lifted her shoulder. "The city wore me out. Too expensive. Too ... much. Beaver Creek felt quieter."

"Most people don't pick a tiny Vermont town off a map just for the scenery," he said casually. "What brought you here specifically?"

Celeste hesitated for a moment. Not long, just enough for Ethan to catch it. "I looked for a place with a good spa. Somewhere I could keep doing the work I love." She rubbed her arms. "Emily took a chance on me."

"And before Boston?"

"Different places," she said lightly. "Nothing exciting."

It was a vague answer, but Ethan didn't think he was going to pin her down today. "Interesting you were close enough to overhear Emily talking to Morgan," he said. "You were at the front desk?"

"Yes. Cleaning."

"Did Jennifer talk to you at all before she left?"

"No." Celeste shook her head. "I don't think she even noticed me."

"But *you* noticed her," he said casually.

She clenched her fists before relaxing them. "She struck me as someone looking for something," she said. "Not a massage. Something else."

He cocked his head. "You tell Emily that?" he asked.

"No, it wasn't my place."

Ethan gave a slow nod, but his Spidey Sense was on alert. It was almost as if she'd practiced what details to drop. He couldn't prove anything. Not yet anyhow.

"Thanks for coming in," he said, closing his notebook. "If I need anything else, I'll let you know."

Celeste stood, smoothed her sweater and left.

The door clicked shut.

Ethan sat back. Something about Celeste's story didn't sit right. And he'd learned long ago that whatever didn't sit right usually mattered.

He'd circle back to Celeste when the time was right.

CELESTE WALKED out of the sheriff's office around ten thirty, her heart thudding in her chest. Ethan was getting too close. He'd picked up on something; she could feel it. He was way smarter than a lot of these small-town sheriffs for sure. She had to be careful.

Thankfully, he had her come down before work. She didn't need anyone asking leading questions. She wondered where that reporter was, the one who came in as Mr. Jacobs. Was he still around? What knowledge did he have? Had Ethan interviewed him yet?

Back at the spa office, she slipped in, hearing Morgan's voice at the front desk. The spa smelled faintly of eucalyptus and the new citrus scent that replaced lavender. Scents that calmed the clients. Celeste wanted to laugh. Calm was an illusion. Nothing about this place was safe anymore. She collected her rags and a bucket and drifted closer just in time to catch the tail end of a conversation about a fundraiser tomorrow night and Adam missing it because he had to work.

Celeste smiled. Tomorrow night. Emily would be there.

Alone.

A slow coil of satisfaction unfurled in her chest. No Adam hovering, no protective shadow. And if Emily lingered after the event, she'd be coming home to her apartment afterward. She could already imagine a weak porch light casting shadows, Emily fumbling with her keys, blissfully unaware danger was so close.

Celeste wiped down the reception area. Emily and Morgan greeted her absentmindedly before going back to their conversation about the fundraiser. Perfect. They didn't suspect a thing.

She had plans to make. The cameras were an issue, but she could circumvent them. Nobody said it had to be done indoors. There were shadows everywhere if you knew how to use them. Bushes. Corners. Blind spots. The kind of place no one looked at until it was too late. All she'd have to do was wait.

Thirty-One

Emily rushed down the stairs from her apartment into the spa. Olivia would be picking her up at five thirty to drive them to the fundraiser.

"Wow," Morgan said, looking up from behind the computer. "You clean up nicely."

Emily laughed and twirled. "What do you think?"

It had taken her forever to decide what to wear. The bodice was sleek and black with short, fluttery sleeves. The full skirt flared out in a swirl of black brocade threaded with gold and soft lilac roses. She'd paired that with a pair of simple black pumps and put her hair into a loose chignon. She felt like a princess and only wished Adam were going with her.

"It's beautiful, Em, and it's so you. Soft, feminine and ... if I were a guy ... sexy," Morgan said with a wink.

"Thank you. I love it."

Just then, Olivia popped her head in. "Ready?"

"Yup. Let me grab my coat and we'll be off."

The drive to the Green Mountain Lodge didn't take long, and the women spent it catching up on everything from work to town gossip.

"You ever been to the Lodge?" Olivia asked as she turned onto the gravel road.

Emily shook her head. "First time. This fundraiser has grown so big that the community center can't handle it."

"You've done a wonderful job getting everyone together to build the baskets," Olivia said. "People are still talking about how creative they were last year."

They approached the Green Mountain Lodge, headlights sweeping across the long driveway. Even before they reached the main entrance, hundreds of tiny white lights twinkled in the trees and wrapped around the front porch columns.

"Oh my. It looks like a fairy tale," Emily whispered.

Olivia grinned. "Wait until you see inside. I heard they went all in with decorations in the ballroom. Piper went early to photograph before the crowd arrived."

They parked and stepped into the crisp, cold air. Emily inhaled deeply. The night smelled of woodsmoke with a hint of snow on the way. All the things she needed to get the spa ready for winter flashed through her mind, but she pushed them aside. Tonight wasn't about work.

"Look at this," exclaimed Olivia as they reached the wide front steps.

Emily followed her inside and paused. Rustic beams soared overhead, strung with strands of golden lights. A fire in the massive stone fireplace crackled, and the scent of burning oak scented the air. They passed a large dining room filled with guests laughing and clinking glasses.

They followed the signs toward the music and chatter. The mouthwatering aroma of Ivy's cooking filled the air with rosemary, sage, and something buttery that made Emily's stomach growl.

Inside the large ballroom, dozens of round tables were covered with white tablecloths. Crystal glassware shimmered under the glow of crystal chandeliers. Each table held vases brimming with autumn's bounty. Clusters of glossy red apples and pomegranates were nestled among sprays of scarlet berries and bright green buds. Russet red and burnished orange maple leaves mingled with pinecones, creating a formal yet warm arrangement. Soft music played in the background.

A huge sign in elegant gold script stretched across the platform at the back of the ballroom and read *Harbor Haven Fundraiser Gala*. Along one wall was framed photos of the auction baskets with handwritten notes explaining their purpose. The winning bidder would donate that basket to a woman at the shelter, a reminder that she mattered and wasn't forgotten.

Emily paused in front of the display, remembering the hours of organizing, the laughter and chatter of her friends, wrapping baskets in cellophane and finishing with pretty bows. Now, seeing it all come together, she realized it wasn't about the glittery evening or the auction items—it was about hope. A future for those who lost everything through no fault of their own.

Silent auction tables lined the opposite side with everything from handmade quilts to gift certificates for vacation homes, while the larger items were reserved for the big auction later in the evening.

"Oh, Em," Olivia said softly. "Look what you made happen."

Emily blinked a tear away. "It's beautiful. More than I ever imagined."

She glanced toward the doorway, wishing Adam was here to see it with her. But even without him, she knew he'd be proud. She ran her hands down the sides of her dress, smoothing the fabric. Everyone was dressed to the nines. She was proud to be here, although this wasn't the type of venue she normally attended—not at two hundred fifty dollars a ticket. Her employees couldn't afford to be here. This wasn't their world, and she felt the difference keenly.

Clusters of guests were standing around nibbling on hors d'oeuvres and drinking wine or beer. Emily thought she knew a lot of people in town, but there were many faces she didn't recognize. It appeared the fundraiser had reached donors in Burlingham and some of the surrounding towns.

Savannah waved her over from a table near the front. Dylan sat beside her, talking to Jane and Ethan. Across the room, Piper darted from table to table, taking pictures. Olivia was already in a corner interviewing a couple. This was going to be great publicity in tomorrow's news, Emily realized. And all good publicity for Harbor Haven.

The president of the Chamber of Commerce walked up to the stage and cleared his throat, reminding everyone that dinner was about to be served and to take their places.

Emily slid into her seat next to Savannah and noticed the place cards for Olivia and Piper. It was a table for eight, and the only one missing was Adam, which made her chest ache. She could almost picture him here, tugging at his tie and muttering under his breath about formal dinners, not unlike Ethan, who looked like he'd rather be investigating a crime than sitting at a fancy dinner.

On each table was the menu for the night: rosemary chicken, balsamic pork tenderloin, or butternut squash ravioli drizzled with sage butter, all locally sourced with seasonal vegetables and salad. Dessert was a choice of maple crème brûlée or apple tart with cinnamon ice cream. Emily resisted the urge to ask if she could start with dessert. They both sounded delicious.

Water and bottles of wine from Fallen Timbers were already uncorked on the table. The rich aroma of roasting meat and herbs filled the air as waitstaff in black carried trays of steaming plates to each table.

Conversations buzzed around her as donors sipped wine, interspersed with laughter and the hum of voices. Olivia leaned over with her notebook.

"Give me a quote, Em. Just a few words for the article."

Emily smiled faintly, shaking her head. All she would say was that this wasn't about her but about the community coming together to make another person's life brighter, to give them hope when they needed it most.

Dinner passed in a blur, then the bidding began.

Emily sat back, listening as the numbers started climbing. The quilt sewn by Cecelia Whitcomb fetched eight hundred dollars. A week in a cottage on an island in Maine went for two thousand. Even the gift baskets she'd helped assemble brought in staggering amounts. Two hundred here, five hundred there, so much more than last year at the community center. Then there was all the money from the advertising in the program. The Lodge and Ivy were paid from ticket sales. It was a win-win for everyone.

Every time the auctioneer's gavel came down with a resounding *sold*, the room erupted in cheers. Emily's cheeks ached from smiling so much. It was surreal.

By the time the last item was bid and dessert plates were cleared, the ballroom started to empty. Ivy had come out to say hello while the staff whisked away plates and napkins.

Olivia appeared at Emily's side. "Ready?"

"Oh, my. Yes." She said her goodbyes, and the two friends walked to Olivia's car.

The drive back was quiet. Emily leaned her head back against the seat and let out a long breath.

"It was a good night," Olivia said softly, glancing at her.

Emily smiled. "Better than good."

They finally pulled up at her apartment. "Thanks, Olivia. I've got it from here."

Olivia waited until Emily pulled out her keys before driving away, her taillights disappearing toward town.

Emily slid the key into the lock, shoulders relaxing for a second. It was so quiet, so peaceful. So ...

A horn beeped lightly behind her. She startled until she saw Adam's cruiser parking in front. Relief loosened her shoulders.

He climbed out, tugging his jacket tighter. The sight of him in uniform, solid and steady, made her heart sing. He gave her a quick kiss and then broke away. "How was the gala?"

She gave a little laugh. "It was amazing. I'm sorry you missed it."

"Me too."

"Liar," she teased, then noticed Adam wasn't laughing.

His gaze drifted past her, sweeping the shadows. Every muscle went taut.

"What is it?" she asked, glancing around and seeing nothing out of place.

"Go on inside, Em, and lock the door," he said softly, still scanning. "I'll wait until the lights are on."

She frowned, searching his face, but didn't argue, just walked inside and locked the door.

Adam stood there until the lights came on, then glanced around again before finally heading back to his cruiser.

FROM THE SHADOWS behind a row of shrubs, Celeste eased her way back, her breath coming fast. Too close. The deputy's instincts were sharper than she'd planned. She hadn't expected him to swing by tonight.

But he'd felt her. Almost seen her.

Emily's laugh still echoed in her ears. Celeste's jaw tightened. She'd been seconds away from making her move, from slipping out and greeting Emily with the surprise she deserved.

Instead, she was pressed against the cold, damp ground, holding her breath like a thief.

Next time, she promised herself. Next time, she'd make sure Adam wouldn't be there to interfere.

She watched Adam leave, placed the knife back in her tote and adjusted the strap, easing back into the shadows. Emily thought she was safe tucked into her little cocoon, but safety was an illusion. And Celeste was more than happy to shatter it.

Thirty-Two

Adam gave up on sleep Sunday morning when the first pale streaks of dawn slipped through the tall windows of his A-frame. The house was quiet, just like he liked it—usually.

He padded barefoot across the wooden floor with a mug of coffee warming his hands, but his mind kept circling back to last night and the spa lot—Emily unlocking the door, a feeling that something was off, a flicker of movement in the bushes gone before he could pin it down. Could've been a stray cat or a raccoon. Could've been nothing. But his gut told him a different story.

Today he'd go back in the sunlight and look for telltale signs of an animal or a human one. Besides, he told himself he wanted to see Emily, make sure she was safe, and bring her home with him. Yes, home with him would be perfect. They could have lunch, a long afternoon on the couch kissing, cuddling, making love. That sounded good to him. A perfect way to spend the day.

A while later, he showered, pulled on jeans and boots, poured coffee into a travel mug, and grabbed his keys. If it was nothing, fine. But if it had been someone hiding in the bushes, he wasn't going to forgive himself for ignoring it. No sense in checking the cameras since they only covered entrances and exits. Maybe he should ask Levi to cover the whole facility. Something to think about. Although Emily hadn't been thrilled with them in the first place.

His truck lights cut through the morning fog as he drove toward town. The roads shimmered with frost. The town was quiet with only a few souls out and about for breakfast or a walk. A couple of cruisers were parked at the station, and Adam was happy to have the day off. He turned onto Firehouse Road. The spa came into view. He parked at the far edge of the lot and got out. He walked the perimeter slowly and easily, scanning bushes and the tree line. Nothing obvious. No footprints. No little note stuck in the bushes saying, "I was here."

Nothing.

He crouched by the bushes where he thought he'd seen movement last night. Empty. No proof. Just his gut telling him he saw what he saw and the hair at the back of his neck prickling.

The sun was high in the sky when he finished scouting around. He was just about to call Emily when he heard the door click open behind him. She stepped outside dressed in a blue wool pea jacket and jeans with a scarf wrapped around her neck. Her hair was twisted into a loose bun.

"Hey. This is a surprise." She smiled when she saw him and then frowned. "Is something wrong?"

"Couldn't sleep," he said. "Thought I'd check things out."

"What things?" she asked, then her eyes widened. "Does this have to do with last night?"

Adam hesitated. He thought about what he wanted to tell her without scaring her. He could sugarcoat it, but he didn't want her to write off danger if there was any.

"Yeah. I thought I saw movement in the bushes. I came back this morning but couldn't find any footprints or indication that it was a person. Could've been an animal."

She relaxed for a moment. "Oh."

He reached out for her sleeve. The touch steadied him more than it did her. "So, want to come back with me, have lunch?" He winked.

She laughed. "I can't. I'm having lunch with Savannah and Claire at the Twisted Fork."

"Oh."

"But I'd love to see you later. I'll stay the night." She leaned close and whispered in his ear. "I'll text when I'm on my way."

Adam was disappointed but instead nodded. "I can handle that."

He watched her walk to her car and waved as she pulled out of the lot. Only when her taillights disappeared did he climb back into the truck, the sense of unease still there.

ETHAN DROPPED into the chair opposite Jane at the kitchen table and studied the morning sky. Salmon and light gray clouds fought for space over Elephant Mountain. It promised to be a sunny day, and he looked forward to spending a few hours with her.

The fundraiser last night had raised a lot of money, judging by what people were bidding on, but formal events like that made him antsy. Give him a shootout or burglary any day over standing around at a formal event, making small talk with people he didn't know. Still, seeing the room full of people coming together for a good cause felt good.

He sipped the hot coffee in his mug and glanced toward

Tanner's farm, then checked his watch. Tanner would be asleep now since he milked at 3:30 a.m. and again twelve hours later. It was the life Ethan knew when he was growing up. Not the life he wanted for himself now. But Tanner made it work and loved it. His girlfriend, Leah, was right there alongside him.

"Hey." Jane's warm breath teased his ear.

"I thought you'd sleep a little later since we got in late last night," he said, putting the mug down and tugging her onto his lap.

"Oof," she said. "You need to warn a girl if you're going to do that."

"What fun is that?" He put his arms around her and kissed her, softly at first, then deeper until she laughed and tugged him closer. "Upstairs?" he finally asked when they broke apart.

"In a little while," she replied. "I need to fully wake up." She got up and poured herself a cup of coffee and refilled his. "Why are you looking so pensive this morning?"

He blew out his breath. "It was good to see Emily so happy last night, but this case is driving me crazy. Three suspects—one with a solid alibi, one with a shaky alibi, and one I don't know about. And then, there is the unknown. Another person to add to the mix."

She leaned forward, her elbows on the table. "Why don't you tell me what the problem is? I do have experience, you know."

"Jane, you promised ..." He gave her a very stern look. Jane only smiled at him.

"I told you I wouldn't get involved in this," she replied, although he heard her mutter "yet" under her breath.

"Besides, Eddie McDermott and Aaron Stone are really popular with the Beaver Creek crowd for their crime-solving abilities. People make the connections themselves."

Ethan snorted. "The citizens of Beaver Creek are not dumb. They know exactly who you're writing about."

Jane smirked and shrugged. "Not my fault." She leaned back. "So, tell me."

"It all boils down to the left-handed angle." He rubbed the back of his neck. "Morgan has an ironclad alibi for that night. Unless her friend is lying. But people saw them together. Daniel Cross is a journalist and was in Burlingham that night. A student ID'd him, plus his credit card shows charges there. It's unlikely he could have driven back and forth although not impossible." He tapped the table. "Cross won't divulge why he's here except to say he was following Jennifer Bishop, trying to get ahead of a story about this spa in Boston. And then there's Celeste."

"Celeste?" Jane's brow arched. "She's short and middle-aged."

Ethan shrugged. "Doesn't matter how tall or old you are if you have the element of surprise. She's left-handed and has keys to the spa. I think she's hiding something, but it may not have anything to do with Jennifer's death."

"That's true." Jane took a long sip of her coffee. "Does she have an alibi?"

"No." He shoved a hand into his hair. "And I can't arrest a person without cause."

Jane leaned back in her chair. "The one thing I learned from all my research and talking to experts in the field is that it's about asking the right questions."

"So, enlighten me," Ethan said with a grin.

She arched an eyebrow. "Who benefits if Emily's business is gone?"

Ethan opened his mouth, then closed it again. He wanted to argue it was too broad, too vague, but Jane was right. "The spa," he said finally. "The land."

"Go on," she prodded.

"The train station renovation!"

Why hadn't he thought of that before? Sometimes it took talking to a disinterested person to rattle the brain cells. "That end of town could be worth a lot more than it is now. Property like Emily's could be prime real estate."

Jane tapped the table. "It doesn't have to be personal, Ethan. People have killed for less."

He let out a short, humorless laugh. "Great. So now we can put greed on the list."

She reached for her phone, scrolling through her contacts. "Every story has red herrings. Maybe this one does too. I'll call a friend in Boston, see if she has any information on that spa. There has to be a connection." She thumbed a number and left a message when it went to voicemail.

"You'll tell me if you hear anything?" Ethan asked.

"Of course, sweetie." She gave him an easy smile. "You're the sheriff."

Ethan mentally groaned. His mind kept circling questions, and he was eager for just one hint that would make everything line up. There was trouble and danger in Beaver Creek, and it was bad enough Emily was caught up in something. He didn't need her friends caught up in it too.

All thoughts of danger and trouble receded when Jane stood and kissed him. "I'm ready," she said in a low voice. He let the worry drift away and told himself he'd deal with it later.

Thirty-Three

Rain battered the windows early Monday morning as Emily slowly woke up and stretched. The clock on the end table read 6 a.m. Adam was curved up against her, his arm over her chest, his cock tucked warm and insistent between them. She felt warm and safe. For a delicious second, she thought about pulling the covers back over both of them and pretending the world could wait, but clients didn't care about cozy mornings.

She lay there for a few minutes replaying yesterday's lunch at The Twisted Fork with Savannah and Claire. She hadn't been there in a while, so it surprised her to see Savannah's paintings on one brick wall opposite the vintage photos of Beaver Creek scenes. Emmy Walters seldom changed the interior, so the art stood out. The girls were sitting at a wooden table looking out a window by the falls. They spent the hour laughing until their cheeks hurt and rehashing the fundraiser. When it was time to leave, she texted Adam. The rest was history, as they say.

"Hey, heavy thinker over there," Adam murmured, his voice low.

Emily laughed. "How did you know I was awake?"

He nuzzled the back of her neck. "I'm a cop. I know things."

She turned in his arms, fingers trailing slowly over his chest. "Well, I know things too." She kissed him, hot and messy, the kind of kiss that made them both smile.

He laughed. "You sure do. Now let an expert do his thing."

AN HOUR later they were sitting in the kitchen with steaming mugs. "What do you have planned for the day?" she asked.

"Oh, the usual. Run down suspects, give out tickets, break up bar fights." He sighed. "The glamorous life of small-town police work."

She smacked his arm. "Any big plans beyond saving the town?"

He got serious. "Honestly. I'm going to ask Levi to do a sweep of the property, check the ground, the bushes, see if he notices anything off from Saturday night. Do you mind?"

"No, I don't mind. I'm glad there's backup. I have clients coming in at ..." She glanced at her watch. "Crap. I have an hour to shower, dress and get to the spa."

"I can help with that," he offered, eyebrows up.

"Not on your life, bud. I don't need any more distractions." She grinned. "Besides, you'd probably give me a ticket for indecent exposure."

He smirked. "Well, missy, that would be a Code One citation punishable by a stern lecture, two coffees and mandatory making up. I'm totally prepared to do my duty."

Emily laughed, finished her coffee, already racing through her to-do list.

On Monday morning, Olivia was at her desk at the *Beaver Creek News* surrounded by the familiar sounds of keyboards clicking and the scent of stale coffee. She'd come in early to write up the fundraiser piece and made a note to call the event chair to pin down the final total.

She'd been so impressed with everything that night. The Lodge looked gorgeous in the photos, with the ballroom strung with twinkling lights, the long tables of silent auction items and more people than the town usually saw on a Saturday night.

Piper sent over a folder full of photos. Candid pictures of people laughing, a tight shot of the winning bid paddles, one that caught the mayor mid-toast, groups of people ogling the auction baskets and other items, and Savannah and Dylan's paintings, which fetched a good price.

But when she was finished and read what she'd written, she stared at her screen. Emily was in deep trouble. She was sure of that. It wasn't anything Emily had done. But trouble had come to her. Jennifer Bishop had brought it, whether she meant to or not. The woman's questions, her sudden appearance in Beaver Creek, her connection to Boston all pointed to something that didn't belong here. Ethan clearing Emily of the murder was a big step, but it only raised new questions about Jennifer Bishop and how she wound up in Beaver Creek.

Why had she come here? Was she after a story? If so, what story? And what was the man's name that Emily mentioned? The one Ethan asked if she knew.

Daniel.

Daniel Cross. Was he from Boston too? What role did he play in this?

She typed his name into the search bar and waited. Not more than a few seconds later, she had more information than she knew what to do with. Nothing too personal. Bylines, profiles, a handful of solid pieces. The picture of him didn't set off any alarm bells. He was a freelance journalist. From the number of articles she read, a good one. So was Jennifer.

She sent a quick email to a friend asking for information on Cross. Maybe he was working on something big if he came to Beaver Creek. Although what that could be escaped her. This was Beaver Creek—just a small town in the country.

If it was really big, though, she wanted to find out. Then she added a quick note to pull public records and check local court dockets later, just in case.

Her training as an investigative journalist was lost in this small town, but she moved here for a reason. The endless search for the big stories, the thin moral victories had gotten old. She craved a small-town atmosphere like the one she grew up in. Friends who had each other's back, a community that came together to help the less fortunate. That was what fed her soul.

But if there was a real story hiding here, she wasn't walking away.

Olivia tapped her pen against her notebook, circled the name Daniel Cross twice. She hoped she'd get more answers from her friend.

The one thing she knew for sure was that Ethan was hunting answers too.

AROUND THE SAME TIME, a few blocks away, Ethan left the station to check with the clerk at town hall. It helped to talk to Jane, get a different perspective. He'd never considered the train station renovation as a motive, but it made sense. It also made sense that the surrounding properties would be valuable.

He pulled on his rain jacket and walked to the town hall a couple of blocks over. Too close to drive, and besides, the fresh air felt good, even in the rain.

Sue, at the clerk's window, set him up with a stack of recent permits, and he even spotted a council member to ask about outside developers sniffing around the railroad station.

Nothing. No filings. No interest. Not even a whisper of an offer on Emily's block.

He left there with nothing but disappointment. Either he was chasing shadows, or someone was covering their tracks too well. And he hated both options.

Ethan stepped back out into the rain, frustrated as hell.

NOT LONG AFTER, while the storm pounded the roof, Emily had just finished a massage and walked out to talk to Morgan when the lights in the reception area blinked. For a second, she thought it was the weather. Lightning and heavy rain hammered the town all morning.

Then, the faint metallic scent of something burning drifted through the air. *Please don't let it be the wiring*, she prayed to the gods of good fortune, knowing they had already abandoned her and were laughing. The wiring in the building was old. She knew it when she remodeled, choosing to fix what people could see, not what was underneath. Rewiring the whole building was on her to-do list when she had extra money.

"Do you smell that?" Morgan asked, her brows narrowing.

Emily nodded and walked down the hall to the breaker

panel next to the back door. The little red tester light was dead.

Morgan followed her. “Em, the heaters are dead.”

Emily’s mind jumped in a dozen directions at once. Was it a frayed wire? Oh God, please don’t let it be the furnace on top of everything else. Then one word flashed through her mind. Safety.

Clients, staff, equipment, supplies—everything hinged on that one word.

She could only shake her head.

“Em? What do you want to do?” Morgan asked.

What she wanted to do was bury her head in the sand. But she couldn’t. This was her business, and it was her responsibility to keep everyone safe.

“We need to close the spa. Why don’t you get the staff out, and I’ll talk to the clients?”

Within minutes, people were getting their things together and clearing the building. They stood in the lot in small groups, pointing at the building and clutching coats and purses. Emily’s hands shook as she pulled out her phone and dialed 911.

“This is Serenity Spa on Firehouse Road. We’ve got a power outage, a smoke smell, and possible electrical issues. The building’s been evacuated.”

She hung up after the dispatcher confirmed the fire department was on the way. She immediately called Adam.

“I’m on my way,” Adam said. “I’ll be there in a few.”

She walked around to the front door after asking Morgan to encourage onlookers to leave.

Moments later, the blare of a siren could be heard over the thundering rain. In no time, a fire engine rumbled to the curb, red lights reflecting off the wet pavement. Behind them was a police cruiser and Adam’s truck.

Adam raced over, holding an umbrella. He patted her from head to toe. "Em, are you okay? Hurt anywhere?"

She shook her head.

Two firefighters walked over to them. "Adam, fancy meeting you here," said one.

Adam shook hands with them both. "Emily, meet my good friends Nic Garcia and Reed Samuels. Two of Beaver Creek's finest."

They shook hands with her.

"Hell of a way to get us to visit the spa," Nic teased.

"Whatever works," Emily quipped, trying for humor even though her voice shook.

Reed gave her a nod before the two disappeared inside, followed by two more firefighters.

Adam wrapped his arm around her shoulders as she spotted Ethan walking toward them.

"Emily. Bad things keep happening here," Ethan said, shaking his head. "What's going on?"

"Don't know yet. The fire department is figuring it out."

What felt like hours but in reality, was only half an hour, passed before Nic emerged first. "Good call clearing the building. No fire, but your breaker panel is toast. Shorted clean out. You're lucky it tripped before the whole wall went up."

Reed added dusting ash from his palm. "Plastic's melted. You'll need a new box, rewiring in places and an inspection before you can flip anything on. Furnace is fine. This is all electrical."

Her stomach sank. "How long are we talking?"

"Inspector will need to see it first," Nic said. "It could take a few days, maybe a week, depending upon what needs to be done and if you can get a licensed electrician over here. Then he'll have to sign off with the town before you reopen."

Emily closed her eyes and shook her head. Perfect. Just perfect. As if things weren't dicey enough, now she'd have to cancel appointments, refund anyone who paid up front, pay idle staff and lose clients to Aspire Day Spa. She was already bleeding money, and now ... coming up with more to pay an electrician was overwhelming.

Adam slid an arm around her shoulders. “One step at a time. At least everyone is safe.”

She nodded, but she really wanted to cry. But she forced her chin up. “It’s not the end of the world. We’ll get through it.”

Adam gave her a squeeze. “That’s my girl.”

Adam’s steady arm held Emily close as she tried to breathe through the smoke smell. She hoped the worst was over.

ACROSS THE STREET, under an umbrella, Celeste knew better.

She stood watching the fire truck’s red strobes flash across the wet pavement. The spa’s door was flung open. Staff and clients huddled nearby under umbrellas. Emily stood in the middle of them, pale and stricken, with the phone pressed to her ear.

A delicious ripple of satisfaction coursed through her body as she remembered how simple it had been. No one noticed her drifting down the hall. The breaker box was old. She opened the panel, pretending to wipe the frame clean.

She’d planned it perfectly—a loosened screw on the neutral bar, a strip of copper wire shaved bare, just enough to arc against the metal plate. Not enough to spark a blaze. They’d call it bad wiring, age. She left everything looking untouched, every wire back where it belonged. Almost.

She didn’t want Emily dead. Yet.

She wanted her to lose everything first.

Movement caught her eye. Adam had arrived and put his arm around Emily, his head turning as his gaze swept across the sidewalk. Then Ethan joined in, both scanning the crowd, and for one moment, Celeste felt their focus on her.

Her pulse jumped. Did they suspect? Could they see through her?

She adjusted her umbrella and pretended to fuss with the strap of her bag. When she turned to look at them, she widened her eyes in feigned surprise. Then she turned away, slipping back toward the group of staff gathered nearby.

Across the street, Adam muttered something low. Ethan replied, his gaze narrowed. They might have suspected someone in the crowd, but there was no proof.

The spa was Emily's pride and joy. Without it, she was nothing. Now Emily would know how it felt to lose everything, just like she did when the Boston spa went under and Marcus killed himself. Clients would drift away, her reputation would be shot, and soon Emily would be begging for business.

Celeste's lips curved. *Let's see you charm your way out of this one, princess.*

She tugged her hood lower and turned away, leaving the flashing lights and Emily clinging to that deputy's arm. Soon Emily's whole life would implode, and when she was at her weakest, Celeste would finish the job.

Thirty-Four

There was nothing more Emily or anyone could do, so she quickly sent all the employees home, promising to guarantee their paychecks. She noticed Adam and Ethan talking quietly by the front door. The fire truck was leaving, its lights fading into the rain. And now it was just her. Standing alone in the rain with the cold seeping into her clothes, wondering what the hell she was going to do next.

Adam broke away from Ethan with a quick squeeze to his shoulder, then jogged toward her.

"Sweetheart." He ducked under the umbrella and pulled her into his arms. "This really sucks, but I have a friend who's a licensed electrician. I'll give Mike a call and see if I can get him over here ASAP."

"Thanks." A tear dripped down Emily's cheek. Adam brushed it away.

"It's going to be okay, I promise."

"Humph. You can't promise that."

"I can, and I did." He looked around the area. "You can't stay here. Go upstairs and pack what you'll need for a while. I'll make sure everything is closed here."

It didn't take Emily long to pack a few things. She thought about the deserted spa, her heart breaking. Why? Why was all of this happening right now? What if this problem couldn't be fixed? She couldn't afford to start over. And it wasn't just the business. Her home would be gone too. Then what would she do?

Emily sat on her bed and looked around her apartment at some of the mementos she'd carried from Boston—the framed photo of her parents, her massage therapy diploma from the Tranquil Path Institute hanging beside a Restorative Yoga certificate from the Lotus Path Wellness Collective, a funny birthday card signed by her friends there. All memories of happier times.

A tear slipped down her cheek, then another. She couldn't stop the flow. All she could do was go with it. She buried her head in the pillow that Jane had given her that said *Home is where you find your peace.*

What peace? Her spa was dark. Her home was on the edge of being ripped away. It was just too much, especially after leaving everything behind in Boston. The career she'd built, the friendships she'd lost, the fear she ran away from and the promise she made herself that she'd never let herself fall apart again. She'd thought Beaver Creek would be a safe place to heal. A second chance to start over.

Now even that dream was crumbling.

She clutched the pillow tighter and let the sobs come. For once, she didn't try to be strong. She didn't try to pretend everything was fine. Just for once, she let herself fall apart.

The bed dipped beside her, and a warm hand rested on her back. Adam didn't say anything, just rubbed slow circles between her shoulder blades.

Finally, she took a deep breath, hiccupped a couple of times and then looked at Adam. He brushed her tears away with his thumb. The gentleness of his touch soothed her.

"Sweetheart," he murmured. "You are not alone. Not anymore."

Her lips trembled. "I feel like I'm losing everything."

"You're not losing me or your friends," he replied. "The spa can be repaired. But you? You're what matters."

Her chest tightened, and she leaned into him, letting his strength wrap around her.

He stood and offered her his hand. "Come on. Let's get you settled at my place."

"Thank you," she said in a small voice, barely a whisper.

Adam shook his head. "You never have to thank me. I'm here for you. Now come on, let's go. Tomorrow we'll deal with the electrical."

He placed her suitcase in the back of her car and opened the driver's-side door. "I'll meet you there."

She nodded and watched him get in his truck. The ride out of town was quiet. Emily followed Adam's truck past town and then onto the gravel drive.

The A-frame slowly came into view. She parked beside him and for a second just stared at it.

Adam was waiting beside her car before she even shut the door. He grabbed her bag from the back seat. "You're here for as long as it takes." His eyes held hers. "And don't bother trying to negotiate."

She swallowed the lump in her throat and gave him a small smile. "Bossy."

"Only when it comes to you." He leaned in and gave her a quick kiss on the mouth.

Inside, the living room smelled of cedar and burning pine, the familiar scent rising to meet her and chasing away the acrid memory of burned wires clinging to her skin. The place always felt like Adam, but tonight it felt like a sanctuary.

She shed her coat onto the hook by the door and glanced around. "It feels safe."

He put the suitcase down and pulled her into his arms. "It is safe. And I intend to keep it that way."

"Guess we're roommates," she mumbled into his chest.

He gave a little huff. "Roommates with great perks."

Her laughter caught in her throat when she looked up into his eyes and saw the desire burning there. Heat curled in her belly, and the air shifted. Her heart gave a wild thump, and before she could think, his mouth was on hers. He didn't give her time to doubt, only to feel. He took her hand and led her upstairs. She followed, trusting him with everything she hadn't been able to trust in herself.

EMILY WOKE a little after eight and reached for Adam. But his side of the bed was empty and cool. She blinked at the sunlight streaming through the naked branches outside the window and then stretched. Maybe this was an omen of brighter days ahead. She could only hope.

The door eased open, and Adam walked in with a steaming mug in hand.

"I figured you'd be up," he said, passing it to her. "Called my friend Mike Ferguson. He's a licensed electrician and knows his stuff. He'll meet us at the spa in an hour."

Emily took a long swallow of coffee, letting the warmth spread through her chest. "That's terrific news. Let me drink this, then I'll shower and be ready."

Adam winked. "Need help in that shower?"

"Humph." She arched an eyebrow at him. "If you help, we'll never meet up with Mike on time."

"True. When you're ready, come downstairs. I'm making eggs and toast."

Emily set the cup on the nightstand and stood, only then

realizing she was still naked. Adam's gaze swept over her as if she were his favorite meal.

She put her hands on her hips. "Pull your eyeballs back in, buddy. No time for hanky-panky right now."

Adam laughed as he tugged her in for a kiss. "Maybe not now. But I don't have to work today, so hold that thought."

EMILY TRIED to sit quietly in Adam's truck as he drove them to the spa, but she couldn't stop twisting her hands on her lap.

"Em, it's going to be fine. Stop fidgeting."

"I know, but I can't imagine what he's going to say. What if he says he can't fix it? What if it's beyond repair? What if the insurance won't cover it? What if…"

Adam reached over with his right hand and covered hers. "Whatever he says, we'll deal with it. Okay?"

Her throat tightened. She nodded, trying to draw calm from the warmth of his hand.

She glanced out the window as the spa came into view, looking deserted.

Adam gave her hand a gentle pat. "Breathe, sweetheart. We've got this."

By the time they pulled in front, Mike Ferguson's van was already there.

Adam parked and squeezed her hand once more before climbing out. "Come on, we'll know something shortly."

Emily unlocked the spa. She showed Mike where the breaker box was and let him get to work. Adam stayed with him while Emily opened her office and sat in her chair staring out. The spa was eerily quiet except for the men's voices. The faint scent of eucalyptus and lemongrass hovered in the air.

The worst-case scenario was that the whole building

would need rewiring. She didn't have enough money for that. And once that thought landed, her mind was skipping straight into every other disaster it could think up.

Thankfully, she was startled out of all her negative thoughts.

"Em, Mike wants to talk to you."

She followed Adam down the hallway and found Mike crouching in front of the breaker box with a flashlight, muttering to himself.

He stood when they came in. "Wish I had better news for you."

Emily's stomach clenched. "Better news?"

Mike angled the flashlight toward the open panel. "This isn't normal wear. Someone stripped the casing, pulled wires and crossed connections. That's not an accident."

"You mean ..." She took a deep breath and let it out. "Sabotage?"

"Clear as day," Mike confirmed. "If this had gone on much longer, you'd have been dealing with a fire."

Emily swayed, and Adam put a steadying arm around her waist.

"Can you put it in writing for her insurance?" Adam asked.

"Already started," Mike said. "That should cover your claim. They should reimburse you for repairs and downtime."

Adam and Mike shook hands. "Appreciate you coming on short notice, man."

"Thank you," Emily said.

"Don't thank me. Thank Adam for dragging me here," Mike said, giving Adam a pointed look. "Keep the spa closed until I've checked every inch of wiring. Promise me."

"I promise," she whispered. Her voice sounded hollow even to her own ears.

Mike packed up and left, leaving only silence and the echo of a slamming door.

Adam rubbed his hand over his jaw. "He's got a point," he said quietly. "Thankfully, no one was hurt."

Emily turned to Adam. "I can't believe someone is trying to destroy everything I've built."

She wanted to argue, to insist it couldn't be that bad, but knowing the whole place could have caught on fire, perhaps even killing people, stole her breath.

Adam's jaw flexed. "You're not staying here until this is resolved, Em. I'm not taking any chances with your safety."

Emily wanted to protest, wanted to tell Adam she was a grown-ass woman who could take care of herself, but right now she was scared. And for the first time since Boston, she decided to let someone else help shoulder the weight.

Still, her life was in this spa. "I left some things upstairs—my laptop, some personal things," she said. "But after what Mike found, I'm not going up there right now. I'll come back for them later."

A chill slid down her spine. If someone had done this on purpose, they could still be watching.

Silently, she prayed Adam could keep her safe from whoever wanted to ruin her life.

Thirty-Five

Ten days, a safety inspection, and thousands of dollars later—oh, and she couldn't forget the state health inspector, who stopped by with some expensive suggestions—Emily was finally able to walk back into her spa. Ethan and Adam had called everyone they knew to expedite the process. Mike, the electrician, gave her a small discount, which helped, but until the insurance check came in, she was out-of-pocket for almost all her savings.

She had to keep reminding herself that she didn't have a mortgage, but paying salaries, losing customers, having the whole place professionally cleaned cost more than she anticipated. Even so, the what-ifs kept her awake at night. What if clients didn't come back? What if the spa couldn't recover? Even thinking about the numbers made her stomach ache, and it felt like a weight chained around her neck, and panic set in. Through it all, Adam had been her rock.

Tonight, she refused to think about bank balances or busted breaker boxes. She was meeting some of her friends at Lily's farm. Rustic Roots was just down the street from Jane's place, and for the first time in days, she could feel herself relax. Feel normal. Maybe even hopeful.

At half past dusk, she got into her car and followed Mills River Road past the small white church and cemetery, past the Old Mill, Tanner McQueeney's farm, Jane's house and finally Lily's farm. The gravel drive crunched under her tires. The early November air smelled of woodsmoke and made her think of roasting marshmallows over an open fire.

The small white farmhouse sat back from the road, surrounded by hoop houses, fruit trees that were now bare, and a small barn where Lily kept some chickens. Emily pulled beside Jane's car and stepped out. The air was brisk, and silence settled around her, cool and still. Steady, peaceful. She took a deep breath, letting it cleanse her lungs. Laughter spilled through the windows, and Lily's old Labrador, Doodles, stood, barked once from the wide front porch, and then flopped back down.

Emily climbed the steps, stooped to greet Doodles, scratching behind his ears until his tail gave a lazy thump, and then opened the door.

Inside, she hung her coat by the door and glanced at the small fire crackling in the fireplace. She followed the voices into the kitchen. Savannah, Jane, and Claire were clustered around a long wooden table, papers and half-empty glasses of wine scattered around. Olivia and Leah had their heads together in a serious conversation, and Lily was pulling something out of the oven that smelled delicious.

"Hi?"

"Oh goody, you're here and just in time," exclaimed Claire.

Emily blinked. "In time for what?"

Savannah grinned. "Oh, just a little planning session."

"Planning session?" Emily repeated. "For what?"

Lily handed her a glass of white wine. "Your grand reopening, of course."

Emily froze. "My what?"

Jane stood, arms crossed. "Sweetie, you didn't really think we were going to let you reopen without a proper party, did you?"

Her throat tightened. Sure, she thought about reopening. Just open the doors and business would get back to normal. Or maybe not. What if her clients stayed away for good? What if the spa's reputation sank with the murder? Actually a reopening party sounded wonderful.

"Ivy couldn't make it tonight, but she volunteered to cater it," said Savannah. "Piper said she'll take photographs. Olivia will write it up. Oh, I contacted Taryn Keene. She promised to be there to support you."

Emily took a long swallow of her wine. She needed a moment to collect herself. Otherwise, she'd start crying. These were her friends. Her tribe. The ones who refused to let her stand alone when life kept trying to knock her down.

But Taryn? Why her? She was a competitor. Although when they'd spoken at the Chamber, she'd been surprisingly friendly. So ... why not her? She was an influencer and might have some great ideas to help get people to come back. Because the truth was, the murder and closing of the spa had hurt business more than she wanted to admit. And the whispers and rumors were still out there.

"So, what have you planned so far?" she asked.

The girls threw out suggestions all at once until Savannah whistled. "Let's spice things up with a male stripper." She waggled her eyebrows. "Anyone willing to volunteer a male friend?"

Jane groaned. "For heaven's sake, this is Beaver Creek, not Vegas."

Claire snorted into her wineglass. "Can you imagine if we hired a farmer to peel off his flannel shirt in front of half the town?"

"I was actually thinking more along the lines of a sheriff or deputy," quipped Savannah, staring at Jane and Emily.

Emily couldn't help herself. She giggled, then it turned into a full belly laugh. The other women followed until Olivia finally threw up a hand. "Stop. I'm gonna pee my pants if this conversation continues."

Which set them off again. Emily drew in a deep breath, surprised by the sound of her own laugh. It'd been too long since she'd heard it, but God, it felt really good to let it loose. Adam's ears were probably burning. She'd mention it later to him. He'd get a good laugh out of it. Maybe even volunteer.

"Okay, no to a stripper. And no to Adam stripping or any other member of the sheriff's department," Emily said, wiping her eyes. "But I love the idea of inviting the town, having some good food, some music, and just enjoying ourselves."

"Done," Lily said firmly. "Rustic Roots can handle the flowers and produce. Between all of us, you'll have the whole town behind you before you know it."

The mood was broken by the cheerful ding of the oven.

"Oh my." Leah wiped her eyes and rushed over. "I'm trying out a new recipe for an autumn apple pie with a crumb topping and maple glaze."

The rich scent of apples, cinnamon, and maple filled the air as she pulled the pie from the oven. The women groaned in unison. It'd be hours before it would be cool enough to eat.

"No worries," added Leah. "This one is for Lily. I brought two more that I made earlier so we can enjoy them now."

"Coffee's almost ready," said Lily. "Let's go over the specifics and timeline, and then we'll have pie."

Emily sank into a chair, her wineglass still in her hand. For the first time in days, she didn't feel she was waiting for the next disaster. Surrounded by her friends and their laughter, she felt almost light. Maybe this really could be a new beginning.

Thirty-Six

Saturday afternoon, the grand opening was in full swing. The spa sparkled, soft music floated through the air, and the calming scent of eucalyptus and lemongrass drifted from diffusers.

Ivy had outdone herself with a simple spread: warm butternut squash soup served in tiny espresso cups, cheddar and cranberry bites on crackers, and baskets of cinnamon-sugar-dusted apple cider doughnut holes. She paired those with a choice of sparkling cranberry spritzer in glass pitchers or apple cider.

Lily had filled the space with flowers from her greenhouse. Potted white, red and orange mums were interspersed with small pumpkins and colorful gourds.

People Emily hadn't seen in months—some since she first opened—came by to wish her well, sample the spritzer and apple cider, and also sign up for ten percent off a yoga class or massage. She still felt the sting in her bank account, but at least insurance would reimburse her, eventually.

"Over thirty people have signed up for the special so far," Morgan whispered, eyes shining. "Congratulations!"

Wow, Emily had braced herself for ten sign-ups, maybe fifteen if luck was on her side, but this was beyond her imagination.

She took a deep breath, let it out, and raised her voice enough to carry over the chatter and music. "I want to thank everyone who signed up today. Your generosity and support make me glad I moved to Beaver Creek—a small town with a big heart."

Cheers went up, echoing off the spa walls. Then Taryn stepped forward. "As a special bonus, we've put together spa day packages, including massage, hair, nails, and facials, for just two hundred dollars to the first ten people who sign up. Lunch included. Aspire Day Spa wants to support all local businesses, and I'm lending Emily four of my technicians to help that day."

The crowd reacted with laughter and applause. Piper pushed forward to take snapshots of people signing up. Olivia had her notebook open. Emily's friends jostled each other in line, mock-arguing about who would get in first.

Emily stood there, heart pounding. Tears threatened as her friends and others literally lined up to support her dream.

Taryn sidled up to her. "I know I didn't check with you first, but I took a chance it would be okay. I hoped it would generate more interest. I'm donating my technicians' time as a gift. Although lunch is on you."

"I don't know what to say. Thank you," Emily sputtered. "Lunch is a small price to pay."

"No thank-you is necessary. I still feel bad about poaching some of your massage therapists."

Emily smiled and pulled her in for a hug. For a fleeting, petty moment, she allowed herself to be irritated all over again about losing staff to Aspire. But today, Taryn had gone above and beyond, and that made up for any lingering resentment.

Taryn had turned away to talk to some women when

Celeste came over. "Emily, this is marvelous. The spa looks brand new. You must be proud."

Emily gave her a grateful smile. "Thanks, Celeste, and thank you for sticking with me."

Celeste leaned closer. A faint, powdery floral scent drifted over her. It was pleasant in an old-fashioned way, and Emily realized Celeste didn't wear perfume when working. "It's my pleasure. You deserve all the happiness that lasts." She gave Emily's hand a soft squeeze before drifting toward the refreshments.

Across the room, Emily noticed Olivia pause mid-conversation, her gaze narrowing on Celeste. She tilted her head, studying her. When Emily caught her eye, Olivia smoothed her expression and gave her a quick smile before making her way over.

"Who's that?" Olivia asked casually, nodding toward the gray-haired woman.

Emily glanced at where she had been staring. "Oh, that's Celeste Miller. She's new. Came on as cleaning staff a few weeks ago. Why?"

Olivia shrugged. "Just curious. I thought I knew everyone here, but she was unfamiliar. Don't think I've seen her around town."

Emily blinked. It was odd, but there was no time to dwell on it. The room was alive with chatter and bursts of laughter. The scent of soup and cinnamon mingled with the sweetness of Celeste's perfume. Whatever flicker of unease Emily thought she saw in Olivia's eyes was gone, and she told herself she was imagining it.

More people arrived just as one group left. Emily accepted their congratulations. She looked around the bustling spa filled with friends, clients, and neighbors. This was her community. She wasn't just reopening, she was rising.

A COUPLE OF HOURS LATER, Adam was raising a glass of beer to his mouth at the Log & Lantern when Ethan and Dylan walked in. A fire crackled in the massive stone fireplace, throwing heat across the room.

Today was the spa's grand opening. He'd asked Emily if she wanted him there, silently praying that she'd say no. Spending an afternoon in a spa with groups of women chatting about yoga and massages didn't sound like his idea of a good time. Still, he would have gone had she asked.

"Speak of the devil," Dylan said, shrugging out of his jacket. "Why aren't you at Emily's side handing out scented candles and cucumber water?"

Adam smirked. "Well, for one, I don't do girly shit like candles or cucumber water. And for another ..." He stared at Dylan. "Your sweet girlfriend volunteered Beaver Creek's finest to do a striptease."

Ethan laughed and dropped into the seat across from him. "Figures Savannah would come up with that idea." He shook his head as he glanced at Dylan. "I don't want to even know what goes on at your house."

"I'll never tell." Dylan mimed zipping his lips closed.

"That just makes my eyeballs burn," groused Adam. "Anyhow, the girls had everything planned, and Emily was ... moderately excited. I think she's afraid no one will show up."

"We drove by earlier, and it looked like a good crowd," said Ethan. "Boy. She deserves all the best."

A server came over and took their orders. The room hummed with murmurs of conversations, the clink of glasses, and an occasional burst of laughter from a corner where a group of hunters sat. The air smelled of grilled meat and fried onions.

"Yeah, she'll be fine," Adam said. "I'll head over later and help her close, stay there tonight."

"You guys still on for tomorrow?" Dylan asked, looking at each of them. "Game, burgers, beer?"

"Emily and I will be there," Adam replied. "Wouldn't miss it."

Ethan tipped his beer toward Dylan. "Count Jane and me in. Besides, somebody's gotta keep you honest when you start calling burnt burgers 'smoked.'"

Laughter rolled around the table.

Beers were placed in front of them, and Dylan lifted his glass in a toast. "To football and Emily."

"Damn right," Ethan said, clinking his glass against Dylan's and then Adam's. "At least Cross has been cleared. Guy was a pain in the ass." He leaned back. "But we still have Celeste. I don't know what her story is yet, but I know the public likes simple answers. They see a hothead or drifter and point fingers. Nobody looks twice at a middle-aged woman with a polite smile who folds laundry and mops the floor."

Adam met his gaze over the rim of his glass, a silent agreement passing between them. They'd keep an eye on her while investigating who else had a grudge against Emily or the spa.

He took a swallow, but his mind drifted to Emily and the spa. They still hadn't caught the person who messed with the breaker box, and until someone was in cuffs, he wouldn't rest easily. There were no usable prints. Whoever did it wiped it clean. It wasn't an accident. Someone knew what they were doing.

He glanced toward the massive stone fireplace, flames leaping and snapping against the logs. It was a beautiful sight, but all he could think about was how quickly a fire could get out of hand, how fast safety could turn into chaos. He set his glass down a little harder than he meant to. Tonight, he'd be right where he belonged. Beside Emily.

Thirty-Seven

The sun's rays hit Adam in the eyes, dragging him from sleep. He cracked one lid open, groaned, and rolled to his side. Emily was curled toward him, her blond hair spilled across the pillow, her breathing slow and even. For a moment, he just stayed there, staring at how beautiful she was even sleeping and letting the quiet of the apartment wrap around him.

Last night, or was it closer to this morning, he and Emily made love. Easy, unhurried, the kind that carried more promise than urgency. They hadn't talked about the grand opening yet, and he was anxious to hear how it went. When he arrived yesterday afternoon, the girls had just finished cleaning up and were sprawled around with wineglasses and leftover appetizers. He'd said hello and left them to go upstairs. It had been Emily's moment, and he wasn't about to steal it.

His bladder was urging him to get up, so he eased his way out of the bed, trying not to disturb Emily.

"Adam?" Her voice was soft and groggy.

"Shhh. I'll be right back."

"'Kay." She closed her eyes again.

After the bathroom, he thought about making a pot of coffee. But when he looked over at the bed, Emily opened her eyes again.

"Come here," she murmured.

Coffee or a warm, sexy woman? He weighed his options for all of a nanosecond. A warm, sexy woman won, hands down.

He crawled back under the covers, and Emily immediately curled closer, resting her arm around his waist. Her lips brushed his neck, then his ear, before her hand wandered lower.

That was all it took. In the next heartbeat, he pulled her into his arms, and the rest of the morning melted away in soft sighs and tangled sheets.

He lay there satiated until he glanced at his watch. Damn. Eleven o'clock already.

"Em," he said, brushing a strand of hair off her face as he gently roused her. "It's time to get up. Dylan's expecting us around one."

She groaned and waved her hand as if she were shooing him away.

"Come on, lazybones. We promised to bring the rolls. If we don't show, Dylan will be hunting us down."

Emily cracked one eye, a sleepy smile tugging at her lips. "They can eat burgers without rolls. It's healthier."

Adam laughed. "Try telling the guys that. They'll never invite me again."

"Fine," she huffed. "Coffee first, shower and then store."

"Shower?" He waggled his brows.

"In your dreams, Casanova. If we shower together, we'll never get there, and for sure you'll never be invited again."

He grinned, leaning down for a quick kiss. "Worth the risk."

She pushed his chest with a laugh. "Coffee, Adam. Go start the coffee while I shower. Then it'll be your turn."

"Bossy," he muttered, grinning as he headed toward the kitchen.

A SHORT TIME LATER, Emily and Adam were on their way after a quick stop for rolls and a fun argument about which was better—New England hot dog buns with the slit on the top or the other kind, slit on the side. They got some of each.

The road took them past the town, the Callahan B&B, and over the Callahan River, where Dylan's red barn came into view. They parked on the gravel driveway next to a few other cars. Adam grabbed the bag of rolls, and they walked toward the modern glass entrance. In the background, they heard voices and then Moose baying at their arrival. The scent of grilled meat and charcoal permeated the air, and Emily's stomach growled.

"I hope they have that dog on a leash," groused Adam. "The last time I was here, the damn dog had rolled in mud and thought it would be fun to jump up and try to lick my face."

Emily giggled. Moose had become a favorite of their group with his antics and protective streak toward Savannah, but he was a puppy—well, a rather large puppy—who didn't quite understand boundaries. Yet.

They stepped into the open-concept living area, the smell of herbs and something savory drifting from the kitchen. Ethan, Tanner, Nic, and Charlie were spread out, drinks in hand, on the leather sectional that faced the windows. Across from them, Jane and Piper were deep in conversation. Ivy, Leah, Savannah, and Lily were chopping, stirring and laughing in the sleek, modern kitchen filled with colorful pots of herbs.

In the back corner, Olivia leaned close to Levi. When she spotted Emily, she broke away and came over for a quick hug.

"Looks like you have a new friend," said Emily, nodding toward Levi, who was moving toward the couch.

"No chemistry," Olivia replied. "I find him interesting, but that's all."

Emily smiled but couldn't help thinking Morgan would be devastated if she'd seen the two of them laughing like that. Then again, Morgan was too young for Levi. Whatever spark he might have, though, wasn't for Olivia.

Adam disappeared outside to deliver the rolls to Dylan, while Emily slipped toward the kitchen, offering to help.

"Nah, we're all set," said Savannah. "This is supposed to be easy and relaxing."

Just then, Dylan and Adam walked back in. "Okay, folks, we have burgers and hot dogs and, lucky for us, Adam remembered the buns," quipped Dylan.

"Fuck off," Adam declared.

"I will if you will," countered Dylan with a grin.

Savannah stepped between the two of them. "What? Are you boys two? Because you're acting like it."

Dylan pointed at Adam. "He started it, Mom."

"Did not."

"Did too."

Savannah shook her head. "You two are hopeless. Next time I'm bringing a whistle, and you're both getting time out."

"Ohhh, you're in trouble now, Adam," said Dylan, lightly punching his shoulder.

The plates of burgers and dogs were placed on the massive butcher block island next to potato salad, green salad, pots of beans, bowls of chips, and every condiment imaginable, from ketchup and mustard to a mason jar of Ivy's homemade pickles.

The air was filled with the clatter of plates and the hum of conversation as everyone lined up. "Ladies first," yelled Ethan.

The women filed through, piling their plates high before heading toward the oversize wood table decorated with pumpkins and fall leaves down the center, a table Adam knew Dylan's friend Jack Monroe had built. It was a beauty, twelve feet long and made out of a single slab of Vermont maple that gleamed under the overhead lights.

"Where's Moose?" asked Emily, glancing around as if the gigantic pup could be hiding under the table.

Savannah laughed, shaking her head. "Did you really think we'd leave him out here with all this food? He's upstairs in his crate with his favorite chew toy and a bunch of treats. Otherwise, we'd all be eating beans out of a can."

The hum of voices rose as silverware clinked against the plates. Emily took a bite of her burger. "Delicious, Dylan."

"It's probably the rolls," quipped Adam.

"Who made the potato salad?" asked Levi. "It tastes just like my mom's."

"I did," Leah replied. "Thanks. Old family recipe."

"Well." Dylan lifted his bottle of beer. "Here's to friendship, good food, a great game, and dessert by Ivy. Not necessarily in that order."

The group clinked glasses. Emily looked at her group of friends and thought how lucky she was to have them.

The TV in the corner of the great room was already tuned to the game but muted while everyone dug in. Ethan finished and grabbed the remote. "All right, everybody, place your bets. Who's gonna screw up first, the Patriots or the refs?"

"Refs," Dylan and Adam answered in unison.

Savannah rolled her eyes. "You two sound like an old married couple."

Dylan smirked. "You'll see. We're right."

Laughter rippled around the table, but as the noise settled,

Savannah's gaze slid toward Emily. "So, Em, how are you holding up? The grand opening was fantastic."

Emily's fork paused halfway to her mouth. "It was, although every time I catch my breath, something else happens. First the murder, then the vandalism. I'm just wondering what'll be next."

"Could it be someone with a grudge?" asked Nic.

Adam's voice cut through, firm and sharp. "I don't care who's behind this; they're going to answer for it." He slid an arm around the back of her chair, eyes hard as steel.

The room went silent until Dylan leaned back. "All right, gang, enough crime-solving at the dinner table. Kickoff in three minutes, and I've got fifty bucks that Ethan's team tanks the first half."

"Ha." Ethan snorted. "Keep dreaming."

The room lightened. Laughter filled the air as plates were scraped and drinks were refilled. Adam leaned into Emily's side, letting his warmth and the comfort of her friends settle around her. The shadows still lingered, but for now the noise of football and friendship drowned them out.

THIRTY-EIGHT

Olivia stared at her laptop, the cursor blinking as if it were mocking her. She had a write-up to do for the newspaper about Serenity Spa's opening weekend. It had been a hit, no question about it, and Taryn knew exactly how to play the press. Her headline-friendly gesture helped Emily and certainly didn't hurt Aspire Day Spa.

Clicking through the photos Piper had sent over, Olivia smiled at the familiar faces. There was Emily glowing with relief, Jane and Savannah laughing in the background, Ivy juggling trays of food. She recognized almost everyone by sight, if not by name.

She couldn't place the woman Emily was deep in conversation with. What was her name again? She tapped her fingers on the desk. Celeste. Celeste Miller.

There was something about Celeste that bothered her. What? She remembered that Celeste had come out of nowhere to work at the spa. And then ... things happened. A death, a broken breaker panel.

Did they happen because of her? Or was it just coincidence? Olivia had a feeling all roads led back to Boston and Evolve MedSpa.

She opened a program and stared at the headlines. Nothing connected the dots. Nothing with Celeste's name attached. She leaned back in her chair. Maybe a visit to Daniel Cross was in order. After all, she had researched him. He knew Jennifer, who came from Boston. He might know who this Celeste Miller was.

Olivia thought about calling him at the Green Mountain Lodge. Hopefully, he was still there, but she liked the element of surprise. So surprise it was.

She drove to the lodge, and memories of the fundraiser came back. It was a huge success, and Emily didn't quite get the recognition she deserved. The idea was hers from the beginning, but praise was nice; results were better. Emily probably would never have expected people to line up to thank her. That wasn't Emily. She did what she thought was important, what mattered to her.

A young woman stood at the front desk, and Olivia asked if Daniel Cross was still staying there and, if so, what room he was in.

"Is he expecting you?" the woman asked.

Olivia thought fast. "I'm his fiancée, and I want to surprise him."

"Hmm." The woman looked at her computer. "Room 314."

"Thanks. Please don't alert him. I really want this to be a surprise."

"My lips are sealed."

Olivia's pulse quickened as she took the elevator to the third floor and walked down the plush, carpeted hall, rehearsing how she'd play it once he opened the door.

She knocked once. Nothing.

She tried again, louder this time. Still nothing.

Her brow furrowed. She looked around, saw no one, and stepped closer, put her ear right up to the door and knocked again. No footsteps, no movement.

She straightened and crossed her arms. So much for the element of surprise.

Back in her car, she drummed her fingers on the steering wheel. Cross wasn't here, but he hadn't left town. She'd circle back. For now, deadlines loomed, and her editor wouldn't accept *I was stalking a source* as an excuse.

Still, as she drove away, she tried to figure out why Emily was being targeted. What happened at the spa in Boston felt like a tangled web of lies and deceit. Jennifer was dead, rumors of cover-ups were spreading, and there were too many players who had slipped through the cracks.

She'd be back. Daniel Cross was going to answer her questions.

Thirty-Nine

"Do you want to come over tonight?" Emily asked. Adam was buttoning his shirt and looking all sexy in his uniform.

He glanced at her and smirked. "Em, if you keep looking at me like that, I'm going to be late."

She widened her eyes innocently. "Me? You think I'm staring? I'm just admiring an incredibly handsome, sexy man."

He laughed. "I think you just like the uniform."

Emily shrugged with a grin. "Well ... maybe that too."

"I work until nine tonight, but I'll come over when I'm done."

"That's perfect," she replied, rising to straighten his collar. "I have to reconcile the books, anyway."

"Why don't you hire an accountant to do that?"

She frowned. "I would, but right now I don't have the money."

"Makes sense." He slid his holster into place and checked his gun with the same practiced and precise movements she found strangely comforting. "Make sure you turn the cameras on while you're working. Promise?"

"Of course, I will." She tipped her head toward the kitchen. "I made coffee and eggs. Come eat before you leave. Then I have to get to the spa. I have a ten o'clock yoga class to run."

He hooked an arm around her waist and pulled her close. "I'd do the downward dog with you any day."

She laughed, swatting at his arm. "Go eat your eggs before you make us both late."

After breakfast, Adam helped her clean up before kissing her once more and heading out.

Emily lingered for a moment, watching his cruiser disappear down the street. The quiet of his house settled around her.

Normal. Comfortable.

She glanced at her watch and realized that if she didn't get a move on, she'd be late. By the time she pulled into the spa lot, the morning sun gleamed on the rooftops, casting shadows over downtown. She locked her car and stepped inside.

Morgan was at the front desk talking to a client and nodded, so Emily headed back to the changing room. She removed her jacket and shoes, revealing the burgundy leggings and fitted tank top she'd already put on that morning. She usually just went barefoot in the class, more grounded that way. Pulling a hair tie from her wrist, she pulled her hair into a ponytail and checked her reflection in the mirror. Perfect.

She made her way down the hall toward one of the empty studios. She passed a class already in session, soft music drifting through the door and the quiet murmur of the instructor guiding students into a stretch.

Inside, the mats were stacked neatly against the wall, and the subtle blend of eucalyptus and lemongrass filled the air. She began setting up the room, unrolling each mat across the polished floor. Clients were arriving at any minute.

Emily took a deep breath. Last month's paperwork and reconciliation still loomed, but for now, the spa was alive again. And so was she.

By the time five o'clock rolled around, everyone had left, and Emily sat down at her desk and let her shoulders drop. This was the part of her job she disliked, but it was a necessary evil for a small business owner. The laughter and chatter from the day felt like a lifetime ago, replaced by silence broken only by the faint tick of the wall clock.

Emily sat at her desk, with a mug of coffee beside her and a pile of receipts spread across the surface. She logged payroll hours, flipping through each employee's records. Everyone's record checked except ... where was Celeste's? She frowned and went through the records again. No W-4, no emergency contact, nothing. Maybe it got misfiled, or Celeste meant to bring it back and forgot. She made a quick note on a piece of paper: *Celeste, employee form*. She'd deal with the missing form on Monday.

A new problem arose almost immediately. She couldn't pull the right bank statement. She muttered under her breath. Of course. The file was saved on her personal laptop upstairs in her apartment. She'd have to grab it before she could finish.

Adam would be staying over and had promised to swing by once his shift ended. Just the thought of him eased the knot in her chest. He reminded her before heading out to make sure the cameras were on while she was working, and she had. The little green light on the monitor blinked in the corner of the screen.

Still, the spa felt too quiet. The hum of the diffuser was background noise. She rubbed her arms and told herself not to be silly. This was her place. Her sanctuary. She wasn't going to let shadows spook her.

She closed the computer, stacked the receipts, and sighed.

"Laptop, then dinner, then done," she muttered, standing, then headed upstairs.

Emily climbed the stairs, her footsteps echoing in the quiet hall. She fished her keys out of her pocket, juggling them as she reached her apartment door. The lock clicked smoothly, and she pushed the door open, already picturing that piece of lasagna waiting in her fridge, ready to be warmed up.

Except ...

She stood still. Something felt off.

The air wasn't stale, like it usually was after being closed. A faint, powdery scent lingered. Not lemongrass, not eucalyptus. Something older. More cloying. Familiar.

Her pulse jumped.

She stepped inside slowly, setting her bag down. The apartment looked normal. Everything was in its place.

She took another step towards her desk where her laptop was, exactly where she'd left it.

Still, the hair on her arms prickled. She wasn't alone. She could feel it.

Forty

Olivia had been buried in stories from the school board, a zoning meeting, and the write-up on the spa reopening since Tuesday. Wednesday blurred into Thursday, and by Friday she was juggling page layouts and chasing quotes that never came. Every so often, the image of Celeste and Emily surfaced, but she'd pushed it aside. There was never enough time.

Late Saturday afternoon, Olivia glanced at her desk and the Post-it note scribbled there. *Cross, follow up.* Her gut tightened. Damn, she hadn't meant to let this go this long.

She arrived at the lodge, parked in the same spot as she had on Monday. Thankfully the same woman was behind the desk and recognized her.

This time, Daniel answered the door. His hair was sticking up from running his fingers through it, his glasses were perched low on his nose, and the room was a mess.

"Yeah?"

She introduced herself and asked if she could talk to him for a moment.

"What the hell do you want? Are you looking for a story?

Something that isn't there? Someone to help you win a Pulitzer? I know reporters—you smile, you nod, and then you write something that ruins a man."

Olivia shook her head. "Daniel. May I call you Daniel? I'm here because I need your help. Something is troubling me, and you might know something about it." She put on a pitiful face. "Please."

He nodded and huffed. "Come in."

Olivia looked around the pleasant room, saw scattered papers and empty soda cans, candy wrappers, and a coat thrown on the bed.

She cleaned off one chair by his laptop. He sat at the table.

"What do you want to know?"

"Jennifer was investigating a story about Evolve MedSpa and Emily Harper. Emily is in danger, and I need to know why."

Daniel leaned back in his chair. "I can give you what is common knowledge." He proceeded to give her the background, why it was suspicious and everything he knew about Marcus Vaughn.

"Do you know a Celeste Miller?"

He shook his head. "Never heard of her."

"Who else might have been involved in this fiasco that might have a stake in the outcome?"

He gave her several names, mentioning Emily's roommate Shay, who supposedly was going to the authorities before disappearing, and Bridget Vaughn, who he suspected of being the brains behind the operation, although no charges were made. "It's all in the paper," he said. "Just dig deeper."

"Thanks for the names," she said, already gathering her purse and notes.

"Keep me posted."

She nodded and left. The late afternoon sun was dipping

behind the lodge as she jogged to her car. It took her a little while to get home after being stuck behind an accident.

Finally, her apartment came into view. She gathered her purse and notes and stepped inside. After making a cup of tea, she sat at her laptop and typed *Celeste Miller* into the search bar. Nothing. No DMV record, no property listed, nothing. It was too clean. Too perfect.

She tried a different angle. *Bridget Vaughn, Boston, Evolve MedSpa*.

Images loaded, but they were of the spa and parties. Damn. Was Cross wrong?

Olivia looked at her watch. Five o'clock. She had nothing for her trouble.

Her finger hovered over the keyboard, ready to shut it all down, when another set of images loaded. She leaned closer, her pulse racing.

In the background of a gala shot, a couple stood, arms around each other with perfect smiles. The caption scrolled beneath. Dr. Marcus Vaughn and his wife, Bridget.

Olivia clicked, enlarged the picture, and froze. There she was.

Her hair was darker, sleek, the pearls real. But the face, those eyes, that smile that didn't reach her eyes were the same. The same woman Piper had caught in a candid photo with Emily at the reopening.

Her breath caught. She whispered into the empty room. "Son of a bitch."

Celeste Miller was Bridget Vaughn.

She snatched up her phone and dialed Emily's number. It rang once, twice, three times before going to voicemail.

"Come on, Em, pick up," she muttered, pacing across her living room. She tried again with the same result. No answer.

Her pulse raced. She pulled up Adam's number.

He answered on the first ring. "Sadler."

"Adam, it's Olivia. I'm trying to reach Emily, but her phone is going to voicemail. Do you know where she is?"

Silence. "She's working at the spa. Why?"

Oh God, no. "Celeste is Bridget Vaughn. I bet she killed Jennifer and vandalized the spa. If Emily is there, and Bridget feels the cops are getting closer, she's smart. I think Emily's in trouble."

"Send me a picture." His voice was hard.

"I will." Her voice cracked. "Please just check on her. Something feels wrong."

Adam exhaled. "Text me the photo and stay put. Don't go near the spa; don't chase this. We'll handle it."

The line went dead.

Olivia stared at the frozen smile of Bridget Vaughn on her laptop, fear coursing through her veins.

Forty-One

"Such a shame," a familiar voice drifted from the shadows near the kitchen.

Emily froze, her breath catching in her throat. That voice. Impossible. Not here.

Celeste stepped into view, her gray hair pulled into its usual neat bun. She pushed the door shut with a quiet snick that made Emily's stomach drop. No escape now. "I've been waiting for you. I thought I might be disappointed again." A faint smile curved her lips. "And now here you are.

"Emily," Celeste continued softly. "You've worked so hard to build this little life. So normal." Her eyes lingered on the stack of receipts Emily still clutched in her hand. "But normal can vanish in an instant, can't it?"

"What are you doing here?" Emily's stomach clenched. The papers trembled in her hands. This couldn't be happening. Not again.

Celeste's smile widened, though her eyes stayed cold. "What I should have done a long time ago." She reached behind her and locked the door, her powdery floral scent irritating Emily's nose. "You and I have unfinished business."

"I don't know what the hell you're talking about." Emily's pulse thundered in her ears. "If you had wanted to talk, you could've done it at the spa. You don't belong up here."

Celeste gave a soft, humorless laugh. "Oh, Emily. So brave even when you're in over your head. Just like Boston. Just like Shay."

The name hit like a slap.

"How do you know Shay?"

"Shay thought she could disappear quietly." She tapped her chest. "But I'm the one who helped her along. That email you got? The one saying she needed space and was leaving Boston?" Her smile sharpened. "Shay didn't send it."

Emily's heart thundered in her chest. "What?"

"That girl stuck her nose where it didn't belong. Jennifer too. They both thought they could expose us. And now ..." She lifted one hand in a delicate shrug. "Look where that got them."

Emily's stomach lurched. Shay. Jennifer. Gone because of this woman. Celeste admitted killing them like it was nothing.

"Why me?" Emily demanded, needing to keep the crazy woman talking. Her eyes flicked to the phone on the kitchen counter, so close but just out of reach. "And how do you know about Shay and Boston?"

Celeste's laugh was sharp and brittle. "Shay was going to ruin everything. She asked too many questions. Marcus warned her but she wouldn't stop." She stepped closer. Her eyes gleamed with venom. "And then you started asking, too. Little things at first. Consent forms, Booking blocks. Things Shay whispered to you before she left. Things you shouldn't have noticed."

Emily's pulse pounded in her chest.

"And suddenly," Celeste hissed, "your name was attached to an internal audit trail. Notes. Questions. Patterns. Enough to tell me you were going to do exactly what Shay tried to do.

"Marcus and I had a good thing. But then he killed himself, and you"—her voice cracked into a snarl—"you came here and started over. You have friends. A boyfriend. Hope."

Tears slid down her cheeks. "While I lost everything that mattered."

Emily's stomach turned to ice. Marcus? Marcus Vaughn. Oh, dear God.

The final puzzle piece snapped into place.

"You're Bridget Vaughn!"

Celeste shook her head. "Bridget Vaughn died with Marcus. I buried her. Celeste Miller? She was a dead woman in Ohio whose identity I borrowed. A little data manipulation, a few forged records, and I let the world believe the lie. People see what they want to see."

The phone rang, and Emily tried to answer it, but Celeste lunged, knocking the phone onto the ground.

Whoever it was hung up and rang again.

Celeste gave her a sly smile. "They won't be in time." Her voice softened as she reached into her bag. The metallic gleam of a knife caught the light. "By the time they find your body, I'll be long gone."

Emily's mind raced. The door was behind Celeste. No chance of getting out that way. The windows were too narrow. She needed something—anything—to use. Then, her gaze landed on the ceramic diffuser sitting on the counter.

With a surge of desperate strength, she grabbed it and hurled it straight at Celeste.

It slammed into Celeste's shoulder, shattering, spraying oil and shards across the floor. Hot mist and eucalyptus oil filled the room with a cloying odor. It clung to Emily's throat and made her eyes sting. Celeste staggered, then snarled, her mask slipping. In the blink of an eye, she shoved Emily hard into the counter, the cold edge of the knife pressing against her throat.

Emily froze. The shock stole her breath. She'd never felt

such a mix of panic and disbelief. The blade was real, the danger pulsing against her throat. Her body screamed *move* but her brain said *don't*. One mistake and the knife would slice her like paper. Her pulse thundered in her body. She could smell the oil, sharp and medicinal, mixing with Celeste's powdery perfume and her own sour fear. Her stomach twisted. Cold dread crawled up her spine.

This couldn't be happening. Not here. Not now. She'd rebuilt everything. Her life, her peace, her hope. She couldn't lose it all to a ghost from Boston.

This couldn't be how it ended. Not after everything she gave up. Not after Shay. She wasn't dying in her own kitchen. Not like this.

"Try it. It'll make killing you more interesting."

Forty-Two

The door burst open with a crash.

"Emily!" Adam's voice, fierce and panicked. He charged in, muscles coiled, and for a wild second everything blurred. Celeste whipped around, still gripping the knife in one hand, Emily trapped in the other like a prize.

"Drop it, Celeste!" Ethan's shout followed as he barreled inside.

The kitchen erupted in motion. Adam lunged straight for Emily, yanking her out of Celeste's hold and shoving her behind him, shielding her with his body as Ethan grabbed Celeste's wrist. The knife clattered to the floor, spinning out of reach.

Celeste fought like a wild animal, thrashing and bucking until Adam pinned her arms and Ethan forced her down, snapping the cuffs on her before yanking her to her feet.

Emily stood frozen where Adam had pushed her, breath ragged, heart pounding. Her chest felt so tight she could barely breathe; her hands trembled against the counter. For one second, relief threatened to buckle her knees.

Then Celeste smirked. Cool. Condescending. As if none of this mattered.

Something in Emily snapped. Terror turned to rage. Every sleepless night, every dollar lost, every memory of Shay surged through her. She wasn't just afraid anymore. She was furious. Furious for Shay. Furious for her spa. Furious for herself.

She pushed off the counter and charged, her fist connecting with Celeste's jaw in a sharp, satisfying crack. Celeste's head snapped sideways, the smirk gone in an instant.

"That's for Shay," Emily spat, chest heaving. Adam and Ethan both gaped at her like they couldn't believe what they'd just seen. She drew back and swung again, her palm smacking hard against Celeste's shoulder. "And that's for my spa."

"Emily!" Adam caught her around the waist, dragging her back before she could strike again.

But Emily didn't care. Rage still coursed through her; her whole body was trembling. But she refused to let Celeste see her broken. "You don't get to take anything else from me. Not now. Not ever," she hissed.

Celeste's expression faltered. Emily's pulse was racing, her throat raw, but she squared her shoulders, stood tall, showing the woman who tried to ruin her that she wasn't down. Not even close.

Forty-Three

Adam drove with one hand on the wheel, the other clenched tight against his thigh. He kept glancing at Emily in the passenger seat. She was pale, too quiet, staring out the window, probably reliving the whole scene. He wanted to pull over and hold her, but he knew getting her to his house mattered more right now.

The rescue had been chaos with all the sirens wailing, voices shouting, and the heavy scent of eucalyptus in the air. He'd never forget the sight of Emily pinned against the counter, Celeste's knife glinting under the light. That flash of silver had frozen his heart. For a heartbeat, he thought he was too late.

Now the adrenaline was wearing off, leaving anger and relief tangled tight in his chest. Anger at Celeste for befriending Emily with the thought of getting even. Anger that he and Ethan hadn't dug deep enough. Anger at himself for not seeing it sooner.

Relief too. Relief that Olivia hadn't given up and had found the connection, and because of that, Emily was alive.

He couldn't remember the last time he'd prayed that hard while driving.

He pulled onto the gravel drive, the moon casting shadows through the trees. "Sweetheart," he said softly. "We're home."

She startled, blinking at him. He reached over and caught her hand, needing that connection. Her skin was cold. She felt small in his grip. "Come on, let's get inside."

He let go long enough to step outside and open her door. The porch light clicked on as Adam unlocked the front door and nudged it open, never letting go of her hand. The familiar scent of cedar and pine greeted them, a sharp contrast to the acrid scent of eucalyptus still clinging to Emily's hair and clothes. Home smelled like safety. He hoped she felt it, too. She drew in a shaky breath as if trying to believe it.

Inside, she clung to him, and he pulled her close against his chest. "You're safe."

"I know," she mumbled into his chest. "But I can't stop seeing the venom in her eyes. Like what happened was all my fault."

He eased her onto the couch, sat down, and pulled her onto his lap. "She can't touch you again. She's gone."

Emily let out a long, shaky sigh. "I should feel relieved that Shay's killer is caught. But all I feel is ... tired and sad. That someone could hate enough to destroy everything around her."

Adam tipped her chin to meet his gaze. "You loved your friend. Of course, it hurts. But you're still here. Still standing. And that's all that matters."

Her eyes blurred with tears, but she nodded.

"Come on, sweetheart," he said gently. "Let's get you cleaned up. I'll make coffee or something stronger."

She gave him a small smile, huffed out a breath, but then the tears spilled down her cheeks. She buried her face in his chest and sobbed.

All Adam could do was wrap his arms around her and rub slow circles on her back. He could feel her shaking through his shirt. Every ragged breath cut through him. He'd let her cry as long as she needed. Later they would talk. He'd help her heal. And when she was ready, he'd remind her she wasn't alone anymore.

Soon, he would ask her to marry him, because after tonight he knew he couldn't imagine living a single day without Emily Harper in his life.

EMILY DISAPPEARED UPSTAIRS, the sound of the shower running a few minutes later. Adam busied himself in the kitchen making a pot of coffee, pulling out some cheese and crackers in case she was hungry, lighting the fire, anything to keep himself busy. If he stopped, the image of Celeste's knife at Emily's throat came roaring back.

When she came back down, her hair damp and hanging loose, she wore one of his old shirts over leggings. The sight hit him like a punch—his woman, in his shirt, alive and safe in his house. He sent up a silent thank-you to the universe and vowed to spend the rest of his life keeping her safe.

She curled onto the couch, tucking her legs under her. Adam brought two mugs and a tray of snacks and placed them on the coffee table.

"Tell me how you knew to come to the spa," she asked.

"Olivia. She dug until she spotted a picture of Marcus Vaughn and Bridget together, then tried to call you."

"I was so afraid." Emily nodded. "The phone rang two separate times. I couldn't get to it."

"She called me. I wasn't far away and drove as fast as I could. Ethan was not far behind." He drew a breath and let it out. "I was praying the whole time we wouldn't be too late. When I saw her holding the knife to your throat, I almost lost it."

Emily picked up her mug and took a sip before placing it down. "I can't believe I trusted her. Maybe if I hadn't ..."

He cut her off. "No. You trusted her because that's who you are. You believe in people. Don't let her poison that too."

Silence stretched as Emily stared at the crackling fire. "I don't know what I'd do without you."

Adam kissed her forehead. "You'll never have to find out. Because I'm here with you forever."

For a moment, Emily stared at the floor, then at him. "Thank you. Thank you for keeping me safe and loving me."

He shook his head. "You never have to thank me for that." He gave a small shrug with a glint of humor in his eyes. "Maybe for putting up with you when you're stealing all the covers or eating the last piece of pie."

Her smile widened. "Deal."

She leaned in and kissed him, slow and tender. He kissed her back, knowing with absolute certainty that after tonight he wasn't going to waste another day. Emily Harper was it for him. Always.

Forty-Four

Olivia sat in front of her laptop writing, erasing and rewriting her piece on Celeste Miller (Bridget Vaughn) and Evolve MedSpa. It'd been a couple of days since Celeste's arrest, and her editor wanted the story put to bed. She rubbed her eyes and glared at the blinking cursor, the same sentence mocking her again. Finally, the words came together. It was a good story. Maybe the best she'd written in years.

She wanted the byline, sure. Every reporter did. But this one wasn't hers. Jennifer Bishop had died chasing it. Daniel Cross had researched and tried to fit all the pieces together.

"Damn it," she muttered, saving the piece and turning off her laptop. She poured herself a glass of wine and plopped down on the couch, staring at the ceiling. She knew her editor, Marty, would want more meat, more background, more sensationalism. This was almost the biggest thing that had happened in Beaver Creek in a while. It ranked right up there with Savannah's stalker and the man who tried to kill Jane.

The arrest of Bridget Vaughn—the woman who murdered a journalist and attempted to murder a Beaver Creek business owner—was a big deal. But Olivia had never told her editor the rest of the history. She'd just followed Daniel's leads, doing her own digging, finding enough to know the story went deeper.

Emily was her friend. She'd already had cancellations at the spa because of the murder. One wrong detail could drag Emily right back into the fire. Olivia refused to be the one to do that.

Olivia drained her wine, went back to her desk and copied her notes onto a thumb drive. Then she tightened the language on her draft to just the essentials: Jennifer's death, the attempted murder, Bridget Vaughn's arrest, and slid in a quote from the sheriff. It was enough to satisfy Marty and inform the town without handing them Emily's name on a silver platter.

THE NEXT DAY, Olivia pulled into the lot at Green Mountain Lodge. She'd already checked that Daniel was still there. The mountain air was brisk, pine-scented, hinting that winter wasn't far off.

Inside, the lobby smelled of pumpkin and spiced cider. Staff had started putting autumn garlands along the railing, gold, rust and deep brown leaves twined together with bundles of wheat. A row of bright orange pumpkins and green and gold gourds lined the fireplace hearth. A basket of red apples and pomegranates sat on the counter near the check-in desk.

A cheery sign advertising the Lodge's Thanksgiving buffet was on a stand near the restaurant. Guests lingered around the fireplace or pored over trail maps spread on coffee tables.

Olivia breathed in the faint scent of cinnamon coming from the kitchen. It brought her back to memories of her family gathered around the table with a huge turkey on a platter in the middle. Good times. But she wasn't here for that.

She took the elevator to the third floor and knocked on Daniel's door.

After waiting a minute, she reached up to knock again when the door was jerked open.

"What now? More questions about Boston?" Daniel's eyes were bloodshot. His glasses sat crooked on his nose, and his hair was standing up where he ran his fingers through it.

"Can I come in?"

"Humph. Why not?" He stepped back, and Olivia walked into the same mess of papers, books and empty coffee cups. The room didn't look any neater.

"I'm not going to stay long." She began pulling the thumb drive from her purse and holding it out. "This is the piece you've been looking for."

His eyebrows shot up. He took the thumb drive. "Why?"

"One journalist already died for this. Emily's friend, Shay, who was going to blow the whistle, died for this. You've been chasing this story longer than anyone. It's not my story to tell."

Daniel stared at the thumb drive. "I don't know what to say."

"There's nothing to say. I'll still put something in the *Beaver Creek News* and mention Bridget. She has been arrested for murder and attempted murder. I bet the Boston police will want to talk to her. It'll be a great story. The only condition is that you leave Emily Harper's name out of it. She's not the story."

He cocked his head. "I can do that. Emily never was. She was an innocent bystander."

Her chest loosened. "Thank you." Olivia turned toward the door, tossing a look over her shoulder. "I had better read good things about this exposé."

Daniel's mouth curved into a smile. "Oh, you will." He slid the drive into his pocket as if he'd been handed solid gold.

Olivia left the room before he could say anything else. The hallway was quiet. Outside, the air was crisp and stung her cheeks. She stood there for a moment, watching her breath puff out in little clouds.

The thumb drive was gone. So was the story. But she felt lighter. She hadn't kept the truth hidden; she'd just put it into the hands of someone who would carry it the rest of the way.

She pulled her coat tighter and headed for her car. Daniel's piece would be big. Her own piece would run in the *Beaver Creek News*. And Emily's name would stay where it belonged, out of print.

Olivia started the engine and blew out a breath. Some stories weren't about bylines. They were about protecting the people who mattered.

Forty-Five

It was her first day back at work at Serenity Spa since Celeste had tried to kill her. Emily hadn't known what to expect—whispers, pity, awkward glances—but instead she found warmth. Morgan kept everything running in her absence; her other employees covered massages and yoga classes without a word of complaint.

Emily's hands shook that morning when she unlocked her office door, but the familiar scent of eucalyptus and lemongrass steadied her. Somehow, she made it through the day, even laughing a couple of times.

When closing time came, she and Adam were meeting up with their friends at the Log & Lantern. But right now, there was one more thing to do—face her apartment. She had just started up the stairs when Adam found her.

"You don't have to go back up there," he said. "Come back home with me."

Tempting. But she shook her head. "If I don't walk inside, I never will."

His jaw flexed, but he didn't argue. "Then I'm walking with you."

When the door swung open, she braced for the wreckage —blood, broken glass, fear clinging to the air. For a moment she just stared. The floor was scrubbed. Fresh flowers were on the counter. Everything was neat and in its place. Her friends had been here. They'd erased the worst of it so she wouldn't have to face it alone.

Adam wrapped his arms around her, his voice low against her hair. "The girls came over to clean up. Ethan and Dylan pitched in too. They didn't want you to remember this place as a crime scene."

Her throat tightened. She turned to Adam, pressing onto his chest, hugging him hard. When she lifted her gaze, his eyes were so full of love it nearly undid her.

And in that moment, standing in the place she thought she'd lost, she realized she wasn't just reclaiming her home. She was reclaiming herself. Her future. Her peace.

"Come on," he said softly, brushing her knuckles against his lips. "Let's go meet the others before they send out a search party."

Emily nodded. She could walk out that door, not just to meet her friends but to step forward toward what came next.

THE NOTCH WAS PACKED. Conversations and laughter rolled through the room, and the scent of grilled meat and maple hung in the air. Most of the wooden barrels repurposed as tables were crowded with customers. Soft jazz was playing from hidden speakers in the ceiling.

Emily spotted their friends gathered around a long wooden table off to the side. Getting into the Notch made her smile. The locals knew you had to use a card to get into a back room and then pull a lever in a bookcase to reveal a hidden staircase that was tucked in the cellar beneath the Log & Lantern.

It was part speakeasy and part neighborhood hangout, filled with nostalgia and small-town charm. Hank Talbot, the bartender and local historian, loved to share stories about the original loggers and the bootleggers who once used the place. It was the kind of place you felt instantly at home, even if you'd never stepped inside before.

The last time she'd been here, Ellis Graham had called her up on stage to sing. She could still feel the rush of panic, how her hands trembled as she took the mic and sang a song she'd written. It brought back memories of a simpler life, when her future was rosy until it wasn't.

Tonight was different. The cellar hadn't changed, but she had. She was stronger now, maybe a little scarred, but she wasn't stepping into the unknown. She met it face-on, and now it truly felt like she was home.

"Hank!" Adam called out as he waved to the bartender.

"Hey, Adam." Hank grinned, wiping down the bar with a towel. "You brought your better half tonight."

Adam slipped an arm around Emily's shoulders, tugging her close. "That's right."

Hank winked. "Specials tonight are a maple-bacon burger —smoky bacon with a maple glaze, sharp cheddar and caramelized onions—or the maple-bourbon pulled pork sandwich. If you want something seasonal, I have the Spiced Apple Cider Mule or a Pumpkin Old-Fashioned. As always, I've got the Log Splitter, and the Widowmaker, Ethan's favorite." He smirked at Adam. "Plus anything else you want."

"I'll let you know." Adam guided her to the table.

Emily cocked her head. "Widowmaker?"

He grinned. "Don't ask. Just know I don't let Ethan in my truck when he's had a couple."

Ethan and Dylan were deep in a conversation with Jane

and Savannah while Lily, Piper and Ivy laughed at something down at the far end. Levi leaned back in his chair, and Charlie sat across from him, not even pretending he wasn't watching Ivy.

After hugs all around, Emily slid into the seat next to Ivy. Adam pulled out a chair beside her, his hand brushing her knee under the table.

A server came around with menus and recited the specials again. Emily pretended to study the list, although her attention was on the corner stage and a sign announcing that the Ellis Graham Quartet would be playing later.

She waited for the familiar sign of dread to pass through her. It didn't. Friends, music and Adam's steady presence at her side gave her a sense of calm, a sense that she belonged here again.

"Can you tell me again what's in the Pumpkin Old-Fashioned?" she asked.

"Oh, it's yummy! A classic old-fashioned with a hint of pumpkin spice syrup and orange peel," replied the young woman.

"I'll have that and the cranberry brie burger," Emily said.

"You'll love it. The brie is made down the road at Maple Creek Creamery. June Merritt makes small-batch cranberry chutney, and the arugula comes from Rustic Roots."

Yeah, Lily! Emily was happy her friend was doing so well.

The server took the rest of the orders, and Emily sat back with Adam's arm draped over her chair, listening to happy chatter.

Their meals were served as the quartet started the first set. The music was smooth and familiar, and a few couples got up to dance. Conversation was easy and full of laughter, and for the first time in a long time, the night felt almost perfect.

As coffee and dessert were served, Emily heard her name called.

No. Not again.

She turned, and Ellis Graham was staring at her, beckoning with his finger.

"Ladies and gentlemen, we've got someone in the audience who's sung with us before. A woman with a voice that can still stop a room. Emily, come on up. What do you say?"

Her friends whooped and hollered as Adam whispered in her ear. "Only if you want to."

Her pulse pounded in her ears. Her mouth went dry. And she realized she did. Damn. She used to love singing. But fear had stolen that from her. Not anymore.

Emily stood, and her friends cheered.

She stepped on stage, and Ellis handed her the mic. "You've got this, Emily."

What to sing? She didn't want songs from her past tonight. She stepped over and quietly told the piano player her choice. He nodded, sliding into a playful swing rhythm. The bass joined in, low and steady, with the drummer keeping a soft snare shuffle.

Emily nodded her head to the beat and waited for her cue, then launched into the first playful line of "Hit Me with Your Best Shot."

Not the Pat Benatar version but hers. Imperfect, raw and fun. The trumpet player grinned and jumped in.

The crowd clapped and shouted the chorus back to her. By the second verse, Savannah was on her feet next to Jane, whooping loud enough to make half the room laugh. Adam had his hand over his heart, smiling broadly.

When she finished the last note, applause erupted, louder and rowdier than she ever expected. Emily bowed with a mock flourish, not from fear or sadness this time but exhilaration.

She stepped off the stage, cheeks flushed and heart racing. Adam was waiting, catching her hand.

He leaned close, his lips brushing her ear. "That," he whispered, "was the sexiest thing I've ever seen."

She ducked her head, still grinning. "I wasn't perfect."

"You were fearless," he said softly. "That's better."

For a heartbeat, the laughter, the clinking glasses, the murmur of conversation faded. The room seemed to hold its breath.

Adam took her hand, drew her into the center of the room before she could sit. The chatter faded as people realized something was happening.

"Emily Harper," he said, his eyes locked on hers. "You are the bravest, smartest, kindest woman I've ever known. I don't want to go another day without being the man who stands beside you, through the broken pieces, through the laughter, through every note you sing."

Then he dropped to one knee, pulling a small box from his pocket. "Marry me."

The room went silent, waiting.

Emily's hands flew to her mouth, her throat tight, eyes stinging. For a second she couldn't breathe. Her heart was too full. This man, this life, this moment. She didn't need perfection. She needed this.

"Yes," she whispered, then louder, stronger. "Yes!"

The Notch erupted again. Her friends rushed forward, and Adam slipped the ring on her finger, kissing her like they were the only two people in the room.

As if on cue, the quartet eased into a familiar melody, "At Last."

Emily laughed through her tears, burying her face against Adam's chest. Couples poured onto the dance floor and swayed to the music.

Adam bent his head, whispering in her ear. "Told you your song wasn't over."

She nodded, her voice catching. "At last."

And this time she knew it was.

LATER THAT NIGHT, after all the well-wishes and goodbyes, they were on their way to Adam's house. He'd asked her several times to move in with him, to make it her home, but she had resisted. She needed to feel ready, to stand on her own again.

But now, after conquering her fear of her apartment and singing in public for the first time in a long while, Emily finally was.

Adam's proposal was so unexpected, she still couldn't quite believe she was engaged. It had been the perfect night. Messy, beautiful and completely theirs.

He glanced over at her, one hand on the wheel, the other brushing hers. "You were incredible tonight."

"I honestly wasn't sure I could do it."

"Well, sweetheart, you hit it out of the ballpark."

She glanced over at him, a small smile tugging at her lips. "It's awfully hard to upstage an engagement ask like yours."

Adam laughed. "I've wanted to ask for a while, but the timing wasn't right. Tonight was perfect, and most of our friends were there." He hesitated, glancing her way. "I hope that was all right. Maybe you would have liked something more private."

"It was perfect," she said softly. "I felt so free, unburdened and wanted everyone to feel my joy. It was the icing on the cake, so to speak."

He grinned and gave her hand a squeeze.

Silence stretched between them, comfortable at first, then heavy with unspoken memories. The darkened road stretched out ahead, shadows from the trees flickering across the windshield.

Emily stared out the window, the old ache pressing in, familiar but not as sharp as it once was. It was time to complete the journey. Her pulse picked up, fear and worry stirred in her gut, but tonight she wasn't running from them.

"Adam," she said quietly, "do you know why I stopped singing?"

He shook his head. "No."

She drew a deep breath and let it out slowly. "Back in Boston, most Friday nights I'd sing at a little place off Tremont. Nothing big, just me and a couple of musicians." Emily swallowed hard. "After Shay disappeared and everything happened at the spa, I was terrified. Afraid that if I stood out, if someone noticed me, that Boston would come for me too. It was safer to stay silent, not to attract attention."

Her voice trembled. "So, I did."

Adam's hand found hers again. "Until tonight."

She smiled faintly. "Until tonight."

They pulled onto the long gravel drive, headlights sweeping across the front porch. The porch light flicked on automatically, casting a warm glow over the steps.

Adam killed the engine, and for a moment neither of them moved.

He turned toward her. "You okay?"

Emily nodded. "Yeah, I think I am."

They got out and walked up the path. Inside, the house smelled faintly of cedar and coffee. Scents that felt like safety. Like home.

Adam hung his jacket on the hook and helped Emily with hers. "You don't have to decide anything tonight," he said softly. "About moving in. About anything."

"I already have," she said, stepping closer and resting her

hands against his chest. "I'm ready. I don't want to wake up anywhere else."

He smiled. "Good," he said, brushing a kiss over her forehead. "Because I wasn't planning on letting you go."

They moved together up the stairs. He reached for her, and she melted into him.

For the first time in a long time, Emily didn't feel like she was holding her breath. She wasn't waiting for the next disaster or for the past to catch up. She was here. Safe. Loved.

She whispered against his chest. "I feel like I'm finally home."

Adam traced small circles on her back. "That's because you are."

He kissed her again. Outside, the wind rustled through the trees, carrying the promise of a new beginning.

And Emily knew this was just the beginning of a story she'd been too afraid to sing.

Forty-Six

A month later, Jane and Ethan's farmhouse kitchen was bursting with voices, music and the smell of garlic bread and roasted chicken. The long wooden table was cluttered with half-drained wineglasses and empty plates. All to celebrate Emily and Adam's engagement.

Savannah was teasing Ethan about his lack of culinary skills. Claire was insisting garlic bread counted as a vegetable, and Ivy kept pretending she wasn't sneaking glances at Charlie, who somehow ended up right next to her.

Emily sat near the end of the table, her ring catching the light and sparkling over the whole room. She still wasn't used to seeing it on her finger, and it caught her off guard each time she moved her hand. Every time she looked at Adam, she found him already watching her.

Jane had been fidgeting for the past ten minutes, chewing her lips like she was holding a secret. Finally, she set her laptop on the table. "Okay. Before anyone finds out by accident, I need to run something by you."

Ethan groaned. "Here we go."

Jane shot him a look. "I've started a new book. Working

title *Beneath the Surface*. Small-town secrets, courage, redemption, second chances, you know, the usual chaos."

Savannah grinned. "Can I be the glamorous troublemaker who loves to paint?"

Jane smirked. "I can make that happen."

"I suppose I'll be the handsome and virile sheriff who solves the mystery," said Ethan, preening.

"No way. I've already called handsome and virile sidekick," Adam called out.

Jane shook her head. "You're both wrong. Eddie is the broody sheriff and Aaron the sidekick who keeps taking a wrong turn."

Ethan and Adam groaned.

The group laughed. "Just kidding," said Jane. "This time, though, Ember Hall and Olive Monroe save the day with a little help from the sheriff's department."

Olivia nearly choked on her wine. "Olive? Really?"

Jane tried to look innocent. "Totally fictional."

Savannah laughed. "You just changed two letters."

Jane held up both hands. "Before anyone panics or gets out a pen to autograph, I need to check with Emily." She glanced over at Emily. "I used parts of what happened, but it's fictionalized. Different details, different names. I won't publish it if it bothers you."

For a moment, the table quieted. Emily met Jane's worried eyes and smiled. "You didn't need to ask, but I appreciate that you did. If the story helps someone find their voice again, tell it."

Jane's shoulders dropped in relief. "Thanks. I just wanted to make sure."

Savannah lifted her glass. "To Ember Hall and Olive Monroe, two kick-ass heroines. The fictional versions might save the day, but the real ones already did."

"I'll drink to that," said Adam. Glasses clinked all around.

Across the table, Ivy and Charlie both reached for the same breadbasket, their hands brushing. Ivy froze, her cheeks turning bright pink. Charlie cleared his throat and muttered something about needing more butter.

Savannah leaned toward Emily. "Those two."

Emily smiled. "Mm-hmm. They're either avoiding something or already in trouble." She wondered what was going on between the two of them, what history they shared.

As Ethan refilled glasses, Olivia's phone buzzed on the table. She glanced down and smiled. "It's up."

"Daniel's piece?" asked Jane.

"Yup. It went up in the Boston newspaper. He sent it to me before he published it. It's clean and factual. Bridget Vaughn's arrest, the case history and a short note about the victims. No speculation."

"Good for him," Ethan said.

Olivia nodded. "I ran the local coverage weeks ago in the paper about her arrest. But the *Beaver Creek Gazette* feature this month will be lighter. It'll also include Emily's engagement photos, updates on the spa reopening, and a few words about the town."

Savannah grinned. "Translation: Emily's officially front-page news."

Emily groaned. "Which pictures?"

Olivia grinned. "The one where Adam is kissing you like he's trying to prove a point."

"Accuracy in reporting," Adam shot back.

"Oh, you mean the one where he's sticking his tongue so far down her throat, it looks like he's searching for gold?" quipped Levi.

"Fuck off." Adam grinned. "That's talent."

The table erupted in laughter.

Emily leaned back, soaking it all in. The flicker of candlelight, her friends, the teasing, the warmth. After everything they'd survived, this was what peace felt like.

She caught Olivia's eye across the table and raised her glass. "To fresh starts."

Olivia smiled, lifting hers. "And to stories worth telling."

THE MORNING LIGHT spilled over the table in Adam's kitchen a week later. Emily scrolled through her phone, the headline catching her eye. "Love, Laughter and a Little Music in Beaver Creek" by Olivia Metcalfe.

"Oh, the *Gazett*e is out," asked Adam, leaning over her shoulder, his coffee steaming in one hand.

"Yeah. Look at these pictures." She turned the screen toward him.

The first photo Piper had taken showed Emily and Adam mid-laugh. Then Adam's hand cupping her cheek, the ring glinting between them. The next caught their friends behind them, cheering.

And then there was *that* kiss.

"Oh my," Emily murmured, licking her lips as heat crept up her neck. "That was definitely a kiss."

Adam chuckled, reaching for her phone. "Front-page material, apparently."

She snatched it back. "No one told me my love life was going to end up in print."

He grinned. "Occupational hazard of dating a local hero."

Emily rolled her eyes. "Hero, huh?"

Adam leaned down and kissed her temple. "Well, you are the one who saved the day."

She laughed softly, shaking her head. "No, we all did."

He set his mug down and brushed his thumb along her jaw. "Still makes me smile, seeing you that happy."

She leaned into his touch. "Guess it's hard not to be when you've got coffee, a good man and a small-town headline that doesn't involve police tape."

He laughed. "That's one way to measure progress."

"Mm-hmm." She scrolled down a little farther and caught sight of another photo. Ivy and Charlie stood at the edge of the crowd, both pretending not to look at each other. Emily smiled. "Speaking of headlines, looks like those two have a story brewing."

Adam followed her gaze. "Yeah. Beaver Creek better get ready for another round."

Emily closed her phone. "Oh, it'll never be ready. But that's what makes it home."

Sunlight spilled across the kitchen table. Outside, birds were chirping; a soft wind was blowing through the trees. It was peaceful. A quiet reminder that healing takes time and sometimes, a little courage to start again.

As always, reviews are nice. If you enjoyed the book, please leave one.

Follow me on:

X: @lsferrariwrites
Facebook: @lilaferrariauthor
Private Readers' Group: https://bit.ly/3ilcBw8
Instagram: @lsferrariwrites
Pinterest: @lsferrariwrites

Goodreads: @lilaferrariwrites
Bookbub: @lilaferrariwrites
YouTube: @lilaferrariwrites2774

For more information on books by Lila Ferrari, visit her website here: https://www.lilaferrariwrites.com where you can subscribe to her newsletter to get updates on releases, bonus content, fun facts and enter contests.

BOOK 8 in the Brotherhood Alliance series, *Protecting Mia,* will be available in 2026.

BOOK 4 in the Secrets of Beaver Creek series, *Exposure of Shadows,* will be available in 2026.

Coming Soon

Protecting Mia

Brotherhood Alliance, Book 8 (available 2026)

She thought she left the danger behind.
But it just found another way in.

Mia Whitmore returned to Haywood Lake to care for her father and rebuild her life. Her catering business, Plated Perfection, turned the old family barn into the heart of the community—until the whispers started. Deliveries vanish. Rumors spread. Accidents pile up. Someone wants to destroy everything she's created.

Former Marine and K9 handler **Caleb Jennings** sees the danger others miss—and he won't walk away. But exposing the truth means confronting jealousy, lies, and a woman bent on revenge. When vengeance turns personal, Caleb will risk everything to protect the woman—and the future—they're just beginning to build.

EXPOSURE OF SHADOWS

Secrets of Beaver Creek, Book 4 (available 2026)

Paige Ellison came to Beaver Creek for one reason—safety. After her husband's sudden death exposed his ties to organized crime, Paige packed up her young son and left Boston behind. The small Vermont town promised a chance at normalcy, a place where Colin could grow up without shadows dogging their every step.

But shadows have a way of following. When someone breaks into her home and strange men start asking questions, Paige realizes Derek's secrets didn't die with him. And someone thinks she has what he left behind.

Levi Barrett doesn't go looking for trouble. After years as a military cop, he's content to bartend part-time, rebuild his motorcycle, and keep his demons in the garage where they belong. But when his new neighbor's son wanders into his life—and danger follows close behind—Levi finds himself pulled into Paige's fight.

As buried sins surface and threats close in, Paige and Levi must decide if they're willing to trust each other. Because, in Beaver Creek, even the quietest streets can hide the darkest deceptions—and this time, running won't keep them safe.

Series Order

Each book in these series is a stand-alone and can be read in any order. Reviews are greatly appreciated.

Books in the KnightGuard Security series:

Evidence of Betrayal, Book 1 (Luke and Grace's story)
Evidence of Murder, Book 2 (Ben and Marlee's story)
Evidence of Lies, Book 3 (Pete and Julie's story)
Evidence of Deceit, Book 4 (Joe and Claire's story)
Evidence of Revenge, Book 5 (Sam and Mark's story)
Evidence of Secrets, Book 6 (Hank and Laura's story)
Evidence of Evil, Book 7 (Logan and Maddie's story)
Evidence of Truth, Book 8 (Killian and Anne's story)

Books in the Brotherhood Alliance (Special Forces, Operation Alpha) series:

Protecting Joy, Book 1 (Liam and Joy's story)
Protecting Naomi, Book 2 (Chase and Naomi's story)
Protecting Dani, Book 3 (Ryker and Dani's story)
Protecting Isabelle, Book 4 (Will and Isabelle's story)
Protecting Emelia, Book 5 (Titus and Emelia's story)
Protecting Tessa, Book 6 (Ford and Tessa's story)
Protecting Lainey, Book 7 (Finn and Lainey's story)
Protecting Mia, Book 8 (Caleb and Mia's story) — available 2026

Books in the Secrets of Beaver Creek series:

Exposure of Murder, Book 1 (Ethan and Jane's story)

Exposure of Obsession, Book 2 (Savannah and Dylan's story)
Exposure of Malice, Book 3 (Emily and Adam's story)

New Series, Champlain Security Solutions:
Elimination, Book 1 (Sean and Chloe's story) — available 2026

Preview: Exposure of Murder

Secrets of Beaver Creek, Book 1

Prologue

Warm sunlight poured through Jane Goodwin's office window, casting golden beams across her desk like a shower of congratulations. Life was good. She leaned back in her chair and stared at her computer screen. *Done!*

She smiled to herself, typed the words "The End" and hit save, feeling a deep sense of satisfaction.

Another mystery novel completed.

She wrote about a murder, a tale born from her imagination. The story had everything her readers craved: a sexy hero, a strong female protagonist, plot twists galore, and romance. Oh, she hadn't forgotten the happily ever after. Nope! Her fans would be devastated without a happily ever after.

Jane closed her eyes and exhaled, slowly releasing her breath. The apartment was quiet, just the way she liked it. The hum of the air conditioner was just white noise in the background, and the familiar scent of her husband Mike's cologne lingering in the air comforted her.

She sat there for a while taking in her office—her happy place. A small pink love seat was pressed against one wall. Hung above it was a watercolor of Boston Commons in the springtime and its iconic swan boats, painted by her best friend, Savannah Jones. Pearly pink and fuchsia blossoms of the magnolia and cherry trees popped against the lush greenery in the background.

It was a peaceful scene, quite the opposite of Savannah's chaotic childhood and her outgoing personality.

The painting reminded Jane of childhood memories and the thrill of riding the boats with her grandmother.

Jane ran her hand along the antique cherry desk her parents gifted her when she graduated from college. Its varnished surface reflected the muted light from the window. Floor-to-ceiling bookshelves surrounded the desk, filled with her novels, books from her favorite authors, and family pictures—*lots* of family pictures.

Her gaze landed on the framed photograph of her husband, Mike, front and center on the shelf. His warm brown eyes stared back at her, crinkled at the edges, his infectious laugh captured in the moment, frozen forever. God, Mike loved to laugh. People flocked to him.

He was the one who said hello to strangers, helped little old ladies across the street, and even gave money to the man who spat on his windshield and wiped it with a dirty rag. However, as kind as he was, no one ever mistook him for a patsy. He was the most driven, moral man she had ever met.

Two opposites.

Even their friends in college were surprised when she and Mike hooked up.

Jane was the dreamer, the introverted romantic. Mike was the extrovert, the one who made her laugh, who dragged her out of her comfort zone and encouraged her to follow her dream of becoming an author. In return, she gave him unconditional love and stability—two things that were missing from his life growing up in foster homes.

Tonight, they were celebrating their five-year anniversary with family and good friends. It also marked the launch of her fifteenth novel and Mike's promotion at work. In a stroke of luck, they secured reservations at an upscale restaurant they'd been dying to try. Everything was perfect and going according to plan.

Next on their list would be deciding when to start a family. She couldn't wait to begin that next chapter with Mike and hoped it would be soon. She was so ready to move on to the next phase of her life and settle down in a cozy house in the countryside before she turned thirty-two.

Jane spent an hour luxuriously bathing and washing her hair. Standing in front of her fogged-up mirror and wiping the moisture away, she looked at her reflection and smiled. Her green eyes shone with happiness at how perfect her life was.

The biggest decision she had to make right now was what to do with her hair—up or down? She'd keep her whiskey-brown hair down for tonight, just the way Mike liked it.

Next up was deciding what to wear. Jane opened her closet door and pulled out two dresses: a sexy short black dress she'd recently purchased, as well as a sleeveless light blue cocktail dress gathered on the side with the back down to there.

Hmmm. Mike hadn't seen either dress yet. She decided to surprise him with the blue one—he loved that color on her. She put it on, looked in the full-length mirror, and twirled—yep, perfect.

Jane poured herself a glass of wine, turned on some smooth jazz, and walked into the living room to admire the view from the window, which overlooked Boston's iconic botanical garden and the swan boats gliding by. As she opened the window to let in fresh air, the sweet scent of lilac with undertones of exhaust filled the room. Excited children's voices, cars honking in the distance, and a lone trumpeter playing drifted up from the streets below, vying with the silence.

Jane loved their condo. Right in the center of everything. Could life get any better than this?

Her life was everything she dreamed of and more.

Until a knock on the door—a simple *rap, rap, rap*—changed the course of her future.

PREVIEW: PROTECTING TESSA

BROTHERHOOD ALLIANCE, BOOK 6

Ford McCallum inhaled a deep cleansing breath of crisp autumn air, letting it fill his lungs before releasing it. He took one last look at his family's home before getting into his truck.

The white Cape-Cod-style house with its green shutters was his sanctuary growing up, filled with the comforting aromas of his mother's cooking, the sweet smell of his father's cigar, and the creak of the porch swing on a summer's night as fireflies flickered.

Love and laughter once filled this place. Now it stood silent and dark.

So many happy first memories were made there—the swing set he and his dad built; working on fishing lures together; the birthday parties and holidays; his first car—a sweet Ford Mustang, bought with money he earned; his first kiss under the stars with his crush, Melody; his first sexual experience in the back seat of said Mustang, also with Melody; and finally graduating high school and following in his father's footsteps when he made his decision to join the Army.

Ford had sold the house and carefully packed up anything of sentimental value and placed it in the back of his truck. It wasn't much—a couple of photo albums, his father's watch and service medals, and his mother's wedding ring.

The rest of the furniture and clothes were donated to charity. There was no sense in holding on to the past. Another family would hopefully benefit.

The funeral had been intimate, just friends of his parents and a few close friends of his from the military under a gray sky with threatening dark thunderclouds.

Thankfully, it hadn't rained.

After the twenty-one-gun salute and presentation of the flag in honor of his father's military service, he left.

He had no relatives—both parents had been only children, just like him. Now they were together for eternity, buried in adjoining plots under a sprawling oak in the local cemetery.

Loss seemed to be a constant in his life. First, he lost his parents in a tragic car accident. Then he'd watched Pete, his best friend and brother—not by blood, but still—die in battle. He'd talked Pete into giving up college and joining the service with him. The weight of that never left him.

Now haunted by ghosts, he drove south toward Haywood Lake, Florida, the familiar mountains of his hometown giving way to vast farms and wide-open farmland and finally to palm trees and sunshine. Hopefully, the sunshine would chase away the dark shadows following him.

A while ago, an Army buddy mentioned that a group of veterans was providing protection services in the area. The idea intrigued him. It called on his sense of duty to protect the innocent.

Before the funeral, Ford got the job at the Brotherhood Alliance after a brief conversation with the director, Chase Maddox. He was thrilled to be working alongside men who had walked similar paths as he and to put to good use the skills he learned in the service.

The best part was living rent-free on campus in a cabin

nestled among the trees, which allowed him to splurge on a more secluded place just outside of town, deep in the woods, where he could retreat when life got overwhelming.

The Brotherhood Alliance was a melting pot of backgrounds, yet united by shared experiences. They were a tight-knit group of men, all ex-military. Some had girlfriends, and some were married, a condition he hoped to avoid. The pain of loss was still too raw.

He, Zach Rodgers, and Titus Finch were single and lived on campus. He and Titus had started there at the same time but didn't spend much time together.

Not that it mattered now.

Titus had a woman and would be moving in with her. Ford had helped Emelia Wells move into her apartment above her bakery and then guarded her when she was threatened by her ex-boyfriend. Titus was one lucky man. Emelia was outgoing, funny, smart, a fabulous baker, and sexy. Although he'd never tell Titus that. Not if he wanted to keep his balls intact.

None of that mattered, though; he wasn't looking for a woman.

Eight months later

Ford sat at the long conference table in the command center. It was after work hours at Paws for Caring, so the few employees who worked there had gone home. Titus had just finished giving his update, and Chase turned to Ford.

"How about you, Ford?" Chase asked. "Any issues?"

Ford took his time answering. "No. I got the mom and kids out of their situation and safely to the shelter. The director helped settle them in."

"Any problem with the dad?" asked Chase.

"Nope." Ford smirked. "He might have a case of swollen balls for a while. But yeah, he finally saw the light."

Boy, that had been a stressful case.

He was always amazed how much trouble followed people who least deserved it.

The dad was drunk and thought he'd get away with striking his wife in front of his screaming kids, then threatening her with more of where that came from if she left him.

Ford intervened and got the dad in a chokehold while the woman took her kids and got in his truck. Then dad thought he was a tough guy. A well-placed knee to the guy's balls was rewarding, especially when he curled up on the floor, crying like a baby. Ford left him in the apartment with a few choice threats and got the little family to safety.

The shelter in town was one of the Brotherhood's pet projects. They did a lot of free protection work for women and the occasional man who were in fear for their safety. The Alliance just recently branched out and took on paying projects, which he liked better. Emotions weren't necessary to safeguard a client, only expertise and focus.

In a couple of days, if he didn't have an upcoming job, Ford planned to head out to his cabin. The stress of work and the constant camaraderie with the guys was getting overwhelming. He felt alone in his thoughts and the familiar weight of guilt and the past creeping in.

He needed to clear his head and refocus. Just him and the peace of the woods. Although he'd learned the hard way peace never lasted.

Preview: Evidence of Truth

Book 8, KnightGuard Security

About the Book

Kindergarten teacher Anne Walker dreams of a family of her own. She's been on lots of dates, but no one has met her stringent criteria of the perfect man—someone who is trustworthy, intelligent, protective, wants kids, loves cats, has a good sense of humor, and is sexy as hell.

When Anne foils a child abduction from the schoolyard, her life is threatened. KnightGuard Security assigns Killian Caswell to protect her.

Killian's sole reliable family was the military. Haunted by memories of his abusive father and long-suffering mother, he can't imagine making a commitment to anyone—until Anne challenges everything he believes about himself. He doesn't want kids, hates cats, and doesn't have a sense of humor, but he is protective, trustworthy, intelligent and easy on the eyes. Is that enough for her?

As their connection deepens, a sinister figure emerges and threatens their relationship. Can Killian shield Anne from the threat before they lose their chance at happiness?

Six years ago

Could my life get any worse?

Anne Walker's hand trembled as she swiped at the tears streaming down her cheeks. She pushed back her damp hair clinging tenaciously to her face and sank back on her pillow—her now very soggy pillow.

How did she ever get into this position?

That was a stupid question. She thought she was in looove.

Anne didn't sleep a wink last night because of the knots in her stomach, besides the inability to turn her mind off her problems. She tossed and turned and woke up feeling drained.

Dawn was fast approaching, and she needed to get up soon for class—a class she didn't want to attend today.

What difference would it make if she missed her early childhood development class? Or, for that matter, any of her classes? She just wanted to lie in bed and wallow in self-pity.

"Jason, please don't leave."

Anne's pleas fell on deaf ears. She had been so happy last night. Jason came over for dinner. She presented her joyful news. It didn't go over well.

The painful memory of her boyfriend, the father of her unborn child flipping her the bird before slamming the door closed, getting into his car, then driving out of her life, played on repeat in her head like a bad movie. The pain of abandonment pierced her heart. He left her crying in the parking lot.

He had been upset at first because she accused him of cheating on her. Sure, she accused him, but only because two of her friends confirmed they saw him cozying up with another woman. Anne hoped he would deny it.

Sure, she claimed her pregnancy hormones were going a little crazy, but he couldn't deny he got her pregnant, or so she thought.

Jason's once warm blue eyes turned cold and hard. "I knew you were a conniving bitch, always talking about marriage," he sneered. "Did you really think I want to be tied down at my age, especially with a little brat?"

Anne's stomach roiled. Had Jason dated her so she would pay for things, or was it just for the sex?

He stabbed his finger at her. "You said you were on birth control."

"Jason," she reached out for him and pleaded. "I didn't lie about that. You've got to ....."

"Liar."

Yeah, as if being on birth control guaranteed someone would never get pregnant. Jason stood as still as a statue, his nostrils flaring, his breathing loud, shaking his head like she was the stupidest person alive.

"We used condoms. Remember?" Jason added.

Anne shook her head and sighed. This conversation was going nowhere.

"Remember that one time?" she reminded him, referring to that one time a couple of months ago when Anne noticed his condom leaking.

Jason's answer for the leaky condom—she poked holes in it.

"I would never do something so awful," she angrily replied.

Then he accused her of trying to trick him into marrying her. Riiight. As if she now wanted the lying, cheating bastard after showing her his true colors.

And Jason, the scumbag, turned and walked away, abandoning her when she needed him most.

"You're just leaving? You don't feel any responsibility for me or the baby?" Her voice rose in anger.

Although they'd dated for a year, they never discussed a future together. Anne always assumed marriage was a given. Instead, Jason cheated and lied, and now the douchebag left her pregnant.

The coup de grâce was when Jason stared her in the eyes and coldly told her to get an abortion.

The tightness in Anne's chest cut off her oxygen. Her vision blurred. The parking lot began to spin. She braced herself against the building wall. Did Jason really said that? Get an abortion?

What was she thinking? Did she really expect Jason to embrace fatherhood with welcome arms?

In retrospect, there had been too many red flags.

Jason didn't have a full-time job or his own apartment. He was a mama's boy, living off his parents in their basement.

She overlooked it initially because he claimed to be saving money—for them. Now she knew why she split the bill with him when they went out. *Ha!* What a crock. He lied. Anne saw that now.

What did trusting him say about her?

Was she too willing to give up on what she considered the perfect man just to say she had a boyfriend?

Apparently, yes.

Jason MacIntire was a cowardly, irresponsible, disloyal, disgusting human being.

Having a child out of wedlock hadn't been anything that ever crossed her mind.

Anne's stomach lurched. She ran to the bathroom and hurled last night's dinner. With nothing left in her stomach, she wiped her mouth with the back of her hand. What was she going to do now? She didn't want to burden her parents, who scrimped and saved to send her to college. Sure, they would be disappointed, but they'd never disown her.

Even with grants and her work, she barely made enough to cover her tuition, board, and books. Money would be tight. With a baby coming, she'd have to find a full-time job. Her part-time employment with the little convenience store down the street wouldn't cover her expenses, let alone the hospital bill, a bigger apartment, daycare, diapers, or, or...

Oh God. Anne's stomach churned, and she vomited again. Getting pregnant before she graduated was not part of her long-term plan. Hell, it wasn't even part of her short-term plan. She dreamed of finishing her master's degree and teaching kindergarten here in Florida. She was at a loss whether she could achieve it.

Anne stared at her disheveled reflection in the mirror. Her blond hair looked stringy and unkempt. The dark circles under her eyes made her look like a raccoon. Nothing could be done about that. She splashed her face with water, gargled with mouthwash, and got back in bed, all the while crying big, ugly crocodile tears.

She wondered why she ended up with men who only wanted a good time.

It was her fault for being too trusting.

Anne trusted Jason when he told her he worked nights and weekends. She trusted him when he called to say something came up and he cancelled dates.

She trusted the wrong man again.

Never again. She vowed to be wiser about men in the future.

Jason was now in the column of losers she dated.

Maybe she was a sucker for a good pick-up line and a cute guy. However, she wanted what her mother and sister had. A loyal man. A man she could trust. Someone who put her first and could make her laugh. Was that too much to ask?

Anne took a deep breath. Her life plan needed a major adjustment. She would have this baby. She would secure her teacher's certificate, find a job, save a little money, and eventually marry the right guy who loved her and wanted children—someone she could trust.

The sun shone through her window and heated her face. Anne groaned. Why was the day bright and cheery? Shouldn't it be gray and raining? Shouldn't thunder and lightning shake the ground, promising hell and damnation and maybe shriveling Jason's dick so this never happened to another woman?

One could only hope.

The room she'd lovingly decorated now looked garish and sad—not unlike the way she felt. An eerie silence replaced echoes of laughter. She glanced at a picture of her parents holding her on their second anniversary. Their smiles and looks of love told a story—a story of love and trust, one she'd never have now.

Anne reached out with trembling hands to grab the last Kleenex. She stared at the empty box—empty like her life—and tossed it on the ground. She blew her nose and was repulsed by the sounds of wet snot. Flinging the disgusting tissue into the waste basket along with the thousand other tissues, she wiped the tears away and looked at her watch.

Great. Now she'd be late for class—no more time to feel sorry for herself.

Anne groaned as she dragged herself up for another trip to the bathroom, this time to shower, brush her teeth, and get dressed. She pulled on her favorite black leggings and a blue-striped top. The outfit always made her think cheery thoughts. However, the outfit wouldn't fit her in another couple of months. Anne added new clothes to her growing list of future needs.

She piled her hair into a messy bun and added a touch of

mascara and lip gloss, then fingered the antique ruby necklace her mother given her for graduating college.

Anne's grandmother had given it to her mother when she graduated and became a teacher. Her mother claimed it was for luck and good fortune.

Anne sighed. Not today.

Taking a deep breath, she rubbed her belly and stared in the mirror. "You're safe, little one," she whispered. "Having you now is not the end of the world. We'll get through this. Your mom is strong."

Mom? Anne closed her eyes and hugged her chest. Her heart raced. *Oh God! She was going to be a mother.* She rocked back and forth on her heels, then gave herself a mental slap. *Suck it up, buttercup.* This was now her life.

"Oh," she huffed. She couldn't forget she needed to have a conversation with her parents before too long, no sense surprising them in seven months with a baby in her arms. Gah. Anne was not looking forward to having that conversation.

Class was in a half-hour.

The good news was she didn't have to make any decisions today—or even this week.

Although the way her luck was going, Anne figured next week could bring worse news. Despite the setback, she was determined to move forward, prepare a good life for her baby, and hopefully, the next time, be wiser if or when she dated again and not take any crap from a man.

Acknowledgments

I'm so grateful to everyone who picked up this book and took the time to dive into my story. Your feedback and encouragement have been invaluable in shaping this journey.

Many thanks to Chris Kridler of Sky Diary Productions for keeping me focused and refining every word to make my story shine. Her suggestions made the story pop.

Huge thanks to Dar Albert of Wicked Designs for yet another stunning cover.

A special shout-out to my amazing writing group—your insights and motivation pushed me to be better with every draft.

A heartfelt thank you to Ray Ferrari, my rock and best friend, for always being there with honest feedback that made this book stronger.

To my ARC readers, special thanks. And to beta reader, Mary Moniz, whose sharp eyes picked up things I've missed.

Finally, to every reader who's supported my work, left a review, or spread the word—you're the reason new authors like me get noticed, and I can't thank you enough!

Any errors, blunders, or inaccuracies made are all mine.

Books by Lila Ferrari

Brotherhood Alliance series

Protecting Joy, book 1

Protecting Naomi, book 2

Protecting Dani, book 3

Protecting Isabelle, book 4

Protecting Emelia, book 5

Protecting Tessa, book 6

Protecting Lainey, book 6

Protecting Mia, book 8 — available in 2026

Protecting Norah, book 9 — available in 2026

KnightGuard Security series

Evidence of Betrayal, book 1

Evidence of Murder, book 2

Evidence of Lies, book 3

Evidence of Deceit, book 4

Evidence of Revenge, book 5

Evidence of Secrets, book 6

Evidence of Evil, book 7

Evidence of Truth, book 8

Secrets of Beaver Creek

Exposure of Murder, book 1

Exposure of Obsession, book 2

Exposure of Malice, book 3

Champlain Security Solutions

Elimination, book 1 — available in 2026

About the Author
Lila Ferrari

I love writing, whether I'm writing poems, plays, short stories, cookbooks, grants, newsletters, newspaper articles or full-length novels.

Growing up in New England, where summers are sweet but winters are long and cold, has given me lots of opportunities to expand my creativity.

I have enjoyed: basket weaving, spinning wool, quilting, canning, teaching cooking and traveling.

I have been a recipe tester, sailor, farmer, shepherd, cattlewoman, chick herder and Master Gardener.

Like many women, I have worked full-time, raised two children, and helped my husband's career. Finally, I get to make my dream come true. After all, dreams never die, and new doors open every day.

Today, I live in sunny Florida with my husband, enjoying paradise. In addition to writing novels, I recently took up birding and photography.

My stories are about courage, redemption and second chances. Everyone deserves them. Don't you agree?

Find me on:

• **Website/Newsletter**: LilaFerrariWrites.com

• Amazon author page: amazon.com/author/lilaferrari

• BookBub: bookbub.com/profile/lila-ferrari

• Facebook: facebook.com/lilaferrariauthor

• **Facebook private group**: https://bitly/3ilcBw8

• Goodreads: goodreads.com/author/show/17380860.Lila_Ferrari
• Instagram: instagram.com/lsferrariwrites
• Pinterest: pinterest.com/lsferrariwrites/
• X: x.com/lsferrariwrites
• YouTube: https://bit.ly/3yxV5Mf

Made in United States
Orlando, FL
02 January 2026